THE PARTNERSHIP

A Novel

Steven J. Harper

This is a work of fiction. It is not about any particular lawyer or law firm. In a sense and to varying degrees, it's about all of us. Handling cases throughout the country for thirty years and co-teaching law school classes for the last fifteen, I encountered hundreds of lawyers, judges, law professors, and others who collectively inspired this book's characters and events. Some personality traits may be unique to attorneys; others pervade the human condition and resonate beyond the bar. Based upon conversations with colleagues, friends, and acquaintances working in dozens of the nation's largest firms—known as the *Am Law* 100 and *NLJ* 250—I'm convinced that the book's themes depict what many regard as ubiquitous conditions and unsettling trends. Finding answers is always more difficult than posing questions, but perhaps a great lawyer's observation from long ago is worth remembering: "Sunlight is the best disinfectant." For those contemplating a legal career, here is another: "Forewarned is forearmed."

ISBN 9780984369102

For my family

PART I

"ARTICLES OF PARTNERSHIP FOR MICHELMAN & SAMSON LLP

. . .

ARTICLE III – FIRM GOVERNANCE

A. EXECUTIVE COMMITTEE

1. THE LAW FIRM SHALL BE MANAGED BY AN EXECUTIVE COMMITTEE CONSISTING OF SEVEN MEMBERS, ONE OF WHOM SHALL SERVE AS CHAIRMAN . . ."

CHAPTER 1

"A FISH ROTS FROM THE HEAD," thought Albert Knight as he studied his fellow members of the Executive Committee. He'd arrived first; one-by-one, eyes transfixed to their BlackBerrys, the other six drifted into the oak-paneled conference room on the fifty-fifth floor overlooking Midtown Manhattan and the East River. The firm's dazzling offices in the clouds sat atop the world. Ordinary people walking the streets below were invisible to the naked eye; they were too small to matter. In the building's lobby, mystery dwelled at the spot where only a special access card and clearance from a uniformed security guard permitted entry to the elevator banks reserved exclusively for travel to the Michelman & Samson heavens. Even before the post-9/11 era produced new security measures for most high-rise buildings, it took a magnetic key to enter the M&S workspace. In a profession built on the sanctity of secrets, Knight knew that his firm had plenty of its own.

The magnificent seven, as everyone called the partners on the Exec Com, had reached the pinnacle of M&S. Most didn't like each other, but that was irrelevant. Money was the glue that bound them inseparably, at least until a better offer came along. Having benefited from an economic and political era that became known as America's second gilded age, they made a lot of money and spent even more. Among these self-styled supermen (and one woman) of the twenty-first century, only Albert Knight did not believe his own press releases. At least, not today.

These fleeting occasions of insight unsettled Knight, but he took comfort in the knowledge of his chameleonic character. This moment would pass, and he would lose its revealed wisdom. Sooner rather than later, he'd revert to form. When that happened and someone asked this select group at the top of the nation's most lucrative law firm how much was enough, he'd join the chorus in responding: "More."

"Let's get this over with," began fifty-four-year-old Ronald Ratkin, who, as usual, had breezed into the room last. He looked like his name. A ruddy complexion masked the barely visible remnants of severe acne that had afflicted him throughout adolescence. Although small in physical stature, he carried himself so as to create the unmistakable impression that he was looking down his sizeable nose at everyone. With the long sleeves of a handmade cashmere sweater tied around his neck, he appeared as if he'd just jumped out of an antique MG Roadster in an old Cary Grant movie. In fact, like other wealthy fifty-something baby boomers, he owned the modern-day equivalent: a black Porsche Carrera.

Ratkin fancied himself a bon vivant, a debonair man-about-town. Every morning, he blow-dried, brushed, and combed his thinning red hair until each follicle lay exactly where it belonged. Intelligent, articulate, and an impeccable dresser, the nationally renowned litigator was at the top of his game.

"I have a jury trial resuming Monday morning in Boston," he continued as he approached a marble table that could easily seat thirty but today accommodated only the magnificent seven.

"Relax, Ron," said Charles O. Hopkins III, the sixty-four-year-old chairman of Michelman & Samson's Executive Committee and the one person in the world who could get away with addressing him so informally. "We all know about your celebrated trial. Our PR people have done a nice job getting the press to bite on that one."

A graduate of Harvard's college and law school, Hopkins had been at M&S for forty years. Six-foot-two and strikingly handsome, he'd always been a ladies' man and still retained his movie star aura. A deep baritone voice complemented blue eyes that never wavered or even blinked on their path to the depths of a person's soul. Early in his career, he'd consciously developed the penetrating gaze that mesmerized juries; the longer the trial, the more effective he became, especially with female jurors. His legendary personal charisma created irresistible temptations; he'd been married and divorced twice. Out-of-town trials often occupied months during which he'd kept many different female companions. Rumors abounded that time had slowed but not stopped his dalliances, especially in his hometown of Chicago.

The wily chairman knew that Ratkin bristled when anyone called him Ron. It implied a relaxed informality, the antithesis of the image Ratkin had cultivated since joining Michelman & Samson almost thirty years earlier. Abandoning the nickname he'd brandished since childhood, Ronnie, he still looked younger than his years and corrected anyone who failed to address him properly. Few dared defiance. He retaliated at Hopkins's feigned slip of the tongue by reminding everyone in the room that he controlled the firm's largest client.

"Then I'm sure you can understand why Edelwise doesn't appreciate this interruption in my undivided attention to the biggest case in its history," he said while shooting a glance at Knight, his only rival for the next generation's leadership of M&S's litigation department and, by inevitable extension, the firm itself. Two generations earlier, great trial lawyers had founded the firm, recruiting young attorneys whom they hoped would achieve even more than they had. Lawyers in its other practice groups then built on the firm's reputation to create an international powerhouse that now dominated all areas of the profession.

Smiling at Hopkins's intentional needling of an unpleasant colleague, Knight relished his own build, a physical stature that Ratkin lacked. They differed in other ways, too. Ratkin wore contact lenses; Knight had used the same horn-rimmed spectacles since law school. Ratkin's personal tailor fitted his suits in M&S's offices; Knight's wardrobe came off the rack from Macy's, formerly Marshall Field's State Street store in Chicago. Ratkin's personal barber and manicurist came to his office weekly; Knight made monthly visits to the same downtown barber shop he'd discovered shortly after graduating from law school the year both men joined the firm.

What Ratkin viewed as their most important difference irked Knight: Ratkin considered him an unworthy second-rate intellect. Certain that his superior mind had taken him to the top of Michelman & Samson, Ratkin was equally convinced that Knight had done it the hard way: putting in long hours and playing internal office politics. Ratkin saw himself as a genius; he regarded Knight as a calculating and manipulative grind.

On one point they agreed. Anyone who worked fewer than twelve hours a day, six days a week, was a slacker. Both had grown weary of carrying the firm's lazier brethren and spoke of it often, except to each other. Apart from unavoidable interactions in Exec Com meetings, they had not exchanged a word in twenty-five years. The story of the romantic triangle behind their enmity still reverberated through the halls of Michelman & Samson. Few knew it was just the tip of an ugly iceberg.

Ratkin's decision to announce his entrance with two points that he knew would rattle Knight was premeditated.

He specialized in such prickly tactics with all adversaries, including his partners. Looking for any edge, he knew that catching an opponent off guard was the first step toward disabling him completely. "Freeze Bambi in the headlights, and then run him over," he often said.

So he mentioned his ongoing jury trial to remind everyone that, except for the aging and increasingly irrelevant Charles Hopkins, he was the only real trial lawyer in the room. Knight had taken a case to a jury only once, and that had been long ago. The remaining four committee members came from the firm's other major practice groups: bankruptcy, intellectual property, and the corporate departments. To varying degrees, each sat in awe of any first-rate M&S trial lawyer who could cast spells over a courtroom and just about any other unsuspecting audience.

Ratkin's second cut went deeper. He announced that his case was for Edelwise, a client that had been Knight's before Ratkin stole it from him fifteen years earlier. He'd taken other things from Knight, too, but Ratkin had no idea how his rival was getting even.

"Any additions or modifications to the agenda?" Hopkins offered his usual initial remarks, knowing that his upcoming birthday would be the main focus of the day's meeting. The partnership agreement required that, upon reaching sixty-five, he had to retire as chairman of the Exec Com and from the equity partnership. In three months, someone in the room would replace him. The contestants had spent years girding for battle.

Both front-runners for the job, Ratkin and Knight, had been Hopkins's protégés. He knew their strengths and weaknesses better than they knew themselves. They admired him as his own children never had and never would. Confident that cream always rose to the top, he'd pitted them against each other early in their careers. The surprise was that, somehow, both had survived to this point, at the brink of ascending to a throne on which only one could sit.

"I'd like to discuss the question of leadership for the Beijing office," said sixty-two-year-old John Merritt, sipping a glass of iced tea. Now the elder statesman of the corporate transactions department, he was the only lawyer in the firm who wore a bow tie. The Yale Law School graduate was a brilliant strategist, peering around corners that seemed miles away. Before anyone else saw it coming, he sensed the economic vulnerability of his position as an employee benefits specialist in a world that was heading toward private equity megadeals. So he transitioned himself away from his limited counseling practice to establish M&S's venture capital group. When that area took off during the 1980s, its contribution to the firm's fortunes made him an essential presence on the Exec Com. Even in severe economic downturns, he somehow managed to increase his power and influence. Still, he was too old to succeed his closest friend on the committee, Hopkins, as chairman. Generational change was always the order of the day at Michelman & Samson. Some joked that the firm ate its young and its old.

"Very well," said Hopkins, "we'll add Beijing." M&S had a dozen offices throughout the world, and Beijing, about to become number thirteen, had stumbled for want of a senior partner willing to relocate there. "Anything else?"

"I think we need to address whether last year's budget cuts went deep enough to preserve partner earnings during the current recession," said forty-six-year-old Scott Canby, Merritt's sidekick and an outspoken voice for his corporate equity partner constituents. The most prolific of all M&S lawyers in the art of gratuitous vulgarity, he'd gained weight steadily since his second marriage. A decade earlier, his fellow thirty-somethings ran the venture capital firms that fueled a transactional frenzy. Armed with both law and business degrees from the University of Chicago, Canby became their go-to lawyer. But he always thought it unfair that he hadn't earned as much money on the deals as the clients benefiting from his genius. Making it his personal mission to catch up with them, he'd recently assured Knight that before leaving Michelman & Samson he would have a "fucking personal net worth of fucking $50 million." In another moment of uncharacteristic clarity, Knight responded calmly with a simple question: "What's the point?"

"Fuck you!" came Canby's predictable response.

"Yes," Hopkins resumed the Exec Com meeting, "our progress toward preserving profits remains a critical issue, and we've got to spend more time on it. I can tell you the bottom line: we need to do more, or partner earnings will decline."

The crash had taken a major toll on the firm. Initial rounds of associate and non-equity partner layoffs reduced attorney headcount by ten percent in an effort to keep M&S's average billable hours up. Reductions in all non-attorney staff—including legal assistants, secretaries, and administrative personnel—went wider and deeper, eliminating all bonuses and raises. The Exec Com viewed these as necessary prices paid to preserve the equity partners' seven-figure incomes.

Hopkins continued the session with standard opening fare, requesting a motion to approve the minutes of last month's meeting before turning to the main reason they'd gathered on a sunny Saturday morning: adopting a selection process for Michelman & Samson's next chairman. A knock at the door brought the room to an abrupt and awkward silence.

"Yes," Hopkins boomed. "Come in."

"Excuse me," said the secretary as she entered. "I have an emergency call for Mr. Ratkin. It's the general counsel of Edelwise, and he says it's urgent."

Ratkin had probably orchestrated this episode to humiliate him, Knight thought. Everyone in the room knew that what had grown to become the firm's largest client had once been Knight's. He looked at his watch. Ten-thirty in the morning was too early for a double Tanqueray and tonic, but it sure sounded good to him.

"I'll take it and be right back," Ratkin said briskly as he rose from his seat. He'd dreaded this call for a long time, but he'd also planned for it.

CHAPTER 2

"This is Ratkin," he said after picking up the receiver in one of the nearby private telephone rooms.

"I'll put the call through, Mr. Ratkin," said the efficient female voice on the other end. During Exec Com meetings, all calls came through Charles Hopkins's office in Chicago. Even from eight hundred miles away, his secretary controlled access to the New York conference room. Unbeknownst to Ratkin, she pushed the mute button on her phone and remained on the line. Wearing a headset, fifty-nine-year-old Helen Peterson picked up a pencil and began writing in her steno pad. Shorthand had become a lost art at which she still excelled. As Hopkins's loyal secretary for almost forty years, she knew how to gather and keep secrets.

Never married, Peterson devoted herself to the firm as if it were family. But her life was becoming more difficult. Shortly after widespread staff layoffs earlier in the year, she began to suffer insomnia and recurring anxiety attacks. Having risen to the top of her pay scale, she made a juicy target for any myopic cost-cutter. Close friends counseled her to quit, but she was years away from Medicare eligibility and viewed retirement as presenting new and unknown challenges. She had become a conflicted prisoner in a place she'd once loved, simultaneously craving and fearing release. Even so, Peterson remained fiercely loyal to Michelman & Samson as an institution to which she owed much. Any firm critic seeking a sympathetic ear knew to turn elsewhere.

"Ronald, it's Phil," said Phillip L. McGinty, Edelwise's general counsel. Fifteen years earlier, he'd been a Michelman & Samson non-equity partner who had sacrificed too much for too long as Ratkin's faithful and obedient minion. As reward for a decade of indentured servitude, McGinty earned a decent income but never gained Ratkin's endorsement for promotion to equity partner. That doomed him.

Ratkin had given McGinty the bad news about his future at M&S using the baseball analogies that always peppered his comments: "You're a solid minor league prospect, but you'll never get a call to the majors. You'll have a decent career; it just won't be here."

Fortunately, the economy was booming then and the options for jettisoned big firm attorneys were many. He accepted Charles Hopkins's advice to join a small client, Edelwise Technology. That was a typical career path for involuntarily departing senior associates and non-equity partners: out the door and into someplace where losers in the race to equity partnership became overnight winners in a different contest. As clients, they could steer business back to the firm. M&S threw McGinty a big going-away party at Spiaggia on Michigan Avenue; Ratkin took him to lunch at Charlie Trotter's. By the time the firm had given him its special treatment, the departing thirty-five-year-old reject felt like royalty, just like his out-placed predecessors and the many others who would follow him. No longer a firm pariah, he had become a valued source of revenue.

McGinty's new job became an even more surprising blessing to him and his former firm when Edelwise's explosive growth astonished everyone, especially Phil McGinty. The double-domer—he'd attended college and law school at Notre Dame—was now worth more than $50 million in Edelwise stock options. Hopkins and Ratkin spoke about the phenomenon periodically, usually after work at the exclusive Chicago Club on Van Buren Street just off Michigan Avenue. When in town, neither man ever had any particular reason to rush home at the end of the workday.

"The son-of-a-bitch fell into a bucket of cream," Hopkins remarked. "He's now making more money than anyone in the firm, including me. Let's face it. The guy is a slug."

"Slug is too generous," answered Ratkin, who likewise found it difficult to comprehend that his former underling now held paper wealth vastly exceeding his own. Life is so unfair, he thought. But then he remembered his consolation prize: he and Hopkins had also benefited handsomely from their ability to participate in Edelwise's success.

As it grew to become its industry's leader, the company had generated friends, enemies, and lots of legal work. Now M&S's largest client by far, Edelwise regularly employed more than two hundred of the firm's two thousand lawyers and accounted for fifteen percent of its revenues. It contributed to an even greater share of the firm's profits, thanks to premium billing arrangements that Hopkins had negotiated with McGinty. The special agreement required Edelwise to pay legal fees far exceeding the firm's hourly rates of a thousand dollars for top partners.

Annual client billings that had exploded from $5 million to twenty times that number in fifteen years were the smallest part of the story. Thanks to an opportunity that corporate partner John Merritt had initially developed, Hopkins and Ratkin became large Edelwise shareholders, too. Merritt had arranged many such sweetheart deals that started with direct investments in firm clients when they were start-up companies. After M&S later did the legal work that took the companies public, the partner-investors' earlier stakes converted to large stock holdings.

Edelwise had become the most lucrative of Merritt's private investment opportunities reserved for M&S equity partners. There was only one catch: the law firm's continuing role as its counsel made the law firm partners what the Securities and Exchange Commission called *insiders.* They had to exercise great care in buying or selling the company's stock so as to avoid the charge that they benefited from knowledge that the market lacked. The safest times to execute trades came during management-designated trading windows, but even those did not provide complete protection. All of these thoughts raced through Ratkin's mind as he listened to McGinty's call that threatened everything.

"We have a problem," McGinty said solemnly.

"I know," came Ratkin's dismissive reply. "We've had a problem for two months. It's not going away any time soon."

"It's gotten worse."

"How is that possible?" Ratkin's voice betrayed his irritation.

"Egan's dead."

"Damn it! My star witness has been knocked out of the lineup just as he was about to step into the batter's box. Now who am I supposed to send to the goddamned plate on Monday?"

"No, you don't understand. It's worse than that."

Ratkin never took it well when someone accused him of not understanding something. "Okay, tell me what I don't understand."

"He's more than just the founder of the company; he *is* Edelwise. Investors have been worried for two years about Joshua Egan's health. Every time there's a rumor that he's getting a head cold, our stock price drops ten percent."

"So what? I know all of that. We've created a contingency plan for it. Come on, Phil, we all knew this day was coming."

"Yeah, but you know perfectly well that the timing couldn't be worse. If word gets out that our top guy is dead, investors will panic and the stock will tank. We have a $15 billion credit line up for renewal in sixty days, and the only collateral is company-owned stock. Your people are renegotiating the deal. Without that credit line and the high stock price it requires, we're toast."

"Phil, I don't understand your anxiety," Ratkin said with a calm detachment, remembering why he'd concluded fifteen years earlier that McGinty didn't have what it took to be a Michelman & Samson equity partner. Even when presented with foreseeable events like this one, the guy fell apart. "You know I've already developed the strategy to deal with this."

"It'd better," his voice trembled. "Let me tell you something: if this thing turns sour, you'll be leading the parade to prison."

"Calm down, Phil."

Ratkin began analyzing the potential personal repercussions of this development; none was good.

"Who knows he's dead?" Ratkin continued.

"You, me, and Alvarez," McGinty said, referring to Egan's personal nurse. "I've had him sequestered away from everyone else for the past two months, just as you directed."

"Where's Alvarez?"

"Right here. I mean, she's still in the room with him, but she hasn't gone anywhere, and she won't until I release her."

Ratkin was glad he'd had the foresight to hire a private nurse from Costa Rica whose only relatives and acquaintances lived in poverty thousands of miles away. She could disappear, and no one would notice or care, Ratkin thought. After receiving its commission, the New Jersey employment agency placing her in what it thought was an ordinary assisted-living situation on Manhattan's Upper West Side had lost interest. It had no idea that her real assignment was for a multibillionaire in northern California.

"We've entered the first phase of my plan," Ratkin said with the firm tone that always commanded the respect of his clients and the undivided attention of jurors. He knew it was usually more important to sound confident than to be right. "Don't let her out of your sight. Tell no one about this. Tell her to talk to no one about this. How about the electronic files?"

"Still where we saved them."

Both men knew that the hard drive on McGinty's laptop computer offered the only hope of buying the time they and Edelwise needed.

"The world will learn that the founder and chairman of Edelwise is gone. But only when I decide it should. Take a deep breath, Phil. We'll all get through this. Just follow the game plan and keep a close eye on your scorecard."

Helen Peterson waited for the two men to hang up before disconnecting her line. She removed her headset, put down her pencil, and closed her steno pad. Her job was safe for a while longer, she thought with a smile.

CHAPTER 3

Ratkin hung up and returned to the conference room, where the discussion had turned to the question of Charles Hopkins's successor as M&S's chairman. As Albert Knight studied the white-haired lion's wrinkles that had become facial crevices, he pondered whether his inevitable fight with Ratkin for the top job was worth it. Hopkins had aged far more than his years in the position; people in the firm called them *M&S years*—like dog years. Every year as chairman of the Michelman & Samson Executive Committee was the equivalent of three or four in a normal human life. Maybe the price of success was too high.

Knight's misgivings at such a critical point in his own career didn't really surprise him. Throughout his thirty years at the firm, two dueling impulses racked his psyche as a sense of entitlement battled relentless guilt. Usually, entitlement won because the long hours that all M&S lawyers billed made it easy for him to believe that he deserved the staggering sums shown on his income tax returns. Economic fairness in the lucrative partnership was a relative concept, he told himself. The Exec Com meted out such justice during the annual equity allocation decisions, so that was the destination he needed to reach. Once on the committee, why not become its chairman? Usually, life was as simple as that for Michelman & Samson equity partner Albert William Knight, always referring to this side of himself formally and in the third person—as if he needed the M&S label to establish his identity, as if he were in fact someone else. His efforts had produced power to wield and money to spend. All of that was as it should be.

A rival demon appeared less frequently, but to devastating effect. At such moments, Knight viewed his entire life as hanging from a slender thread. His achievements reflected little more than the confluence of fate, fortuity, and the hand of unseen forces taking him from childhood poverty to incomprehensible affluence. As a first-generation college graduate, he was no better than anyone else, just luckier than most. With frightening clarity, he understood that few things had contributed more to any definition of his success than being in the right place at the right time. That was how he'd advanced to his seat at the table of the M&S gods a decade earlier. Deep in his heart, he knew that he deserved none of his good fortune.

As the years passed, such episodes of paralyzing guilt emerged less frequently. But when they did, their intensity left him increasingly alienated from his colleagues. Maybe he'd never belonged at M&S at all, he thought on such occasions. Today was one of them.

"The first question is process," Hopkins began as he trained his laser-like eyes on Ratkin. "Ronald, let me summarize what we've begun to consider in your absence. Because I was the first chairman in a new management system that we adopted ten years ago, we have no precedent for selecting my successor."

"We don't need precedent," Ratkin interrupted. "We have a partnership agreement that spells out the process. The Exec Com selects its chairman. It couldn't be clearer."

"Yes," Hopkins replied. "That's true, except the question is, which Exec Com? I confess that in drafting the provision myself, I didn't realize the ambiguity I'd inadvertently created. The issue is whether I should be voting on who the next chairman should be, even though someone else will take my seat on the Exec Com in September. On my way out of the firm, I'm not sure my dead hand should be attempting to rule from the grave."

Interesting, Ratkin thought. The old man was getting soft, just as Ratkin had anticipated he might. Hopkins knew that it would take four of the Exec Com's seven votes to elect a chairman. The only two viable competitors for the spot—Ratkin and Knight—had been Hopkins's protégés, and each appeared to have three votes in hand, not counting Hopkins, who would have to break the tie. Ratkin guessed that Hopkins didn't want to choose publicly between his law firm children, although he was also certain that Hopkins favored him. Fortunately, he'd wisely foreseen such a moment of weakness from his former mentor. Before he put his plan into action, he'd listen to what his fellow Exec Com members had to say.

"Start with the basics," the bow-tied John Merritt began. He was one of Ratkin's sure votes for chairman. The crash had crushed his clients and revenues, and he now had difficulty billing seven honest hours in a day. Ratkin thought Merritt had become a pathetic figure, but he was an ally, and that mattered above all else in the Exec Com room, where careers and fortunes were made and broken in almost whimsical fashion. It always came down to who had the votes.

"Let's step back a bit," Merritt continued. "This year, Ronald is up for his third term, and I think we all expect his renomination to be a foregone conclusion. But, as we also know, this year's nominators must fill Charles's seat, too. If he weren't turning sixty-five, he'd have three more years to go in it. So his departure requires that the nominating committee select two people, one of whom presumably will be Ronald. Last month, we picked the nominators."

Yes we did, Ratkin mused as he tried to suppress a smile. He was especially proud of the way he'd worked with Merritt and his unpleasant corporate department colleague on the Exec Com, Scott Canby, to orchestrate the nominating committee's composition. Only equity partners not on the Exec Com could serve as nominators. Ratkin, Merritt, and Canby had stacked this year's group with Merritt's allies. They were certain to choose another of Merritt's protégés—forty-two-year-old corporate partner Karen Morton—as the nominee who would then go to a *pro forma* vote of all partners before taking Hopkins's seat. Merritt and Canby would then make sure Morton became the Executive Committee's fourth vote for Ratkin as chairman.

His prior success had never required Hopkins's help, and his coronation wouldn't either, Ratkin thought. Merritt would score well with this arrangement, too; he'd control the three corporate seats on the seven-person Exec Com. That was a pretty good result for a moribund practice area that had died two years earlier and showed no signs of returning to life.

"As always, the two nominees will be placed before the full partnership at our annual meeting in three months," Merritt continued. "They will probably get elected by acclamation. So if I hear what Charles is saying, one option would have the next Exec Com, presumably including all of us along with Charles's replacement, select the new chairman."

Ratkin wanted things to proceed exactly as Merritt had outlined. With their own areas in an economic tailspin, Canby and Merritt needed what Ratkin had already promised them: protection of their equity stakes in the firm. In return, they'd helped create a nominating committee whose selection of Morton would break the voting deadlock in Ratkin's favor.

"I don't understand why we're wasting our time on this," Ratkin urged. "The rules of the game are set."

"I'll tell you why," interjected Knight. "Because the selection of the next chairman will be the most important event in the history of this law firm for the next decade and beyond. We owe it to our partners and our posterity to get this right."

For his tenth birthday, Knight had asked his parents for a subscription to *Vital Speeches of the Day*. In his ambivalent quest to preserve a shred of the profession's nobility, he often found himself lost in his own rhetoric. The rest of the Exec Com had become accustomed to his soapbox tendencies. As was often the case, he advanced no particular philosophical agenda as he spoke. But today he was particularly unhappy with his law firm and his life. To his delight, he could vent his displeasure with an oratorical gun aimed directly at Ratkin.

"We must exercise the greatest care in the discharge of our fiduciary obligations," he continued. "We must assure that the firm's essential culture remains strong. We must use the same diligence in making this decision that we would for a client paying our highest fees. We must get this right for ourselves and for those who come after us."

As always, Knight waited for applause that never came. At such moments, he endured the frustration that resulted every time his colleagues failed to appreciate the presence of greatness.

"So putting aside the b.s., what's being proposed?" Ratkin asked impatiently.

Hopkins was a lame duck, but he still mastered every room he entered. Besides, most of the people on the Exec Com owed him something.

"Because the partnership agreement is silent on the issue of a retiring chairman's right or obligation to vote on his successor," Hopkins began slowly, "we must adopt a process that assures maximum acceptance among the partners. One option is to do as Merritt suggests. That's somewhat better than the criticisms that could follow if I cast a deciding vote for my successor. But it has a different disadvantage: it could look wired. There is a growing perception that the nominating process has become politicized. Some of our partners now believe that, to borrow Ronald's favored phraseology, the whole ballgame for a replacement Exec Com member is over as soon as the composition of the nominating committee is set."

Of course, Hopkins was right. The process was wired; Ratkin had been counting on its predictable corruption to put Karen Morton on the committee and thereby assure his new leading role. This game was over.

"There is one more alternative," Hopkins continued. "We could put the selection of the next chairman to a full partnership vote. In addition to the nominating committee's selection for my replacement, the ballot would list every current Exec Com member as a candidate for chairman. The person with the highest vote total would win."

Ratkin calculated the possibilities quickly. That approach could work out for him because Merritt and his people should be able to deliver the votes he needed. Then Hopkins dropped his bombshell.

"The election would proceed by secret ballot."

With those words, the room went silent. The idea of a secret ballot made Ratkin, Merritt, and Canby physically ill. It meant they would lose control over people who could vote without fear of reprisal, freeing partners to reject the dominant culture of politics and cronyism. Their previously successful effort to mold a nominating committee assuring Ratkin's victory would go for naught. Ratkin knew he was among the most feared and hated partners in the firm. Although he'd cultivated precisely that image, it meant he wouldn't fare well in the popularity contest that an open election was sure to become. The last thing any law firm needed, especially Michelman & Samson, was uninhibited participatory democracy.

"So, is there a motion to put the various alternatives to a vote of this committee?" Hopkins asked.

"I move that we defer consideration of this matter until next month's meeting," Knight suggested. Some people could analyze complex situations instantaneously; he needed time to map out decision trees. He wanted a yellow legal pad, a pen, and at least three hours. Until he'd considered every ramification of every possibility, he couldn't decide which of Hopkins's alternatives best served his own ambitions—or, today, what those ambitions even were.

"Second," said Deborah Rush, hoping that her quick support of Knight's motion would help score points with him. The first and only female member of the Exec Com, her practice combined litigation and corporate skills in the intellectual property department. Three years younger than Ratkin and Knight, she was disarmingly attractive and struggling for stability in some facet of her life. A member of the first generation of women who tried to do it all, she'd learned that she couldn't in the way she'd planned.

A top performer from the University of Pennsylvania and editor in chief of its law review, she'd married a Wharton Business School student the year they both graduated. A few years later, she had a child whose birth became an immediate subject of Michelman & Samson lore. Rush remained at her desk to finish a client conference during three hours of labor contractions; she was back at work within forty-eight hours at a time when doctors typically kept new mothers in the hospital for three days. Two years later, she had another baby and shortened her maternity leave to a single evening. A full-time nanny raised both kids.

As her children reached adolescence, the family struggled. Never finding that elusive perfect blend of professional fulfillment and personal satisfaction, Rush watched the marriage falter just as the couple's individual careers blossomed. Their divorce became final as her oldest child began high school, about the same time Rush joined the Exec Com. To her, it seemed like a lot longer than four years ago.

Rush's consumption of martinis had accelerated with her career's success. At Exec Com meetings, she sometimes became teary for reasons that Knight couldn't fathom. Maybe she needed an adjustment to her medication, he thought. Most importantly for Knight's purposes, Deborah Rush hated Ronald Ratkin and John Merritt as much as they despised her. She was one of Knight's sure votes on the Exec Com.

"Any discussion?" Hopkins inquired, but heard no response. "Very well. Those in favor?"

All hands shot up. Enemies in all other things, Ratkin and Knight uncharacteristically agreed that the matter should not proceed with the speed that Hopkins seemed to favor. The ramifications of pursuing each possibility required careful consideration. Futures hung in the balance.

"So in three months' time, I will no longer be this firm's chairman," Hopkins continued wistfully, in a way suggesting that his primary target audience was himself. "Nor will I be a member of the Exec Com. Indeed, I will not be an equity partner of Michelman & Samson. We should all consider this matter carefully. Shall we now proceed to discuss the Beijing office and then the budget reduction issues?"

Ratkin couldn't take another minute of such nonsense. His alliance with Merritt remained intact; he had a month to dissect Hopkins's ploy and its implications but no time to deal with the matter now.

"You'll have to excuse me," he said. "I have a plane to catch."

Buried in his BlackBerry as he walked to the elevator that took him to the lobby, Ratkin proceeded through the building's revolving doors. He moved briskly to an idling black limousine whose driver had instructions to take the defendant's lead trial lawyer in *Compucom v. Edelwise* to a private hangar at LaGuardia Airport. Ronald Ratkin always traveled in style; the client always paid the bill.

On the plaza bench, a short, stocky man in his early seventies and wearing a gray fedora stopped reading his copy of the *Chicago Tribune*—curiously out of place in Midtown Manhattan—and calmly folded it as he watched the subject of his latest assignment climb into the car's backseat. Ever eager for the center-stage spotlight, Ratkin remained oblivious to the one person who followed his every move.

CHAPTER 4

While Ratkin rode toward Edelwise's luxurious private jet, the chief enforcement officer for the Securities and Exchange Commission's insider trading division sat at his Washington, D.C., desk with the file he'd compiled over the prior twenty years. A folder labeled "Edelwise/Ratkin/M&S" had grown to fill a cabinet drawer for which only one man had the key. Like Phil McGinty, that man, Daniel Schmidt, had suffered a career setback at the hands of Ronald Ratkin many years earlier. Unlike McGinty's bucket of cream, Schmidt landed in a pile of manure, and it took him a decade to dig out. Now he maintained a personal vigil, waiting for an opportunity to return the favor.

*   *   *

Schmidt's life now bore little resemblance to what he'd expected as a rising second-year law student. Then again, Harvard Law School hadn't been what he'd expected, either. The truth was that, like many of his peers, he considered law school a way to buy some time while he figured out what to do with his life. When he took the LSAT on a lark and scored in the top one percent, his fate was sealed.

The first year in Cambridge had proven to be his most challenging academic experience to date. It took him a while to realize that most pressure came not from the professors or the curriculum but from fellow students, especially the self-formed study groups. They were petri dishes for paranoia. In the end, he did better than he'd expected on the final exams that solely determined his grades and, at the beginning of his second year, signed up for on-campus law firm interviews. Michelman & Samson was on his list for a single reason: upon graduation the following year, he planned to live in Chicago, and that firm was one of thirty on his citywide roster. Beyond the sparse two-sided information sheets in the placement office's notebooks in those days, he knew nothing about M&S or its competitors. Although he'd developed dreams of prosecuting white-collar criminals as an assistant U.S. attorney, the urgency of his student loan repayment schedule moved him toward private practice. M&S's starting associate salaries exceeded their government attorney counterparts by fifty percent, a gap that widened thereafter.

He accepted the firm's invitation for follow-up interviews in Chicago and visited three other large firms on the same trip. For no particular reason, he scheduled Michelman & Samson last. As he completed his rounds, he thought he'd have to flip a coin to decide among them. Then he met Sam Wilson.

"What can I tell you about the firm that you don't already know and that you think no one here will tell you?" asked the forty-six-year-old litigation equity partner. Wilson was Schmidt's sixth and final Michelman & Samson interview before heading to the airport for his evening flight to Boston.

"I've seen three other big firms in the past two days," Schmidt answered. "They all have bad things to say about Michelman & Samson: it's a sweat shop; M&S lawyers are aggressive and obnoxious; they eat young associates and spit them out. What's your response?"

"First, I think it's interesting that they all complain about us, rather than each other. I hope the Michelman lawyers you've met haven't offered any similarly disparaging words about other firms."

"No, they haven't."

"Good. That phenomenon of one-way criticism directed at us is interesting, isn't it? But the more important point is that there is a grain of truth to what they say. We're not the place for everyone. At the same time, that doesn't mean you have to behave in only one particular way to make it here. There are many different paths to success."

As Schmidt surveyed the office, he noticed that it lacked the typical paraphernalia documenting career milestones that he'd seen other attorneys display. Instead, Wilson had covered his walls with photographs of little league teams that he'd evidently coached. In the middle of the credenza behind his desk were a dozen family photos and two identical trophies labeled "WORLD'S GREATEST DAD." The only artifact of his professional accomplishments was a plaque commemorating his election to the American College of Trial Lawyers.

"The truth is that this place offers more flexibility than most firms," Wilson continued. "We operate on a free market principle. There's no central assignment committee. Lawyers are free to turn down work from anyone for any reason. It's a good system. My criminal law professor sometimes represented defendants accused of heinous crimes, but even he had his limits. He used to tell us, 'In our system, everyone has the right to a lawyer, but that doesn't give everyone the right to me.' M&S honors that principle; it gives everyone the right to say no."

A year earlier, Schmidt had had the same professor for criminal law; the line hadn't changed.

"First and always, lawyers are human beings. If we don't respect our core values in what we do, bad things happen to us psychologically. We can't isolate and ignore pieces of our own identity. But a lot of lawyers try to do exactly that. It's one of the reasons attorneys lead all occupational groups in clinical depression. We also rank high on life's other misery measures, like alcoholism and drug abuse. One antidote to all of that is allowing attorneys to choose their work and their co-workers. Everyone craves autonomy."

No one in college or law school had revealed the profession's darker side to Schmidt or his classmates. As he listened to Wilson, he wondered if practicing lawyers had the same secret pact as women who had given birth: if people truly understood the experience, how many would voluntarily undertake it the first time? Do unhappy lawyers remain silent about the aspects of their careers that might drive others away and reflect badly on their own decisions to remain in jobs they detest? He'd think about that some other time.

"How does that play out in real-life situations here?" Schmidt asked.

"I'll give you a personal example. My father recently died of lung cancer after smoking cigarettes for sixty years. It was his decision to be a smoker, but the free choice argument is hard to make when the company's advertising target is fourteen years old, as my dad was when he started. As hard as he tried throughout his adult years, he couldn't stop. Even in his final days, he'd wheel himself to the front porch, turn off his oxygen tank, and light up. After a drag or two, he'd start a cough that morphed into a rumbling gurgle that my kids will never forget. You can imagine why I'd have difficulty defending one of our tobacco clients. Never have and never will."

Wilson's candor impressed Schmidt. Most big firm partners were no-bad-news people; their firm was the best, and everyone should want to join. Rarely did they discuss clients or causes that recruits might find socially or morally repugnant.

"Frankly, one of the reasons I came to Michelman was that I had the freedom to say no to any particular case or client, knowing that I could find other work in the firm. For me, that was one of the big advantages of a large firm. I also knew that I could say no to partners with whom I might not get along. Size creates diversity of opportunity. I didn't want to fail just because I had a personality conflict with some superior who could end my career on a whim."

"That makes sense," Schmidt nodded.

"It makes sense because it's true. But there's another reason to preserve the free market assignment system for associates. Future firm leaders should be people younger attorneys want to work with. When I hear about a lawyer who has trouble getting help for his or her cases, it sends up a red flag. If a lawyer at any level fails to treat co-workers with respect, that tells me everything I need to know about that attorney. If someone is not a good person, he or she is not likely to be a very good partner, either. Oh, I see we're running late. I'd better get you back on schedule."

At that moment, the large law firm sweepstakes for Daniel Schmidt was over. Sam Wilson had sold him on Michelman & Samson.

* * *

Schmidt was only three years younger than Ronald Ratkin, but the difference between them seemed much greater when Schmidt began working at Michelman & Samson. The experience gap between an upstart novice who had just completed law school and a seasoned M&S associate entering his fourth year was akin to the gulf between a seventh grader who still rode his bike to play with friends at the park and a high school sophomore who drove a car to pick up his girlfriend for a date. Especially at

M&S in those days, Ratkin and his fellow associates received opportunities typically reserved for more senior attorneys at other firms. But without the clout that came with being a partner, staffing trial teams became a challenge. Schmidt had been at his new job for only two hours when his phone rang.

"Dan, it's Ronald Ratkin," said the voice on the other end. "I need your help on a big case. It's a major matter and a great opportunity for you. The client is with me right now, and I'll send you the materials I need you to begin reviewing immediately. I've told the client all about you, and he's enthusiastic about your involvement. Welcome aboard!"

Schmidt was speechless. This call sounded far removed from the theme of his interview with Sam Wilson. It certainly didn't embody the free market assignment model that Wilson had touted. Even so, Schmidt had no reason to resist Ratkin's overture and was concerned about the consequences if he refused work on his first day. Besides, for all he knew the experience might be worthwhile.

* * *

It wasn't. Three years after Schmidt signed on to the case, Ratkin had become a non-equity partner and Schmidt was still working for him. So were six other associates whom Ratkin had similarly tapped over a two-year period on their first days at the firm. Most tasks were repetitive and boring, including endless months of document review in the client's warehouse.

Still, Schmidt considered himself one of the fortunate ones. In addition to his responsibilities on Ratkin's mammoth case, he also handled a small lawsuit under Sam Wilson's supervision. Without its respite from the tedious tasks Ratkin assigned, Schmidt would have quit the firm after his first year. The case reminded him why he'd attended law school. It gave him opportunities to interview witnesses, take depositions, confer directly with the client, plan strategy, and prepare for a trial that he eventually conducted himself as a second-year associate. He won the week-long federal jury trial, prevailing against a former Michelman & Samson equity partner who'd left the firm to set up his own boutique practice a few years earlier. The victory made him the envy of senior associates and non-equity partners throughout the firm. Most of them had not yet come close to the lead trial counsel role he'd successfully occupied, much less knocked off a formidable foe who happened to be a respected M&S alumnus.

A week after winning his first trial as lead counsel, Schmidt feared that his experience may have been a once-in-a-generation prize for any associate. Small cases offering young attorneys opportunities to become what they'd always thought being a lawyer meant were rare and disappearing. Even in those days, large firms like Michelman & Samson made most of their money on the big cases. As firm management increasingly emphasized profits in articulating the firm's core mission, less room existed for the cases that made young lawyers feel like, well, lawyers. Interesting courtroom work on the large matters remained at the top of the M&S food chain; layers of equity and non-equity partners separated Schmidt from it.

For most of his days, weeks, and months after that first trial, Schmidt found himself trapped on Ratkin's large case for a client accused of dumping toxic waste near an elementary school. Along the way, he suffered enough verbal abuse at the hands of Ronald Ratkin to ask himself two questions: how did a guy like that continue to advance, and why did anyone put up with such a bully? Schmidt hadn't been there long enough to figure out the answers when an episode that entered Michelman & Samson associate lore became the final straw.

Ratkin had Schmidt accompany him on an out-of-town deposition. When they entered the conference room,

Ratkin didn't shake the opposing attorney's hand. During the first break, Schmidt asked him why.

"I know him; he knows me; we don't like each other," Ratkin told him. "So why pretend otherwise with a hypocritical handshake?"

As the deposition proceeded, it became depressingly clear to Schmidt that his sole function in the proceeding was to hand out specific documents as Ratkin snapped his fingers demanding them. After two hours and several cups of coffee, the opposing lawyer asked Ratkin if he could take a brief bathroom break at an appropriate point in the questioning of his witness.

"Sure," Ratkin replied, but then he proceeded for another ten minutes and began a new line of questioning.

"I still need to make a trip to the rest room," the opposing attorney said cordially as Schmidt observed.

"Just a few more questions," Ratkin resisted before continuing for another ten minutes, at which point his adversary chimed in again.

"Mr. Ratkin, I told you twenty minutes ago that I needed a bathroom break. I still need it."

"Let me just finish these next few questions."

"No, Mr. Ratkin. That's what you said ten minutes ago and again ten minutes before that. The court reporter can read those portions of the transcript back to you while I'm in the bathroom because that's where I'm now going. Meanwhile, I'm instructing my witness that he should not answer any questions while I'm gone. I've been a lawyer for fifteen years, and I've never encountered incivility rising to this level of silliness."

Ratkin smiled as the lawyer left the room and then asked, "Do you accept your counsel's instruction not to answer any question I ask until he returns?"

Properly, the witness refused to answer even that one. When his attorney returned, the deposition resumed. As they broke for lunch, the opposing lawyer asked Ratkin about Schmidt, who'd been dutifully passing out documents in accordance with Ratkin's terse directives.

"When are you going to introduce me to your colleague?" he asked.

"He's nobody you need to know," Ratkin answered abruptly. "He's just my secretary." Then he added his unique brand of humor: "My bat boy."

When Schmidt assumed that Ratkin had been joking and offered his name along with his hand, Ratkin told him to leave the room. Schmidt never returned to the deposition or the firm. Two days later, a messenger delivered two small boxes of personal effects from his former office to his home. Among his friends and acquaintances during three years at M&S, only Sam Wilson phoned to check on him.

"I'll pursue this if you want," Wilson offered after hearing Schmidt's version of the events a week later. "If your description is correct, Ratkin should be leaving the firm, not you."

"I appreciate your offer, Sam. But you know as well as I do that the firm will never side with an associate over one of its own partners. Besides, I've wondered for a while whether I really belong at Michelman. You're a great lawyer and seem to have a life outside the firm. But I don't see many like you in the younger partner ranks. So where am I going in this place, anyway?"

"I think there's room for more than one model of accomplishment at a large firm," Wilson protested.

"I don't know if you're right, Sam, and neither do you. No offense, but the jury's still out on how successful you'll be at M&S."

"I'm as successful as I need to be."

"That's all well and good for you. But it's tough for me to make myself a guinea pig in an experiment involving my own life. This isn't a dress rehearsal. It's the real thing. And I only get one chance to do it."

"I can't argue with you."

Wilson knew he'd lost the debate, as he had with many other promising junior attorneys who feared the firm's workaholic culture and all that went with it.

"I think it's actually a good thing that all this happened," Schmidt concluded. "Without a dramatic event like Ratkin being a jerk and humiliating me publicly, I'd just bounce along like most other lawyers, probably for as long as the firm let me hang around. Momentum and inertia drive most of us for too long. As the saying goes, 'Nothing focuses the mind like a hanging.' Well, I can tell you, Sam, nothing has focused me on my career more than its temporary demise at the hands of Michelman & Samson partner Ronald Ratkin. But this will turn into a good thing for me. Small slights are easily brushed aside, but they accumulate in the victim's psyche. Ratkin did me a great favor: he delivered an indignity too great to ignore."

"So be it," Wilson said with resignation.

Meanwhile, Ratkin lost no sleep over Daniel Schmidt's departure. Without missing a beat, he drafted a new associate, Phil McGinty, to assume a spot on the lowest rung of the team ladder as everyone below Schmidt moved up a step. Attrition looked better from the bottom when it created opportunities for the survivors. M&S prided itself on seamless transitions following the turnover of firm personnel. However indispensable any lawyer regarded his or her role, an equally talented understudy always waited in the wings.

"Associates," Ratkin said often and without regard to who heard or quoted him, "are fungible. They all think they're special, but the truth is that few truly are and all are expendable."

*　　　　*　　　　*

After leaving Michelman & Samson, Schmidt spent the next four years at different small firms before leaving

Chicago to accept a government job at less than half his final M&S salary. He started as a low-level staff attorney in the enforcement division of the Securities and Exchange Commission in Washington, eventually advancing all the way to section chief twenty years later. In that capacity, he reviewed every proposed prosecution of insider trading before the agency filed formal charges. Adhering to Sam Wilson's earlier advice, he'd respected his core values and found a job he enjoyed, and now he eagerly anticipated the start of his workdays.

Although he ultimately embraced his departure from Michelman & Samson as a blessing because it redirected his career, Schmidt never forgot Ratkin's abuse. Year after year, he followed the fate of his old firm in the business sections of the *Wall Street Journal* and the *New York Times*. He watched its annual profits rise to stratospheric levels approaching an average of $3 million per equity partner, according to the *American Lawyer*'s recent listing of the biggest law firms in the United States. He read with interest Ratkin's repeated quotations as Edelwise's lead outside counsel in its various high-profile cases. He learned the company's story: a come-from-nowhere start-up that became one of the largest on the NASDAQ.

He wondered if his old law firm's partners owned a piece of Edelwise. From his brief time at M&S, he knew that special investment vehicles held equity partners' interests in small client companies that sometimes became large. When those businesses became big enough to go public—that is, to issue stock for the public to purchase—M&S partners often reaped huge individual gains. So long as attorneys handled any personal stock transactions properly, there was nothing wrong with rewarding risk capital. If they got careless, Daniel Schmidt was there to protect the little guy. Apart from his profoundly personal interest in Ratkin's connection to Edelwise, Schmidt believed in the fundamental cause that all of his prosecutions for insider trading represented.

"No one occupying a special position of trust in a company should be able to profit from knowledge that is not available to everyone else in the market," he often told new attorneys during training sessions about their work in the enforcement division. "The entire system of free market capitalism requires a level playing field. It's our job to enforce the laws that preserve it."

He regarded lawyers as essential to an orderly society. Confidence in the rule of law and those enforcing it prevented the aggrieved from resorting to self-help that could produce anarchy, chaos, and worse. By their very calling, attorneys labored nobly in the crucible of the adversary system to produce justice for their clients. But if they themselves violated the rules applicable to all, the entire system became a victim. On that essential point compromise was impossible. Once the men and women responsible for upholding the law failed to respect it, civilization's days would become numbered.

So when Daniel Schmidt had a lawyer in his insider trading sights, he was relentless. He knew that greed could combine with competitive aggressiveness to push some attorneys beyond the legal line. When that happened, Schmidt's job was to drag them back and, sometimes, into prison. He was convinced that Ronald Ratkin possessed dangerous characteristics that made him both an extraordinarily successful lawyer and a threat to the legal system's core values. Unlike Ratkin, Daniel Schmidt was a patient man. He'd watch; he'd wait; and he'd pounce.

PART II

"WHERE IT BEGAN, I CAN'T BEGIN TO KNOW IT . . ."

"Sweet Caroline" – N. Diamond

CHAPTER 5

It was a long time ago—thirty years, Knight thought. But he and Ratkin became close friends shortly after their careers at Michelman & Samson began. Single and ambitious, both had been among the firm's twenty summer associates the year they met. It was a large group for those days when everything was smaller, including what were known as "big" law firms. Michelman & Samson's 150 attorneys made it one of the biggest shops in the country. With a Chicago headquarters, it had recently opened its only other office, a small outpost in New York.

Knight hadn't attended law school in the expectation of amassing great financial wealth. People with that primary ambition went to business school and got MBAs. Rather, he'd become a lawyer as many of his peers had: through a process of elimination. From childhood, his parents and teachers had urged him to do his best so he could become something. Like many baby boomers, he assumed that a college degree was merely a starting point for postgraduate education. The most prestigious options were in professions akin to callings: medicine, law, higher education, journalism, or some other specialized field requiring an advanced degree. For a time, Knight longed to become a history professor, but he lacked the confidence to pursue an uncertain academic path leading to questionable rewards. As it had for many of his college classmates, law school became a default solution—the last bastion of the liberal arts major who didn't know what to do next. For those who were a few years older, it had also provided a ready means to avoid being drafted into the army and shipped to Vietnam.

Once in law school, the proper tracks seemed obvious. Upon graduation, the vast majority of students at the best schools accepted jobs at large law firms. Most graduates had little awareness of what their actual tasks there would entail, but all expected to work long hours for decent pay. The very fact that almost everyone wanted such a position created a mystique that fueled herd behavior and student demand. The best firms, as they came to be called, had far more applicants than they could accept. The mere existence of such intense competition—and the large starting salaries—attracted the best and the brightest.

*   *   *

The contest began with summer associate programs employing law students who had completed their second years. Ratkin and Knight prevailed over hundreds of others in gaining offers from Michelman & Samson. They first met during an orientation session that included five other new recruits. After receiving ID cards and completing new employee forms, they toured the firm library occupying the entire fiftieth floor of its Wacker Drive headquarters. Anxiety rippled through Knight as he considered the much better schools that his fellow summer associates had attended: students from Harvard and Yale most intimidated him. He was sure they were learning secrets that future lawyers elsewhere would never know. He'd have to work harder and longer to keep up with them.

Harvard and Yale had rejected Ratkin, too, so he and Knight had that common bond. During their initial encounter, neither had to ask the other about what they both regarded as their first major failures in life. The firm had included law school affiliations in its listing of all summer hires.

"Identified as second-class citizens from the very beginning," Knight thought as he perused the roster.

"Geez," Ratkin whispered to Knight as the Michelman & Samson recruiting coordinator addressed the small group. "I hope there'll be room for us poor peons whose daddies and granddaddies didn't attend Harvard or Yale and donate a lot of money so we could go there. I get the feeling we're not exactly high draft picks for this organization."

Knight laughed nervously. Stern and humorless by nature, he feared there might be some truth to Ratkin's remarks. A relentless researcher, he had prepared for every on-campus interview by memorizing each firm's Martindale-Hubbell legal directory entries for all of its attorneys. From that exercise, he learned that Harvard and Yale were the pedigrees of choice for those who became M&S partners, just as they were for most of the other top law firms east of the Mississippi. Stanford and Berkeley dominated California-based firms.

As Knight resolved to break into that exclusive club, he spent much of the interviewing season wondering if all big firms wanted the same people and none would want him. So he especially appreciated the way Ratkin turned degrees from the nation's top law schools against those who'd received them. He respected anyone who could convert an opponent's obvious asset into an embarrassing liability.

He also agreed with the underlying sentiment, although he considered Ratkin's articulation crude. Knight was certain that the law school application process benefited those who enjoyed advantages that had eluded him. Unlike the Ivy League's children of privilege, he was self-made; that meant he was tougher, if not better. He didn't pause to consider that legacy admissions were on the wane or that, even at Harvard and Yale, most students were similarly self-made and receiving financial aid. Arbitrary unfairness was a more comforting explanation for life's disappointments. Knight also didn't learn until years later that Ratkin's older brother had graduated from Yale or that the Ratkin boys themselves were children of privilege from Manhattan's Upper West Side.

"I guess we'll all find out what we're made of," Knight replied with a slightly defiant tone. Surveying the competition, he resolved to outlast all of them, including his new friend.

When the group took a break for lunch, each new summer hire departed for an hour with a senior associate whom the recruiting committee had selected as an individual mentor. The summer program was the principal feeder for new full-time hires, so it was important to make prospects feel wanted and appreciated. In those days, most would receive offers to join the firm upon graduation the following year, and most would accept.

*   *   *

Ratkin's designated mentor was a recent alumnus of his school, Columbia. Kurt Bronson assured his charge over lunch that he'd made the right decision to spend the summer at Michelman & Samson.

"Here's the thing," Bronson said, "M&S is the best firm in Chicago. Everyone wants to work here. We pay better than any other firm. We provide better opportunities than any other firm. You'll get an offer at the end of the summer to come back as a permanent associate, but even if you don't accept it, you can use it when you interview elsewhere. You'll get offers from other places just because you already have one from us. For them, you're a no-risk deal because M&S has already vouched for you."

These guys never stop selling, Ratkin thought, also concluding that he was far more intelligent than the man who was giving him advice. Ratkin always performed a simple comparative evaluation with everyone he met: am I smarter? If he could have seen himself as he invariably formulated an affirmative response, he would have noticed the corners of his mouth betray an inner smile. The few who observed him carefully enough to notice his subtle change of expression thought he was being smug. In fact, he was just expressing his internal pleasure in confirming, yet again, that he still had not met anyone who could match his brainpower, insight, or cleverness. He was the complete package, he often mused before insecurity began pushing him back the other way: just an unfortunately small package.

Knight's lunch went much differently. Because he was attending a less prestigious school than Ratkin's, caution ruled. His assigned mentor, Doug Johnson, offered more guarded encouragement.

"Well, Albert, the good news for you is you're here," Johnson said. "We made offers to only one person at your school: you. The other good news is that the majority of summer associates receive full-time employment offers. Eighteen out of twenty got them last year. The two who didn't were recruiting mistakes. So the odds are in your favor."

I wonder if I'm a recruiting mistake, Knight thought as he considered what law schools the two rejects from last year might have attended. He eventually learned that neither had gone to Harvard or Yale, but he was relieved to discover that they weren't from his school, either. He was still in the hunt for the prize, he thought. For Knight, every situation quickly morphed into a competition. Life had winners, and he'd be one of them.

* * *

As the summer proceeded, it became clearer what Johnson had meant by a recruiting mistake. One summer associate spent an inordinate amount of his lunch hour reviewing *Playboy* at the newsstand in the building's lobby. The morally upright Knight was surprised at such open and notorious behavior. Ratkin's criticism was more practical.

"What a lack of judgment," he suggested to Knight as the two passed their colleague at his usual noon location. "I can't believe he doesn't go somewhere else to look at that stuff."

Meanwhile, big firm summer programs were famous for their minimal work demands amid aggressive recruiting efforts. Knight, Ratkin, and their fellow summer workers attended Cubs games and dinner parties in partners' homes. The idea was to show them a good time while offering a taste of the even better life that presumably awaited all. Summer Camp Michelman, it was called.

The party at Charles Hopkins's impressive lakefront estate was the highlight event. With massive tents, catered fine food, and live entertainment, the annual spectacle had become famous. The most remarkable aspect for Knight was the fact that Hopkins was only thirty-four years old, yet he and his wife lived like royalty in Chicago's wealthiest suburb.

"She must have money," Ratkin told him. "Or maybe he comes from money. There's no way he could live like this on a lawyer's income. No way."

A memorable disruption in the party occurred when a young Exec Com member arrived in his new Ferrari. Universally acclaimed as a genius, he veered off the driveway, onto Hopkins's manicured lawn, and into the backyard before stopping near the entry to the main tent. He then gunned the engine repeatedly as he laughed at the guests' reactions. The bizarre episode astounded Knight. He was only mildly surprised when, five years later, that same

Ferrari-driving partner suffered a breakdown, divorced his wife, resigned from the firm, and skipped town. Rumors circulated that he'd started a house-painting business in Cleveland and was still driving his Ferrari to jobsites a decade later.

Despite the firm's efforts to keep the summer program a low-key affair with respect to workload, a few found the situation intimidating. One summer associate began to cry during a particularly harsh session with a senior partner. Another worked all weekend on a memorandum that the assigning attorney later told her should have taken no more than three hours.

"How am I supposed to charge the client for the time you wasted on this?" he asked her rhetorically.

The twenty-four-year-old summer associate silently weathered the outburst. She had an answer that she never offered: her assigned mentor had cautioned her to be thorough in completing all tasks and not to concern herself with anything other than generating first-rate work product. She thought she'd done exactly that. As the episode made its way through the gossip mill, Ratkin took it in stride.

"None of us is accustomed to anything but unqualified success," he observed. "In high school, college, and law school, we made the play-offs every year. That's how we all got here. Of course, for some of us, that will be true for the rest of our lives. But it can't be everyone's fate. In the climb up the pyramid, there will be winners and losers—and the higher you get, the more losers there will be. Someone eventually comes out on top. Only one team can win the World Series each year. That's life. Deal with it."

Knight decided he would worry about Ratkin's mixed metaphors later. For now, he just wanted to survive the summer and receive an offer to return as a full-time M&S associate. Among other benefits, the job would allow him to start repaying his student loans. Freedom from financial obligations meant freedom, period. During that first summer at M&S, he learned a phrase that young partners offered in lamenting their own failures to follow this important principle after joining the firm. Ratcheting up lifestyle in anticipation of next year's raise created what they called golden handcuffs. It seemed to Knight that most partners wore them.

CHAPTER 6

Both men received offers at the end of the summer, and both accepted. When they returned after graduation, they took advantage of the firm's program to help assure that all M&S associates passed the bar. They worked at the office during the morning, but the firm paid for a six-week crash review course that met every afternoon in the ballroom of a Chicago hotel. When the course ended, the firm continued to pay the recruits' full-time salaries for the next two weeks, even though no client work was expected from them during that final study period before the bar exam.

Ratkin and Knight developed a daily routine: morning work in their respective offices, lunch together, and then a walk along Wacker Drive to the afternoon class. Both passed the bar on their first attempts. The massive swearing-in ceremony for the hundreds of newly admitted Chicago area attorneys took place on a cold morning in early January at the Arie Crown Theater. Located inside the sprawling McCormick Place complex that hosted national conventions of all kinds, the theater was usually a venue for high-end rock concerts and plays.

"And to think these are just the new Illinois lawyers in the Chicago area alone," Knight said to Ratkin as they surveyed the massive crowd.

"Don't sweat the size of this group," Ratkin responded. "Hardly any of these people will make it to the top. They are irrelevant to those of us who will."

Knight wasn't so sure. The competition to succeed in his chosen profession suddenly seemed even more formidable to him. What gave him the right to assume that he'd fare any better than others in the large group?

*   *   *

For the next three years, Knight and Ratkin lunched together several times a week, usually in the building cafeteria. In those days, a few associates consistently worked late into the evening and on weekends, but most targeted ten-hour days, five days a week. The firm actually counseled attorneys who logged significantly more to ease up.

"Your long-run asset value to us is zero if you burn out," year-end reviewers including Sam Wilson regularly warned both Ratkin and Knight each September, but to no avail. Typically, their billable hours placed them first and second among all attorneys in the firm as they worked the equivalent of six twelve-hour days every week. They even billed significant time on most holidays.

Long before the days of cell phones, voice-mail messaging, BlackBerrys, and laptops, Knight regarded staying home on Sundays as taking the day off. Except on weekends, the days of casual attire were still two decades away at the time of an episode that Knight recounted proudly to associates and young partners working for him years later. He'd been in the office on that traditional day of rest when a colleague walked into the men's room where Knight was standing at a urinal.

"Albert," he asked, "why are you wearing a suit on a Sunday?"

"Well," Knight answered hesitatingly with a forced chuckle, "to tell you the truth, until I got to the office, I didn't realize it was Sunday."

The firm's culture was demanding, but Knight's efforts in that regard surpassed all predecessors. He enjoyed the big annual bonuses that rewarded his long hours, but the extra money mattered only as a measure of his relative standing among M&S classmates. He was out to prove himself, showing the firm's leaders that he was as good as any of their Harvard or Yale graduates.

Ratkin billed long hours, too, but Knight sometimes wondered about them. In contrast to later years, all attorneys in those days worked either in their offices, out of town in someone else's office, or in court. The days of the remote workplace were still far away. Productive activity for a client occurred only in a defined physical space and only to a limited extent at home. On the Saturdays and Sundays that Knight was regularly in the office, Ratkin was nowhere in sight. Yet, somehow, by the end of each year, their total billable hours were about the same. Some years, Ratkin's were actually a bit higher. Curious, Knight thought.

He filed away another incident that occurred when the two young associates worked on the same large case for rising young equity partner Charles Hopkins. That particular lawsuit between corporate giants generated popular sympathy for neither side, but Knight became concerned about the means by which Ratkin satisfied his desire to win at all costs.

"Here's what's happening," Ratkin told Knight over dinner in Wilmington, Delaware. They had spent three days reviewing documents that the opposing party had produced in a dark, dingy warehouse. "The jerks representing the other side are refusing to give us some of their client's most important documents. There's a whole series of reports that they should be making available for our review, but they're not."

"How do you know that?" Knight asked. "How do you know they are withholding reports that you think are relevant?"

"Because they made a mistake," Ratkin answered. "They accidentally let me see a file marked 'confidential and privileged.' It's not on their index of produced documents or on their list of non-produced privileged documents. It was just one file, but that was enough. I'm going to use it to cut off their b-a-a-a-l-l-l-s-s-s."

He used that phrase a lot and always extended the last word—b-a-a-a-l-l-l-s-s-s—with an odd smile. When it came to that word, his cadence was so peculiar that Knight wondered if Ratkin might be gay.

"So you're going to file a motion asking the judge to order production of that file, right?"

"Wrong," Ratkin countered. "I did better than that. I was going to smuggle the file out of their document review room in my briefcase, but they number every page before giving us a copy of anything. So if I just took the documents, they wouldn't have those identifying numbers. Later, if I tried to use them with a witness in a deposition or if Hopkins tried to offer them at trial, the other side would just deny that the documents were theirs or accuse me of stealing them."

Wouldn't the accusation have been accurate? Knight wondered. Wouldn't he have stolen them?

"So, I took that single file and interspersed its pages among thousands of useless invoices in a box of documents," Ratkin continued. "Those invoices have nothing to do with the reports I found. In fact, they're complete garbage to us. But there's no way they'll review all of them, page by page. Someone will open up the box, see a bunch of invoices, and then close the box before shipping it on for processing and copying. Just wait. When we get our copy of that box of invoices, I'll know right where to look for the pages I hid in there. You'll see. They'll miss it. They're using illegal cork in their bats, but they'll still never hit the spitball I've thrown at them."

Ratkin's comments puzzled Knight. On the one hand, he was correct that their adversaries seemed to be refusing to provide relevant documents. On the other, the spitball was an illegal pitch. This kind of self-help sounded like two wrongs in search of a right, but maybe he was just lacking his friend's imagination and creativity in pursuit of the client's interests. In the end, Knight decided that any problems with Ratkin's techniques were for Hopkins to resolve because he was in charge of the case. The presence of two different approaches to a situation didn't necessarily make one right and the other wrong. Law school had beaten that much into him. The entire system depended upon adversaries taking contradictory positions; both couldn't be correct, but the process produced truth and justice. At least, that was the theory.

* * *

Their friendship grew. During their almost daily lunches together, they discussed their cases, their colleagues, and firm politics. Associate compensation remained a closely guarded secret, but after every yearly review, Knight disclosed his new salary and bonus to Ratkin, who then reciprocated; they were always identical, or so Knight believed. When both men worked late into the evening and ordered food delivered to the office, they sat together and ate it. Ronald Ratkin and Albert Knight spent more time with each other than either spent with anyone else in the world. In every way, they were closer than brothers. They had the firm, each other, and little else. In only one respect had they gone separate ways: their limited social lives outside work.

The first woman of Knight's dreams was Fran Connell, a stunning, blue-eyed blonde whose principal attribute was "a body that was made for one thing and one thing only," as he uncharacteristically described it to Ratkin over lunch one day. "And she does it very well," he added. The truth was that Knight had barely summoned the courage to kiss her after eight dates, although they finally made it to bed two months after that. One thing became certain: he loved her.

"I want to know all about the people in your law firm," Fran implored Knight as they became closer. "Every detail."

Over their year-long relationship, he obliged. She memorized attorney names and pedigrees, assessing the prospects for success among Knight's competitors and, of course, Knight's, too. She handicapped the field, separating likely winners from sure losers and trying to determine where Knight fit.

In contrast to Knight's monogamy that was closer to celibacy, Ratkin played the field. The two men rarely socialized together after hours, which is why Knight had been dating Fran for a year before she met Ronald Ratkin. It was their one and only double date.

"You have to meet Nancy," Ratkin insisted. "I think she might be the one for me. After years of sowing my wild oats, I think she could be it."

"We've done pretty well keeping our private lives away from our professional friendship," Knight replied. "I'm not sure it would be a good idea to change that approach."

"That's silly. You should meet Nancy, and I can finally meet the famous Fran you've been talking about for the last year. The one you told me is built for one thing and one thing only."

Knight reluctantly accepted Ratkin's invitation to join him and Nancy for dinner and the symphony. They met in the lobby of the University Club, where the firm in those days paid for an associate's membership after completing four years at M&S.

"Pleased to meet you," Ratkin smiled while extending his hand to Fran. "I've heard much about you for a long time, but Albert has kept you all to himself. I was afraid he'd show up alone tonight and tell me you'd been placed on the team's disabled list for the evening."

Ratkin's grin was beguiling, Fran thought as she smiled politely. He was also the best-dressed man she'd ever met. The crimson handkerchief in his suit's breast pocket matched perfectly the embroidered initials on the French cuffs of his white tailored shirt. She could almost see her own reflection in his well-polished shoes.

"Very funny, Ronald," Knight struggled to match his friend wit for wit, but he knew it was hopeless.

"This is Nancy," Ratkin continued without pause. His date was pleasant but far below Knight's expectation of a beauty queen. She nodded in quiet acknowledgement while offering her hand to Knight.

"Shall we dine?" Ratkin asked as he placed one hand on the small of Nancy's back and the other on Fran's, guiding both women to the elevator. Knight walked alone behind the threesome. Arriving at the top floor, they proceeded toward the main dining room. Stone columns that framed stained-glass windows rising to meet thirty-foot ceilings created an effect that gave the magnificent space its name: Cathedral Hall. A table near the easternmost wall afforded stunning views of Lake Michigan and Grant Park.

During dinner, Ratkin flirted with Fran while Knight and Nancy struggled to maintain a superficial conversation in an increasingly uncomfortable situation. Fran's foot periodically stroked Ratkin's shin, a gesture that neither of them acknowledged. By dessert, things had become unavoidably odd.

"Would you like to feel my sleeve?" Ratkin asked Fran.

"I beg your pardon," she responded.

"My sleeve. Would you like to feel it?"

"Whatever do you mean?"

"My sleeve—you should feel it," he said as he caressed his own arm. "My suit is one hundred percent silk."

"Well, all right."

Fran had previously identified Ratkin as a likely winner in the equity partnership sweepstakes—far more likely than her own Albert Knight. Before the evening was over, Ratkin had persuaded Fran that she might enjoy touching more than his sleeve. Knight pretended not to notice. As they exited a cab near her Lakeview apartment after the symphony, Fran made clear to Knight that she was moving on. Because Ratkin was a step up, hers was an easy trade.

That's when Knight stopped having lunch with Ratkin. In fact, he refused ever again to speak to his former best friend. A year later, Fran Connell married Ronald Ratkin in a ceremony at Wrigley Field. Somehow, Ratkin arranged for Chicago Cubs catcher Jody Davis to receive a pitch that Ratkin threw from the mound to commence the proceedings. It bounced twice before reaching Davis's mitt behind home plate. Pretending that he'd thrown a strike, the groom brushed off his tuxedo and walked toward his bride in center field.

CHAPTER 7

Not long after the Ratkins married, Albert Knight found love again. He first met Catherine Swift at a staff meeting for what he told the group was the firm's most important case. He paid her little notice; she was a junior legal assistant and he was one of Charles Hopkins's principal lieutenants. But she could see he was going places and the ride could be interesting.

When the case ended several months later, they met again at one of M&S's famous victory parties. In earlier days, firm leaders reserved such celebrations for unambiguous wins—usually favorable jury verdicts after a long trial. That yielded to a time when the firm joke became that there were only two categories of client outcomes: wins and developments. The correct spin could transform just about any development into an excuse for a celebration among those who'd worked on the matter. Even settlements that put a client on the brink of extinction justified one final bash. After all, the firm had a bankruptcy group, too.

Nationally renowned trial lawyer Sam Wilson guided the partnership through this era. He'd risen to the top of the firm and, for all practical purposes, ran the place. As its reputation soared to unprecedented heights on the wings of his victories, he urged his fellow partners to maintain equal parts of confidence, pride, and humility in the face of their shared success. His most frequent forum was the monthly luncheons for all litigators, but he said the same thing at firmwide partnership meetings over which he presided. His essential message remained constant:

"It's all right for us to take pride as we review regularly our accomplishments for our clients, as long as people around here don't start believing their own b.s. We're a collection of great attorneys. I happen to believe that we're unique in ways that make us the best trial lawyers in the country. That's because we have a depth of talent that others don't. But none of us should kid ourselves. There are a lot of fine lawyers out there. We're not as special as some people around here think they—or we—are."

Legal assistants, including Catherine Swift, did not attend those lawyers-only luncheons and partnership meetings, but everyone involved in a case was present for its victory party. Joining M&S directly from a six-month specialized training program, Swift was a paralegal, as they were then called. An earlier two years at the University of Wisconsin–Madison had made her far more worldly than most of the male lawyers at Michelman, especially the younger ones. As a group, they were more intelligent than their age peers, but they lagged far behind in all measures of social development. Catherine Swift thought Albert Knight could have been a poster child for them.

When the stunning dark-haired twenty-three-year-old encountered him at the party celebrating the successful settlement of the large case on which they'd worked, she'd already formed her plan. That's why she entered the evening's festivities adorned in a tight black dress suit, her five-foot-four-inch frame perched on classic high heels. After flirting with him over drinks for an hour in the firm's conference center, she looked at her watch with feigned surprise over missing her train to the northern suburbs.

"Where do you live?" Knight asked.

"Evanston, with a roommate."

"I'm heading that way."

He was lying, and she knew it; he lived in the opposite direction. But they also knew that she was stretching the truth, too. Her Metra north line train ran regularly until midnight, still several hours away.

"Would you like a ride home?" he continued the charade.

"I can take a cab," she protested, hoping she wasn't overplaying her hand. Albert Knight was difficult to read in this situation. If he called her bluff, her gambit would fail. He seemed so tentative, almost shy compared to the confident attorney she'd first seen run a staff meeting on a big case. He hadn't noticed her then, but at that moment he became a marked man.

"No trouble at all. I was about to leave, too. My car's in the building garage. Let's go."

They took the elevator to the lobby, where they walked to another elevator that took them to the reserved M&S area of the garage. As they entered the second elevator, she slipped off the top of her two-piece suit to reveal a translucent white blouse with several strategically open buttons. He couldn't resist a quick glance in their direction. Once they reached the M&S parking level, he guided her to a remote corner location. She might have guessed that he chose that spot to avoid dents and dings on his new four-door Mercedes sedan. His recent bonus had gone toward its down payment.

As they made their way to the car located between two foundation pillars for the building, her hand brushed against his. He didn't respond, so she wasn't sure he'd even noticed. He could be impervious, oblivious, or frightened, she thought. As he opened the front passenger door, she used the proximity of a concrete post as an excuse to squeeze her way around him so that her breasts grazed slightly against his back. Completing the maneuver as she circled him, she made sure her right one pressed against his left arm in a way that even he could not ignore.

Blushing with embarrassment, he apologized, "Excuse me."

She could see his hand tremble. Remarkable, she thought. This thirty-year-old man obviously has no idea how to make a move on a girl, or what to do when a girl makes one on him.

"My fault," she said, reaching for his hand. "It was a tighter fit than I realized. I shouldn't have tried to get around you like that."

Knight raced around the front of the car, opened his door, and slid behind the wheel. He fumbled for his keys, accidentally dropping them to the floor on her side of the car. She took control, reaching down to pick them up with her right hand while putting her left hand on Knight's right thigh.

She did that for balance, he thought.

She made an unsuccessful attempt to reach the keys while tightening her grip on his thigh. After what seemed like ten minutes but could not have been longer than fifteen seconds, she lifted the keys in her right hand and exclaimed, "Got 'em!"

She wasn't kidding about that, he thought. As she handed him the keys, they both realized that her left hand was still squeezing his right thigh. He placed his hand on hers and decided to take a chance, leaning toward her in what became a much longer kiss than he'd expected.

"How's the backseat?" she mumbled when he came up for air. He'd kissed her so hard that the inside of her lower lip was bleeding slightly. He didn't get out much, she concluded.

"The what?" Knight asked.

"The backseat. I'd like to see what the backseat is like."

Catherine Swift knew her way around the backseat of a car. She'd just never found herself in a big black

Mercedes like Knight's. The awkward encounter on the car's handcrafted leather took four minutes. Mercifully brief, Swift thought. After a six-month courtship, Albert Knight married Catherine Swift at her parents' summer home on Wisconsin's Trout Lake.

CHAPTER 8

"Congratulations," forty-one-year-old Charles Hopkins told Ratkin and Knight in identical, separate conversations six years to the day after the two had joined Michelman & Samson. "You're a non-equity partner, which means that even though you don't participate in the firm's profits, you're self-employed as far as the Internal Revenue Service is concerned. Starting in January, you'll receive what is called a partner draw, but it's really a salary. Don't spend the final associate bonus that we'll be giving you in December because you'll need it to pay your estimated quarterly taxes in April. Those will go up because you now get to pay both the employer's and employee's share of your social security taxes. So consider the immediate hit you'll be taking in cash flow as the price of trying to get where we big boys play—equity partnership."

Only Hopkins thought his comments about M&S's two-tiered partnership were humorous, but Albert Knight laughed anyway. After all, Charles O. Hopkins III had just become the Exec Com's newest member, along with his friend and corporate partner John Merritt, who was two years younger. Everyone in the firm knew that they comprised the next generation of Michelman & Samson's leadership. Sam Wilson himself had handpicked Hopkins and Merritt for that role.

*   *   *

From the time Charles Hopkins and John Merritt had been senior associates, Sam Wilson had hosted regular lunches with them. At least once a month, he solicited their views as future firm leaders whom he'd first identified when they were in their late twenties. They, in turn, cherished these private opportunities to commune with M&S's untitled but unquestioned leader. Always friendly and respectful, the meetings produced intergenerational consensus on important issues facing the firm. With Wilson's unflagging support, both men had advanced to the Exec Com by the time they all met in the mid-1980s to consider a new and controversial survey of large law firms, one of which was Michelman & Samson.

"This can lead to no good," Wilson began as the three men dined at the University Club. They were discussing whether the firm should cooperate with the editors of a relatively new legal magazine, *American Lawyer,* who were soliciting detailed financial information from the nation's largest law firms. "We're a private partnership. We don't have to supply anyone with anything about how we run our business."

"But our partners make more money than most partners in other firms," Merritt responded as he picked up his glass of iced tea. No one had ever seen him drink alcohol; only members of his immediate family knew that he rarely missed the regular Alcoholics Anonymous meetings that he began attending as a first-year law student. "This listing will provide a data point. Recruiting can use it to help us get the best people."

"Nonsense," Wilson replied. "Starting salaries for all associates in big firms are identical in each city. If law school graduates come here for the money that they hope to make as equity partners someday, they're coming for the wrong reason because we all know most of them will never get there. Even in a strong class, what percentage of incoming associates make it that far—one in three or four?"

"In New York, it's more like one in ten," Hopkins observed as he sipped his Johnnie Walker Black. "That's why the partners there make more than we do. The good news for us is that we get a lot of top recruits who don't like what those odds say about the working environment of the New York shops. But that's beside the point. Other top firms are providing their profits numbers. We'll be left hanging alone if we don't cooperate. It will put us at a competitive disadvantage."

"How?" Wilson replied. "Merritt just told you what everybody already assumes about us—namely, that we make plenty of money and more than most. What's the purpose of greater specificity? The firms that cooperate will be hanging themselves. Whose interest is served if we publish our partner earnings? Partner egos because they can push out their chests and brag to their friends? That's no reason to do this. Clients who will become angry when they discover we're making more than the general counsels who hire us and, in some cases, more than their CEOs? That's a reason not to do it. Prospective associates who think they should join M&S because they'll get rich? Give me a break."

"I don't see how we can avoid it," Merritt continued. "The world is proceeding in a single irreversible direction: disclosure of information, informed choice, deferring to efficient market results. It's all part of the Reagan revolution, and you can't fight it."

"Why not? John, you spend your days advising clients who have to deal with SEC disclosure rules and issues because they are public companies with no choice in the matter. We're private, and now we're thinking about volunteering our most sensitive information. Once upon a time, people didn't even mention their incomes in polite company. Now we're supposed to put it out there in a legal rag for all the world to see?"

"The 'once upon a time' that you're talking about is slipping away, Sam," said Hopkins. "It's a new world of free and competitive markets."

"You think the select group of big firms like ours functions in a free and competitive market? Don't kid yourself. We're an oligopoly with pricing power. We've convinced clients that our top attorneys from the best schools are a limited commodity that deserves to command premium rates. Part of our mystique lies in the fact that no one knows for sure how much we make, just that it's a lot."

"So what's wrong with confirming their suspicions?" Merritt offered.

"Because you don't know where it will lead, and neither do I. But I'm pretty sure the widespread awareness of such detailed information won't bring out the best in any of us. It could open up a Pandora's box of behavioral consequences. None of us will be able to close it."

Wilson broke the tension with a return to his indefatigable sense of humor.

"More importantly, don't either of you come crying to me when your relatives read about your wealth and invite you to share it with them."

All three laughed, but Hopkins and Merritt exchanged knowing glances. For the first time since joining the Exec Com, they were going to vote against their mentor's position. Two days later, Wilson suffered a rare defeat when the Exec Com rejected his plea for continued privacy with respect to M&S's financial performance.

So it was that the *American Lawyer* breached the previously impregnable wall of secrecy that Michelman & Samson had erected to protect its financial results from public scrutiny for half a century. Like other firms following suit, the voluntary behavior made the resulting longer-term wounds self-inflicted. For the first time, all lawyers in what was then the *Am Law* 50—the nation's biggest firms—learned what their competitors were earning.

At the first Exec Com meeting after the story's publication, Hopkins and Merritt proudly observed that M&S fared well in the first survey, placing fifteenth with average profits per equity partner of $350,000. The top-rated firm reported more than double that amount; the fiftieth came in at $170,000. Clearly, Wilson had missed this one, the other members of the Exec Com concluded. What could possibly go wrong with the simple act of providing the market with better information?

As first-year non-equity partners, Ratkin and Knight earned $100,000 annually, but the now public information allowed them to understand more clearly than ever the stakes in the race to the next level. To the outside world, both men and many like them were partners; to the world inside M&S, they were still hired hands in a leverage calculation that classified them as employees. Everyone knew that not all of the new M&S non-equity partners would advance to equity participation in the firm three or four years later, but the historical odds of one-in-three weren't bad.

*　　　　　　*　　　　　　*

Catherine Knight swooned at the opulence as the firm's partners and their spouses or significant others gathered in the Board of Trade Room at the Chicago Art Institute for the Ratkins' and Knights' first Michelman & Samson formal dinner dance. The men wore tuxedos; the women, formal gowns. As they finished dessert, Sam Wilson offered biographical summaries to introduce each of the new partners.

"Albert Knight has been the most surprising associate Michelman & Samson has ever hired," Wilson began. "The first graduate of his law school to become a partner in this firm, he's living proof that there can be diamonds in any rough. He's certainly established himself around here as the 'go-to' person—that is, if you're looking for someone to 'go to' when you're in the office on any Sunday morning, Christmas Eve, Thanksgiving, Yom Kippur, New Year's Day, Labor Day, Memorial Day . . ."

The room erupted in laughter, although Knight didn't find the line particularly humorous.

"I kid Albert because I love him," Wilson continued. "In some ways, he's been like a son—the one who ignored my plea that he *not* go to law school."

Another laugh line at my expense, Knight thought. But Wilson soon redeemed himself.

"I can say without equivocation that I look forward to the day when Albert Knight's efforts will be funding my retirement checks from this firm," Wilson concluded. "He's a keeper. He's the best of what M&S should always be: committed to our common mission of excellence in the service of our clients; aware of his calling to a noble profession; keenly sensitive to the fiduciary duties that go with being a partner; and firmly resolved to leave the firm better than he found it. Albert Knight, please stand and accept a well-deserved round of applause and acceptance from your new family."

As he sat down, Knight realized that Wilson wasn't really describing him. Rather, he was exhorting the partnership to help Wilson hold unstable ground that was shifting beneath his feet. Hoping that Knight and his contemporaries would join his crusade, Wilson was offering a mission and a map. But Knight wasn't sure he wanted what Wilson wanted for him or the firm because that would require suppressing his own competitive impulses. If someone else was higher, Knight's instinctive goal had always been to match and then surpass that person. There was first place and everyone else. That ethic described Michelman & Samson's essence, its culture, its core, didn't it?

Wilson then introduced Ratkin. "Ronald Ratkin graduated at the top of his Columbia Law School class," Wilson began. "He had to be at the top because otherwise he wouldn't have been able to see over the rest of his classmates."

The laughter began anew.

"I know people have said that good things come in small packages. When I think of Ronald, several other half-pints come immediately to mind: Napoleon, Harry Houdini, Jimmy Hoffa, Benito Mussolini. Come to think of it, Ratkin shares qualities of character with several of these remarkable men, although Mussolini was a lot taller. He was five-foot-six . . ."

The crowd roared, but Knight heard the special meaning embedded in Wilson's comments. Napoleon was a megalomaniac; Houdini made a career out of illusion; Hoffa believed any means justified his desired ends; Mussolini's countrymen eventually lynched him. Knight hoped Ratkin understood the knife that Wilson was cleverly sticking into his former friend and now mortal enemy. But then Wilson let Ratkin off the hook as he ended his remarks.

"But say what you will about Ronald Ratkin," Wilson concluded. "He gets the job done. As an associate, he's tried more cases than most of the litigation partners in this room. He charms juries in ways I've never seen. We have to keep him challenged; we have to keep him happy; and we have to keep him from ever becoming what he would call a free agent because I, for one, never want to enter a courtroom and find him representing the other side. Ronald Ratkin, please rise and accept your welcoming ovation into the M&S family."

There it was again, Knight thought. At the end of every introduction, Wilson asked each new partner to accept his place not only in the partnership but also in the family it was. That sentiment captured the feeling Knight had possessed seven years earlier during his on-campus interview for a summer associate job. Two M&S partners, including Sam Wilson, first spoke with him for twenty minutes before extending an invitation for another round of questioning in Chicago. The firm was a little smaller then—about one hundred and fifty attorneys compared to the two hundred it now numbered as he made non-equity partner. But it was still a family. If all went well, they'd spend more time with each other than with their respective spouses and children.

*   *   *

After the formalities of the evening ended, the band started playing and the dance floor became crowded. Catherine Knight had watched the scene for twenty minutes before seeking her husband's attention.

"That's the oddest thing I've ever seen," she said.

"What do you think is odd?" Knight asked his new bride as she fixed her gaze on Fran and Ronald Ratkin.

"Take a look at the short guy and the blonde on his arm. Watch what happens," she said.

Catherine didn't know about Knight's tortured history with Fran and Ronald Ratkin. But when she identified them as the short guy and the blonde, he knew without looking that they were the subjects of his wife's observations. He scanned the dance floor to locate the Ratkins. As they danced, she whispered something in his ear. As soon as the music stopped, he walked over to a senior partner and his wife, chatted briefly, and began dancing with that senior partner's wife when the band resumed. When that song ended, he returned to Fran, who had gone back to their assigned dinner table. After she again spoke to him quietly, he rose and went to dance with the wife of a different senior partner.

"That woman is telling her date, or whoever he is, who to dance with," Catherine laughed. "It's unbelievable. She's telling him how to work the room!"

"I don't want to discuss them," he said.

"No, wait, Albie. Here's what you have to do. You have to go dance with her, whoever she is. Go over there, introduce yourself, and tell her that you'd like to dance with her."

Knight could feel his shirt dampen as beads of perspiration formed on his forehead.

"No. That's a bad idea. I shouldn't do that."

"Please, Albie. Please do it for me. Come on, have some fun. Play with her mind. She's nice looking. It won't be that hard for you to fake having a good time. You could even try flirting with her a little bit. She's too comfortable right now. You need to shake her up."

If only Catherine had a clue, Knight thought.

Catherine knew her husband had no idea how to flirt with a woman, but she thought her suggestion might flatter him. She had no concern that the blonde was any threat. Against his better judgment, Knight honored his wife's request and walked slowly in the direction of Fran Ratkin's table. They had not spoken in three years.

"Hello, Fran," Knight began nervously.

"Why Albert, how nice to see you," Fran said coolly while remaining seated. "How have you been?"

"Why don't we take a spin on the dance floor, and I'll tell you all about it," he said with an uncharacteristic flair that surprised even him.

Visibly stunned, Fran knew that she had to respond in a socially appropriate manner, which meant accepting Knight's invitation.

"Why not?" she said, rising from her chair.

Knight cast a quick glance toward Catherine, who gave him a wink and two thumbs up. He couldn't believe the scene.

The two made their way to the edge of the dance floor as the band finished its cover of "Sweet Caroline." After they stood in painful silence for a few seconds, "Yesterday" began oozing from the speakers. The song's symbolism was arresting, Knight thought. There was no turning back now.

He put his right palm at Fran's waist, maintaining a safe distance as he held her raised hand in a formal position. As she pulled herself closer to him, he remembered why he'd loved her.

"So, what were you going to fill me in on?" Fran asked. "I see you have a date."

"She's my wife, Fran."

"How wonderful for you. She has a lovely frock and seems marvelously pedestrian. I assume you'll introduce us."

"I don't think that would be a good idea."

"Why not? I don't bite."

Oh, yes, you do, Knight thought.

"Maybe some other time," he answered.

"However you want it," she said. Knight wondered whether she had intended the double entendre. But as her body moved closer to his, her meaning was becoming clear.

"I've never stopped loving you, Albert," she whispered in his ear. "I can still be yours, if you want me."

"I'm taken," he whispered back sternly, "and so are you."

"Details," she grumbled before erupting in a cackle of false laughter.

When the song ended, he escorted Fran back to her seat and returned to his table, where Catherine was smiling. Obliviously dancing with yet another senior partner's wife, Ronald Ratkin hadn't even noticed his wife's adventure with his former friend.

"That was great," Catherine said with pride to her husband. "You totally knocked her off her game."

Sure, I did, Knight thought. Sure, I did.

CHAPTER 9

After their reunion dance together, Albert Knight tried to push Fran Connell out of his thoughts. His antidote was an endless workday that persisted through every evening and weekend. Developing technology aided and abetted his effort. His only relief came at day's end—from a bottle of Tanqueray combined with just the right amount of tonic water.

During his early years as an attorney, even Knight's minor revisions to a document required his secretary to retype it completely on her IBM Selectric typewriter. Then came word processing, a special department of former secretaries who used computers and bulky video screens to take especially lengthy documents, make requested changes, and turn a job around in hours. A few years later, that department began to disappear as the firm equipped all secretaries with desktop word processing equipment and, eventually, computers. Everything happened more quickly, leaving Knight less time for dangerous introspection.

Paralleling innovations in the tools generating his written work product, a new phone system permitted callers to leave audio messages that Knight could access from outside the office. The concept of a working vacation took on new meaning, which is to say that the vacation part disappeared. Finally, quantum leaps in technological innovation fueled any workaholic's predilections: attorney desktop computers, laptops, e-mail, and cell phones. What others saw as a prescription for a miserable life fed every beast within him.

More hours brought more money—the only measure of his relative worth and competitive standing. But clients became a two-edged sword. While countering certain of his insecurities, they created new anxieties revolving around fears that they might someday leave him for another lawyer. One thing was clear: the ceaseless intellectual and physical demands of his job enabled him to avoid the distractions of life, one of which was Fran Ratkin.

*　　　　*　　　　*

Sam Wilson occasionally drew Knight away from his own propensities.

"The law is a noble profession," Wilson said as they worked together while Knight was a non-equity partner. "But it will also suck the life out of you. If you don't draw lines separating your work from everything else, no one else will draw them for you. The easiest thing for any lawyer to do—especially in a place like M&S—is bill another hour. Once you get on that treadmill, it's hard to get off."

Knight considered Wilson's advice but ultimately opted in favor of Charles Hopkins's irresistible career opportunities that took him in a different direction. A new client, a big case, and the prospect of advancement conspired to fuel ambition. Ever the pragmatist, Knight also understood that Hopkins's enticing invitations to work with him were really the velvet glove adorning an iron fist. Stated simply, no one in the litigation department ever said no to Charles O. Hopkins III, M&S's newest prodigy.

Before he realized what had happened, Knight had reverted to twelve-hour workdays. He knew exactly how

Sisyphus felt, with one important difference. Knight never minded the tumble back down the mountain because the promise of more money and the prospect that he, too, might someday join the Exec Com awaited. By the time each of Hopkins's great opportunities ended, Knight was always physically and psychologically exhausted. Invariably, he returned to Wilson for sustenance. The beacon, as Knight liked to call him, never dimmed.

* * *

After ten years at the firm, Knight and Ratkin became equity partners. At the time, annual equity partner evaluations for litigators focused on a few self-evident criteria: trials won or lost, new cases brought into the firm, and younger lawyers mentored. Just as Wilson had said at Knight's first partner dinner-dance, M&S attorneys seemed united in their common mission: excellence in the delivery of legal services to firm clients. Whatever their personal disagreements, Knight and Ratkin felt part of a special Michelman & Samson family. Like all families, disagreements at times led to periodic dysfunction. But as a firm, the M&S boat moved forward as all of its oarsmen rowed in the same general direction.

"A good law firm is a circle," Wilson often told Hopkins and Merritt as their University Club lunches together continued. "Top lawyers get great results for their clients; that attracts more clients with interesting and challenging problems; that enables us to recruit the best and brightest lawyers from the nation's top law schools. Profits become the by-product of the approach—but not its central purpose."

"You're right, Sam," Hopkins agreed. "It's all about quality lawyers doing quality work. Attorneys here should never focus on anything else."

"No argument from me," Merritt echoed. "But you have to admit that it's nice to know that our partners on average make more money than almost every other firm's."

"To be honest," Wilson replied, "I think it's actually destabilizing. When dollars alone become the coin of the realm, institutions like ours change—and not always for the better. And I worry about retaining top people who make enough money to retire early. That's not a good thing for the firm."

Hopkins and Merritt exchanged knowing glances in the realization that, with his own words, Sam Wilson had unwittingly confirmed that his days as Michelman & Samson's dominant player were coming to an end. How could too much money be a bad thing for anyone?

*   *   *

The final bell began to toll for Wilson when his close friend, then forty-eight-year-old John Merritt, led a corporate department rebellion while Knight and Ratkin were still working their way up the equity partner ranks. Threatening to take his clients, billings, and attorneys with him, he began the battle with an address to a frightened Exec Com. Michelman & Samson had lost partners before, but never an entire practice group. Merritt's power play in the confidential Exec Com session became the worst-kept secret in the firm. His goal was to increase the power that he and his practice group wielded. That meant increasing his fellow corporate transactional partners' equity stake.

"As a group, the firm's litigation partners receive a share of firm profits that is disproportionately high compared to the revenues they bring in," Merritt told the Exec Com. "Only a fundamental realignment of the equity partnership will restore fairness."

"How are you proposing that we measure fairness?" Wilson asked him slowly and deliberately as the other members of the committee, including Hopkins, watched the titanic battle commence.

"Objectively. Every partner's self-review memorandum that is now used as the common baseline for compensation discussions should also require a detailed analysis of billings, hours, and leverage, meaning the number of non-equity attorneys working for them. This purely objective data would define each attorney's contribution to the firm. His or her appropriate equity allocation would follow as a matter of simple arithmetic calculation."

"Objectively, you say. And who gets credit for what billings?" Wilson asked.

"Presumed credit would go to the attorney who sends the client the bill."

"So as an example, let's take the large case that I just won for your corporate client. That would be credited to you because you sent out the bill, even though I tried the case with a team of M&S litigators and you didn't devote five minutes to it, right?"

"I said 'presumed credit,' Sam," Merritt believed his lawyerly nuance highlighted the flaw implicit in Wilson's criticism.

"Yes, presumed credit, and in the example I just gave, the burden will be on me to rebut the presumption in your favor. Otherwise, I'll get only as much credit as you deem appropriate for the millions of dollars in billings on a case I tried, right?"

"Correct."

"In this new system of yours, the firm's equity partners would compete against each other for billing credit, right?"

"Yes. Competition is always good."

"Do you compete with the members of your own family, John?"

"Of course not, but M&S isn't a family. It's a business."

"We can debate another day what M&S has become and what it should be, but we can agree that this new process you're proposing will take a lot of time and effort on the part of the firm's most senior partners to sort out, correct?"

"You know, Sam, I'm not a hostile witness in one of your courtroom cross-examinations."

"Do I seem hostile?" Wilson said with his disarming grin. "I'm just asking questions in an effort to understand what you're asking all of us to approve, John. You don't have a problem with that, do you?"

"No, not at all."

"Then how about telling us all whether you agree that this new system of yours, with partners competing against each other over who should get credit for what, will take a lot of time and effort to sort out."

"It should take no more time than the current system. In fact, because my proposal relies on objective data, it will probably take less time. Numbers don't lie, Sam."

"Did you ever hear the phrase 'lies, damn lies, and statistics'? Someone has to analyze all of that so-called objective data, right?"

"Sure. You're quoting Mark Twain. He wasn't a businessman."

"Someone has to resolve partners' competing claims to particular clients and billings, right?"

"Of course."

"And in our growing equity partnership, it's going to take someone or a group of someones a long time to do all that, isn't it, John?"

"What's your point, Sam? That's part of what we on the Exec Com have to do in fulfilling our responsibilities to award appropriate compensation, however we do it."

"Yes, it's the Exec Com that has the final say, isn't it? And, at the end of the day, the decisions of the Exec Com become final, binding, and non-appealable, don't they, John?"

"Sure. The buck stops here."

"And when there are disputes between two of our partners over billing credit, and one is on the Exec Com and the other isn't, who do you think is going to win? The person outside this room, or one of us?"

Merritt paused. Everyone on the Exec Com knew that there was only one obvious answer to Wilson's question, but Merritt refused to give it as he shifted in his chair and reached for his glass of iced tea. "I would hope that we would always operate fairly and in good faith, regardless of whether an affected partner sits in this room with us when such decisions are made."

"Fairly and in good faith like a family would but not necessarily as a business would, right, John?"

"I think most businesses operate fairly and in good faith."

"You think most businesses look past the numbers on their balance sheets when it comes to making decisions? Is that what they taught you in business school when you were getting your MBA?" Wilson's tone had become firmer. The smile was gone, and his eyes blazed.

"Well . . ."

"Well, what? You can't have it both ways, John. You can't say that the system you propose is better than the current one because it introduces supposedly objective data that fairly dictate all results but then reserve for yourself the position that some other concept of fairness and good faith can somehow save the day by trumping everything whenever it has to. Let me ask you a different question: as a billing partner for a client, what incentive do I have to introduce you or any other equity partner to my client, knowing that once I let your nose into my tent, I've invited controversy over my year-end compensation?"

"That's up to you, Sam. But if you can serve your clients with non-equity partners and associates, the firm's equity partner earnings will be greater because you'll be creating better leverage. Right now, we have three non-equity attorneys for every equity partner. Just imagine how earnings will soar if we can move that leverage number to four, five, or six!"

"So it's not about matching a firm's client with the best lawyer for the task, is it, John?"

"All of our lawyers are first-rate."

"In fact, under your system, none of our clients will be firm clients anymore, will they?"

"What do you mean?"

"Each equity partner will seek to control his or her own clients. What you're proposing makes that inevitable."

"I disagree."

"As a billing partner for a client, what incentive do I have to part with my billings to create smooth transitions to younger partners over time?"

"That's up to you, too."

"You say it's up to me, John, but your proposed compensation system is really telling me what to do, isn't it?"

"What do you mean?"

"Your economic incentives will lead every rational equity partner in this firm to fight hard to gain and retain every dollar of revenue that comes in. Rather than introduce clients to our best and brightest fellow partners, our lawyers will try to develop self-contained, portable practices. That's how they'll control billings; that's how they'll come to wield special prerogatives when it comes to promoting their people. It will undermine the meritocracy that we brag about. We'll all eat what we kill, along with whatever else we can successfully claim to have killed. And the people at the top—in this room—will always have the last word in making those determinations."

Wilson had made his point, but he continued.

"You're offering the false illusion of objectivity in return for a process that will increase acrimony within the partnership, undermine incentives for partner-like behavior, and exacerbate the infectious politics of our compensation and promotion decisions. The mission of the Exec Com should be to leave future generations with a firm that is better than the one we inherited, not to entrench ourselves in ways that undermine the very fabric of what it means to be a vibrant professional partnership. We should develop policies that encourage our fellow partners to regard themselves as trustees for the young people we recruit to this place, not to squeeze out of M&S for themselves every last dollar they can in any given year. Words can't describe the intensity with which I oppose your approach."

"I think words have described your feelings pretty well, Sam," Merritt said. He knew he had the votes to win, even though Wilson had bested him on the merits of the debate. Most members of the Exec Com feared John Merritt, but they feared losing his economic contribution to the firm even more. "I guess we'll have to agree to disagree."

Merritt then moved the conversation to different ground: "Michelman & Samson has to adapt to the new times. In all large law firms, the profession is becoming a bottom-line business. The *Am Law* 50 of ten years ago has grown to 100. Someday it will grow to 200. Every large firm in the United States measures itself by its average-profits-per-partner ranking on the *Am Law* list. Last year, we averaged $750,000. I think we all agree that more would be better. We have to make hay while the sun shines. The way to do that is to maximize revenues and increase leverage. We then have to divide the crop fairly according to who's contributing."

Wilson scanned the room, discouraged at the realization that Merritt's words resonated with the rest of the Exec Com. Refusing to make eye contact, Charles Hopkins pretended to look for something in his briefcase.

"Let me also say that I regard our requirements as non-negotiable. To remind everyone, there are three. First, there will be no new equity partners in litigation for the next two years. Two, thereafter, the litigation department will be allowed to make only four new equity partners per year for the foreseeable future."

"And what will happen to the remaining fifty non-equity litigation partners who will be up for equity partnership consideration in the next four years alone?" Like all great litigators conducting a cross-examination, Wilson asked only questions for which he already knew the answer.

"Forty-two of them won't make it," Merritt continued, "unless your department develops billings that warrant revisiting the issue. Or you can prune your ranks of current litigation partners to make room for others."

"You call that a business plan for a strong future?" Wilson muttered.

"There's one more requirement," Merritt persisted. "The entry-level compensation for all new equity partners will be lowered and their progress up the ranks from that level will be slowed. We don't need to pay new equity partners as much as they're getting. They can't go anywhere else and make what they're making here."

"None of us can," Wilson interjected. "But you've got yours, and you're damn well going to keep it, aren't you, John? That's what this whole thing is all about, isn't it?"

Merritt ignored him. "All of this will add fairness and precision to the review process as we transform our calculations to actual partner compensation each year. The newly proposed data collection process will facilitate each of these elements. The end result will be higher-quality lawyers in the equity partnership and greater wealth for all of us."

"Can we agree to delay voting on this until our next meeting?" Wilson concluded with disgust. Merritt thought he owed him that much, so he acquiesced.

*　　　　　　*　　　　　　*

Hopkins briefed his two protégés, Knight and Ratkin, an hour after the meeting ended. He solicited their views, but he already knew they'd stand with him on this and just about everything else.

"Sounds like Sam Wilson is tilting at windmills," Ratkin said with a grin after Hopkins described the remarkable Exec Com session. "Merritt's economic power makes his demands a done deal."

Hopkins closed his eyes, nodded, and smiled. The entire episode bothered Knight. Perhaps it was the tragedy of marginalizing a man who'd been such a dominant figure in the firm and who remained one of the leading lawyers in the profession. Or perhaps it was Knight's reluctance to voice disagreement with Hopkins and Ratkin as they celebrated the decline of Sam Wilson, a mentor who'd been a loyal friend to all of them.

*　　　　　　*　　　　　　*

Wilson knew that Merritt's threat to leave the firm was empty. His corporate group had ridden the litigation department's international reputation to great advantage. Without it, they would wander in the wilderness for years, if not forever. The consummate poker player, Wilson was willing to call their bluff. But he needed votes on the Exec Com that he knew he didn't have. His only hope was to go down in respectable defeat so he could still claim to represent a significant constituency within the firm. That meant persuading his protégé Charles Hopkins to side with him.

The night before the Executive Committee meeting at which a final decision on Merritt's demands would be made, Wilson urged Hopkins to resist. They met privately in Hopkins's corner office, where his longtime secretary, Helen Peterson, sat just outside his open door. Pretending to be invisible, she heard every word. Even in regular conversation, Hopkins's booming baritone carried far beyond his office. Obsessed with the significance of symbols, he had insisted that Wilson come to him. He poured himself a glass of ice water from a Waterford pitcher as Wilson sat across from his desk.

"Charles, put all the pieces together," began Wilson, who always marveled that nothing in Hopkins's office betrayed a hint of humanity. Lucite cubes memorializing case outcomes, leather-bound volumes of pleadings, and fine eighteenth-century artwork graced the walls and shelves. There was nothing to suggest that Hopkins had any existence beyond his work.

"Some law schools increasingly require that applicants have real-world experience before beginning their legal studies," he said. "So those new associates now come to us when they're in their late twenties. Six years later, even graduates who took the express path from college to law school won't become non-equity partners until they're in their early thirties. If we adopt Merritt's proposals, we'll soon see the day when fewer than ten percent of all new associates advance to equity partnership, and many will be forty years old when they get there. If, as Merritt wants, they then get equity increases only in the paltry maximum increments that he proposes as the new standard, no litigator will ever get to your level of equity participation in the firm."

Hopkins didn't care: "Maybe they shouldn't. I've worked hard to achieve my position in the firm. If someone else wants to match my success, then that person should expect to sacrifice as I have. Take a look at Albert Knight and Ronald Ratkin. They're doing well and will likely continue to progress."

"You're missing the point, Charles. Of course, you deserve all that you've received. But you did it under a compensation and promotion regime that will cease to exist if you go along with Merritt's proposal. Adopting his metrics view of the firm will result in fewer and less-powerful litigation equity partners. The handful who make it will wait longer to get there, and, once inside, they'll advance at a snail's pace. Knight and Ratkin would never be where they now are if this new system had been in place when they started. And neither would you."

"I disagree, Sam. We're a meritocracy. If deserving litigation equity partners warrant acceleration through the ranks, they'll get it, just as I did."

Wilson knew that further debate with Hopkins on the issue was pointless. Once he couched any position as the reasoned product of his own Horatio Alger narrative, Hopkins stopped listening. When he reached that point, he regarded himself as special in ways that no one else could be.

The next day, John Merritt's proposed revisions to the Michelman & Samson partnership review and promotion system passed the Exec Com with only a single dissenting vote. When he heard about it, Knight was sad for Wilson but more concerned with whether Wilson's setback would affect the progress of his own career.

*   *   *

The fateful Exec Com meeting became what Wilson forever called the MBA takeover of the firm. Merritt and his colleagues with those degrees accompanying their JDs had followed business school principles in developing what they called the firm's new metrics. Wilson received a harsh introduction to the new order three months later, when Hopkins formally proposed reducing Wilson's compensation for the year. Merritt had privately put the idea to Hopkins, who quickly warmed to it as a way to curry favor with Merritt and his corporate group.

"Your hours are down, and your billings have not kept pace with the firm's growing revenues," Hopkins said as he gave his aging mentor the bad news. As always, he forced Wilson to visit his office for the brief and unpleasant message that Helen Peterson overheard. "It's as simple as that." Shifting gears abruptly, he concluded the discussion. "Now, if you'll excuse me, I really need to get some 'strange.'"

Wilson knew that "strange" was Hopkins's code for sex with a woman he'd yet to meet. Before this evening ended, he'd find someone with whom he'd become intimately acquainted, and then he'd never see her again.

"So tell me," Wilson asked as he left Hopkins's office, "I've always been curious about something. When you find these women—the ones you call 'some strange'—and check into hotels with them, do you use a false name or what?"

"Better than that," Hopkins answered with a chuckle, "I use yours."

Sitting outside Hopkins's office, Helen Peterson pretended not to hear them.

CHAPTER 10

So it was that Sam Wilson's twenty-year tradition of hosting regular University Club lunches for Charles Hopkins and John Merritt came to an end. It was one thing to disagree over firm policy, as Wilson and Merritt periodically had over the years. Their friendship even weathered the storm that Merritt's threatened departure had created when he successfully pushed through the MBA takeover of the firm. But Hopkins went too far when he made it personal. Voting on firm policy was one thing; wielding the axe that sliced the compensation of a productive mentor was something else. That Hopkins made himself the bearer of the bad news was more than Wilson could stand.

Still, Wilson recognized at once the career slide that now lay ahead of him. Already sixty years old, he accelerated his planned exit from the firm by a few years. He'd always vowed not to hang around while the Exec Com severed his digits individually until he bled to death. The time had come for him to make good on that promise to himself. Shortly after his unpleasant session with Hopkins, he had lunch with John Merritt.

"You've won," Wilson began as they sat in the Chicago Club's main dining room. By then, he'd figured out that Merritt had persuaded Hopkins to be the point person for cutting back Wilson's compensation a month earlier. "I'm going to retire early. I want to have an orderly transition and an appropriate disengagement from the firm. I'll begin the transfer of my major client responsibilities next year and continue that process until I leave three years from now."

"That sounds agreeable to me," Merritt said as he lifted his glass of iced tea. "What about your compensation level during that period? Have you given any thought to that?"

Wilson knew that M&S corporate lawyers negotiated best when they faced a tough adversary. So he removed their most potent weapon: opposition.

"You and the Exec Com can make that determination," Wilson said. "You've already set it for the coming year. Whatever you decide beyond that will be fine with me. I'm sure you'll treat me fairly."

It was a bold move. Other retiring equity partners had negotiated detailed arrangements whereby their compensation declined slowly over as many years as they could squeeze out of the firm. Never had someone of Wilson's stature and equity stake put his fate so squarely in the hands of the Exec Com. His reasoning was simple, as he later explained to Knight.

"Here's the thing, Albert. They can do whatever they want to me, and there's nothing I can do about it anyway. So the best thing is to let go. When people approach retirement in this place, they often become unhappy. Why? Because they think the firm in some monolithic sense is screwing them on their way out. They become desperate to hang on to their positions because they had to sacrifice too much to get them in the first place. It's defined who they are. The whole process of transition to the next phase of life gets bound up with the loss of their identities as M&S equity partners. Humiliating cuts in pay during the final years of a career unnecessarily complicate the whole thing."

"But shouldn't you try to hang on and make as much as you can for as long as you can?" Knight asked.

"Why? My wife and I have lived well but relatively modestly. We have enough money for our needs. So what's the point?"

"But you and I both know that equity positions translate into power and respect. Below a certain level, you become irrelevant around here."

"You've fallen into the trap this place sets. I've always led the life I wanted to lead inside and outside the firm. As I enter my so-called golden years, am I really going to let my self-image turn on arbitrary determinations that a group of self-interested lawyers makes about me? I don't like most of them. I've lost respect for their politicized decisions. Why should I give them any power over my aging psyche?"

"It seems like a dangerous way to play it."

"Not really; it's liberating. When I say I don't care what they decide about my compensation for the next three years, I mean it. But that doesn't mean I'm without leverage in all of this, Albert. They have to worry about how happy or unhappy they want one of their reasonably accomplished alumni to be. They also know that I still get calls from headhunters looking for a seasoned veteran willing to accept big bucks to anchor a new Chicago office for some other big firm headquartered outside the city. Most members of the Exec Com are for sale to the highest bidder, so they think I am, too."

Wilson's analysis turned out to be correct. The Exec Com knew that whatever precedent it set for him could easily become the template for their treatment in the years ahead. His three-year package assured him a million dollars annually, far more generous than he'd expected. Undoubtedly hoping for a similar fate when their times came, they also wanted to keep him in tow. After a lifelong career as one of Michelman & Samson's top trial lawyers,

Sam Wilson was still in a position to write his own ticket with any competitor, even though he had no desire to do so.

* * *

Charles O. Hopkins III eagerly pursued the firm's new mission: running M&S as a short-term profit-maximizing business. Jettisoning Wilson, he tied his fate to Merritt and the other joint JD/MBA degree holders who ran the corporate group; in return, they elected him the Exec Com's first chairman. Thereafter, when they demanded a pound of flesh from litigation equity partners because distorted calculations continued to show the litigators as a group to be overcompensated relative to their corporate counterparts, Hopkins quickly obliged. As he threw others under the bus, he feathered his own nest and protected only a few of his favorites. Ratkin and Knight fared well; he left all others to fend for themselves, twisting in the wind.

Merritt's predictions of remarkable wealth for the survivors came true. When he and Hopkins had entered the equity partnership, the top lawyers at M&S made about three times more than he did. Thereafter, the size of that chasm more than doubled while the absolute dollars they all earned skyrocketed. Before long, entry into the Michelman & Samson equity partnership ranks assured million-dollar annual incomes to such winners.

Hopkins pulled up the ladder, especially in his practice area. The numbers told an unhappy story for most. Attorneys who survived to achieve a lower entry level of equity partnership waited years longer to get there. Then the path became slow, slippery, and uncertain. Eventually, those who found limited success became victims of the arithmetic that Wilson had described. The result: Ratkin and Knight were the only litigation members of their generation who held any possible hope of achieving Hopkins's rarified heights. There would be none among the generations following them.

Just as it should be, Chairman Hopkins often thought as he annually reviewed the growing list of casualties—younger attorneys he'd abandoned. Just as it should be. Ratkin and Knight, his favored sons, concurred.

CHAPTER 11

"It's a simple formula," Hopkins told the gathering of all equity partners at their first meeting where he presided as the firm's chairman. "The total hours all attorneys bill times the hourly rates charged generate our total revenues. Subtracting costs from those revenues results in our profits. If total attorney hours and hourly rates continue to rise as we keep our costs down, our profits will increase. If the firm maintains a strict limit on the number of new equity partners elected each year to share in that wealth, we in this room will continue to get richer."

Perennially thereafter, Knight and Ratkin listened as he repeated the marching orders for the new age.

"Bill your time promptly; send out your bills promptly; follow up on collections; prepare your clients for the next cycle of rate increases; and then prepare yourself to do it all over again," he concluded. "Because the firm reviews all equity partners annually, every year we are a new and different partnership."

*　　　*　　　*

The strategy applied to boom times and bust. It also followed the law of unintended consequences with respect to partner behavior. A month after the equity partners' meeting inaugurating Hopkins as the first chairman, Albert Knight received a call from a client he'd brought into the firm several years earlier.

"Albert, it's Phil," said the new general counsel of Edelwise. Phil McGinty had recently joined the company after learning that his career at M&S was over. For a decade, he'd worked exclusively for Ronald Ratkin, who then single-handedly killed McGinty's chances for promotion to equity partner. Knowing that McGinty's days at M&S were numbered and that Edelwise was looking for an in-house lawyer, Knight set up an interview with Edelwise's president, who hired McGinty on the spot.

"Here's the thing," McGinty continued his conversation with Knight. "I just received a call from Edelwise's chairman, Joshua Egan, who told me that he went to high school with Ron Ratkin—sorry—Ronald Ratkin. He said that he wants to involve him in our cases."

An adrenaline surge caused Knight's hands to tremble.

"I don't like it one bit, but when the chairman says I have to involve someone in a case, I have no choice," McGinty complained.

"What about the president? How does he feel about this? After all, I've bailed Edelwise's chestnuts out of the fire more than once. That's why your president listened to me when I told him you were the best person for the general counsel job. Ronald Ratkin hasn't done anything to help you, that's for sure." Knight hoped that a twinge of guilt might give McGinty the guts to push back on Ratkin's client grab.

"I know, Al. I hate it. But I'm really caught in the middle on this one. I don't see how I can refuse a direct request from the chairman. He also demanded that I make sure our M&S legal bills come from Ratkin. He said something about Ratkin enjoying a greater status at your firm and that we'd be better off with him as the billing attorney. I'm truly sorry about this. Really, I am. I know how Michelman works. I know that losing the Edelwise billings will cost you money at the end of the year. I feel helpless."

"I understand, and I'll start the process. But understand one thing, Phil: I'm no longer Edelwise's lawyer. If Ratkin wants to run the show, that's fine. He'll run it. But I'm not a second-stringer on this team or anywhere else. The transition will be smooth. You and I know Ratkin is a talented lawyer. All of this saddens me at many levels, but in the end, Ratkin will be more your problem than mine. Good-bye, Phil."

"Wait, Al . . ."

Knight hung up the phone as McGinty struggled to continue his apologetic groveling.

CHAPTER 12

It was not the worst day that Albert Knight had ever spent at the office, but it was right up there. He'd just lost a $5 million client to the man he hated most in the firm and, perhaps, the world. There was one small consolation: the way Ratkin staffed and billed clients, Edelwise's legal fees next year would double for about the same amount of work. He knew as much from the way Ratkin threw billable bodies at every problem.

So as the law firm benefited from Ratkin's manipulation, Edelwise itself would pay the price. Although corporate clients increasingly required their outside law firms to develop and adhere to budgets for legal fees, the superficial appeal of such targets yielded to their attorneys' expressed views of unbending and unpredictable reality. How much should a company incur to prosecute or defend a major case? No one really knew because every lawsuit was unique; litigation expense comparisons were rarely meaningful. Outcomes mattered most, and Ratkin had the talent to win the vast majority of his cases. No general counsel wanted to report defeat to his management. In such a regime, only the company's shareholders and customers bore the true burden of excessive fees, and they were in no position to realize it.

Prior to the MBA takeover, Knight had used a different approach, priding himself on lean staffing that he'd learned from Sam Wilson.

"Fiduciary duty means treating a client's money as if it were your own," Wilson often told younger attorneys at monthly luncheons of all litigators. "Consider whether the activity you contemplate will really add value. If it won't, don't do it."

Knight had taken that admonition seriously, but implementation required a confidence that he sometimes lacked. When it came to making tough decisions about cost-effectiveness in the deployment of M&S's legal manpower for his clients, he wasn't as bad as Ratkin, but he wasn't as good as Wilson, either. How could any lawyer decide whether another hour or two editing a brief would be a waste of time? Didn't it make sense to do everything possible to win every motion in every case? Shouldn't he explore every potential path to victory? Didn't his obligations as an attorney require that he leave no stone unturned? Pick up every rusty nail? If he didn't, how could he be certain that he hadn't missed something important?

Before the MBA takeover, Knight regularly wrestled with these questions in an effort to do the right thing by Edelwise and his other clients. After that watershed event, the questions themselves disappeared. More billable hours for the firm meant ever-higher status on the *Am Law* 100's annual profits-per-partner list. Moving up those ranks had become Michelman & Samson's principal mission. When in doubt, assemble more underlings and keep them busy. Ratkin had just been ahead of the curve on that one.

Meanwhile, Knight resigned himself to the economic hit that the Exec Com would deliver at his next compensation review. It would note his loss of client revenues and penalize him accordingly. The MBA takeover had made Michelman & Samson an unforgiving place, even when a partner's only sin was the loss of billings as a result of another partner's scheme. In fact, Ratkin's ploy seemed to work out particularly well for him. He soon was named the newest member of the Exec Com. Hopkins and Merritt had become M&S kingmakers, just as Sam Wilson had originally planned.

*   *   *

As always when faced with major setbacks, Knight tried to put things into perspective as he walked to the special spot on the M&S level of the parking garage where he still kept his most recent black Mercedes sedan between two of the building's foundation columns. He'd been married to the same woman for more than ten years. He had tried to live a frugal life, but Catherine decided that the way to make her husband pay for his inattentiveness was to spend his money faster than he could earn it. As he slid behind the wheel, he noticed a small sheet of paper under his windshield wiper. He assumed it was another flyer for the garage car wash that he never used. He reached around and grabbed the note. The handwriting looked familiar:

"Hey, tall, dark, and handsome, I know it's been a long time, but I still miss you. Call me. Fran."

He looked around, not knowing whether he should expect to see her or someone else who might reveal his new secret: he had an admirer. Once the paranoid impulse passed, he focused on the perfect symmetry of his day. As Ronald Ratkin was stealing a client, Ratkin's wife was giving herself away. He got out of the car, walked to a nearby trash bin, and tore the note into tiny pieces to prevent its reconstruction. He thought about eating the fragments but decided that was unnecessary. Such peculiar things happened to him in that solitary parking spot on the M&S level of the garage.

CHAPTER 13

Most evenings, Knight worked late at the office, rarely getting home before ten o'clock. If he planned to arrive before eight when Catherine was in town, he'd call ahead to tell her so they could dine together. He didn't know how she filled her days, and he never asked about her nights. They also had established a routine of Saturday evening dates with friends involving the opera, theater, or client dinners. They were happiest together in the company of others; it made playing their respective roles easier.

On the rare nights that he and Catherine were both home for dinner, Knight ate quickly so he could resume work in his large oak-paneled den. For the short time that the couple sat at opposite ends of a formal antique mahogany dining table, they barely exchanged a word. The marriage had been respectful but ultimately unrewarding for both.

Catherine had always thought she wanted to marry a rich professional who could provide a life to which she dreamed of becoming accustomed. The first year of their marriage had gone well. Reluctantly, Knight had agreed to forsake his work in favor of a two-week honeymoon in Europe. But he kept hotel FAX machines humming day and night to keep up with him. The following year, she wanted to vacation in the Far East, and, once again, he billed time as if he'd never left the office. After that trip, his career trumped every request she made of him.

"I won't make equity partner unless I bill at least 2,500 hours a year," he explained to her. "That means working sixty-hour weeks. Then I have to maintain that pace if I want to advance in the equity partner ranks."

"So no one in your firm has a life?"

"We have a life, Catherine. Look around you. Look at our house. Look at our investment portfolio. Look at how we live."

Their purchase of a vacation home the year he made equity partner gave her new hope. Promising her the time she wanted and deserved, he said they'd spend long weekends there throughout the summer. Foolishly, she believed him, although their first and only trip there together told her everything she needed to know about how that experiment would end. As she drove the car, he sat in the passenger seat tapping away on his laptop computer. The vehicle and his typing stopped only for restroom breaks. Every year thereafter, she left for their summer home in May and returned in September, leaving Knight behind in Chicago and freeing him to work unfettered into the early-morning hours. She stayed busy, too—alternating her evenings with her private tennis instructor and the landscape architect.

She acquired all the accoutrements of a successful life: the big house in the suburbs, a new BMW sports car every three years, designer clothes, a country club membership, and the summer home. She filled her days in the company of like-minded girlfriends until they started having babies. Parenthood was not for her; the last thing she wanted or needed was a young version of Albert Knight. He wasn't a bad person, she concluded; just hopelessly dull and wedded to his job. She was convinced that the single moment of spontaneous excitement in his entire existence had occurred at the beginning of their relationship—the four-minute entanglement in the backseat of Knight's Mercedes. She couldn't get enough of that sort of thrill; for him, once was sufficient for a lifetime.

Catherine spent every December through March at a luxury resort in Palm Springs. Knight typically joined her there for three days at Christmas. Even after almost twenty years at M&S, he still found no rush matching that of a client who viewed him as indispensable. He couldn't bear the thought that another M&S partner might bring in a case that was properly his or, even worse after the MBA takeover, bill it.

"Better than sex," he'd tell his closest colleagues, who were following similar paths at the firm. Better, that is, until he decided to call Fran Ratkin a week after she'd left the note on his windshield.

* * *

"I got your note," he spoke haltingly on the phone in his Chicago office. "I was quite surprised, Fran."

"Albert, we need to talk. I made a terrible mistake, but I can't talk about it on the phone. Where can we meet?"

"What do you have in mind?"

"It can't be a public place."

"That leads me to think it has to be a public place."

"Come on, Albert, I really need to speak with you. How about the Four Seasons Hotel in two hours?"

"Are you kidding? My schedule is packed. I can't possibly get away that quickly."

"All right. How about when you're done with work tonight? Can you meet me then?"

"I suppose. Catherine is out of town for another three months, so it's not like anyone is holding dinner for me," he said, sensing how pathetic his life must have sounded to her.

Catherine's extended absence was the critical information she needed to prepare for their evening rendezvous. "I'll meet you in the lobby at ten o'clock tonight. I truly appreciate this, Albert."

"I'll see you then."

That evening, he reported as requested to the four-star Michigan Avenue hotel. Fran sat in an overstuffed chair in a remote corner. She looked as beautiful as he remembered.

"Hello, Fran."

"Albert, thank you so much for coming," she said while reaching for his extended right hand. "Please follow me."

She knew Knight would always respond to firm direction from a woman in charge. In that respect, he hadn't changed. Obediently, he accompanied her into the elevator that took them to the guest rooms.

"Where are we going?"

She brought her left index finger to her lips and then his. The doors opened at the fortieth floor, and she led him to a room she'd already reserved. She turned the knob, and they walked inside. He saw a bottle of Tanqueray waiting for him on the nightstand. She still remembered important details, Knight thought.

"Okay, I give up. I thought maybe you had a surprise birthday party planned for me," he said with ineffective sarcasm. "What's the deal?"

Fran removed her outer coat to reveal that, underneath, she was wearing items that only Victoria's Secret carried: a red push-up bra, lace panties, a garter belt, and fishnet stockings. She then threw herself at him in an embrace that he resisted for only a few seconds before melting in her arms.

"Oh, Albert, I made such a mistake," she moaned. "It should have been you. It should have been you . . ."

In the lobby below, a short man wearing a dark business suit and grey fedora sat in an overstuffed chair as he finished reading the *Chicago Daily Law Bulletin*. Chewing on an unlit cigar, he folded his newspaper, slid the cigar into the inner breast pocket of his coat, and walked into a private booth.

"Outside line, please," he said in a gravelly voice after picking up the house phone.

CHAPTER 14

As Fran Ratkin guided Albert Knight through the first of their biweekly Tuesday evenings at Chicago's Four Seasons Hotel, Ronald Ratkin familiarized himself with his newly acquired Edelwise cases. Knight considered the trade to be fair, although his nemesis had no awareness that he'd lost anything in his acquisition of the firm's large client. Both men had long ago forgotten about Daniel Schmidt, who'd advanced through the ranks of the SEC's enforcement division.

Schmidt's personal file of all media reports mentioning Edelwise or Ronald Ratkin had become voluminous. On the same evening that Fran Ratkin was reacquainting herself with Albert Knight, he sat at his office desk in Washington, D.C., reviewing the highlights to date:

1990: The start-up company began with venture capital that included an investment from an entity called M-S Direct Investment Fund IX.

1992: Edelwise announced technological breakthrough resulting in a pioneering anti-virus computer program.

1995: Edelwise issued its first public stock offering. Required SEC filings revealed that M-S Direct Investment Fund IX retained ten percent ownership interest through restricted stock. Separately, individual investors Charles Hopkins, Ronald Ratkin, Albert Knight, and three other specifically named Michelman & Samson partners each owned two percent. On its first day of trading, the stock doubled from an initial offering share price of five dollars to ten. Six months later, it was at twelve when senior management declared its first trading window. M-S Investment Fund IX sold its stock at that time, as did Albert Knight and all individual partners owning Edelwise stock, except for Charles Hopkins and Ronald Ratkin. Those two men bought more during the window period—a lot more.

"Hopkins and Ratkin have double downed on Edelwise," Schmidt muttered to himself. "They must have borrowed to make those purchases and leveraged themselves beyond any reasonable level. They've made a staggering gamble. Watch and wait . . . watch and wait . . ."

He picked up a pen and scribbled a note that he placed in the file: "Watch Edel insdr trds & trdg wndws, esp Hop and Rat."

*　　　*　　　*

Losing Edelwise as a client might have destroyed lesser men, but not Albert Knight. He redoubled his efforts at what the firm called client development. He and Catherine entertained corporate executives and in-house lawyers from the largest companies in the Midwest. Occasionally, he got lucky and snared a New York or California contact, too. Through his relentless efforts and with his always-charming wife at his side, he managed to replace his lost Edelwise fees with those of several other large corporate clients. In some ways, he thought, he was better off because he'd now spread his eggs among many baskets. It was always dangerous to rely singly on anything, although he would have enjoyed sharing at least some credit for the millions that Edelwise was paying the firm throughout the period.

* * *

Knight got a big career boost when Sam Wilson retired early at age sixty-three and transferred all billings to him, thereby doubling Knight's total revenues and positioning him for a spot on the Exec Com. Hopkins and John Merritt reviewed his candidacy during one of their weekly meetings for after-work drinks at the Chicago Club.

"Ratkin is a remarkable talent, but he's also dangerous," Merritt said softly, sipping his glass of iced tea. "He's the personification of unrestrained ambition, and that's not always a good thing, especially for you, Charles."

"I agree. We need a counterweight to Ratkin," Hopkins nodded as he drank his Johnnie Walker Black on the rocks. "He's been on the Exec Com for two years, and we need someone his age to maintain the appropriate balance of power on the committee. Knight is the only viable candidate."

"Charles, you're a genius," Merritt said. "He's the perfect choice. You'll have no trouble playing Ratkin and Knight against each other to strengthen the firm and enhance your own power."

Hopkins knew that supporting Knight was also good politics for another reason: now both Knight and Ratkin would owe him.

A few days later, Hopkins met with Knight to outline the broad support he'd enjoy in his quest for Wilson's seat on the Exec Com. In that conversation, Hopkins confirmed that he'd lost respect for the aging mentor who'd once championed his career at Michelman & Samson.

"Wilson is a slacker," Hopkins told Knight over drinks at the Chicago Club. "He's not even that great a lawyer. The only reason he achieved his success is because he had outstanding young people like you, me, and Ratkin working for him. Without us, he would have been nothing. I don't know how he got all those clients and all those trials. Even worse, he never worked at anywhere near his potential. He could have brought millions of dollars more into the firm. You know, the Exec Com reduced his compensation several years ago in an effort to jump-start him with a kick in the pants. Instead, he said he wanted to retire."

Knight remained silent throughout the diatribe. He saw no reason to antagonize a more powerful partner over an issue that, in the end, had nothing to do with him anyway. Even so, the intensity of Hopkins's vitriol surprised Knight. After all, Hopkins had won it all: he was the first chairman of Michelman & Samson. What could be better than that?

* * *

From Knight's initial Exec Com meeting, he observed firsthand the evolution that followed the MBA takeover of the firm. Those who had the numbers prospered; those who didn't were at the mercy of others. For average partner profits to rise every year—M&S's doubled in a decade—the annual promotion and review process required the Exec Com to make the correct decision as to each attorney. Only two metrics mattered in that analysis: billings and leverage. Wilson's prediction came true: equity partners ate what they killed, along with what they could successfully claim to have killed.

As the firm increased in size, any other evaluation of individual attorneys became impossible. In promoting lawyers into the equity partnership, Michelman & Samson clung to the rhetoric of meritocracy as reality gave way to horse-trading at the highest level. Politics displaced quality as the essential criterion for advancement. If a young non-equity partner worked for the right senior attorney, promotion and progress occurred if that senior person so decreed. Those in the wrong camp, working for partners whose billings didn't give them the clout to protect anyone other than themselves—and sometimes not even that—eventually saw the exit. The vaunted free market assignment system that had allowed associates and non-equity partners to decline any senior partner's request to work on a matter disappeared. No one could resist the firm's most powerful partners without serious career jeopardy.

Knight learned the lessons that Ratkin's theft of Edelwise had taught him. Rather than empower those working for him with the autonomy that came from client billings of their own, he maintained a tight grip on every revenue dollar he touched. That gave him stature in the Exec Com's deliberations while also positioning him to tell his minions, "I brought you into this world, and I can take you out, so keep your hours up."

*　　　　　*　　　　　*

The Michelman & Samson profits machine assumed a life of its own. In an interview appearing in the *Wall Street Journal* immediately after the firm announced a round of non-equity partner layoffs during a still-booming economy, Hopkins acknowledged the firm's relatively swift transformation that was still under way.

"We are now among a select group of the most profitable law firms in the country—in the world, for that matter," he was quoted. "For us to succeed, we have to stay there. That means keeping our stock price high. Barring some cataclysmic event, I see no reason why we can't continue our current profits growth for the foreseeable future. Are the changes challenging? Sure. We're in the midst of a sea change in the way large firms operate. Every M&S lawyer should wake up in the morning feeling just a little bit vulnerable; it keeps everyone on their toes."

Hopkins had summarized the new governing mantra that was not unique to Michelman & Samson: keep the firm's stock price—stated as average-profits-per-partner—high; keep everyone feeling vulnerable; keep people on their toes. Predictably, even those at the top guarded their client billings. Every partner feared introducing clients to other partners because Ronald Ratkin's legendary theft of Edelwise from Albert Knight had been real, as were the consequences. It had become common knowledge that Ratkin's compensation went up the year of his client coup and that Knight's went down. Those things happened because the institution's incentives made such behavior essential for economic survival, even as an equity partner.

* * *

Throughout this transformation, the firm properly boasted a large stable of talented attorneys. How could it be otherwise? Every year, the nation's top law schools produced too many graduates wanting to start their careers at the enormous salaries that M&S and other big firms offered. Of the country's forty thousand new lawyers annually, more than half of the seven thousand from the so-called top schools took initial jobs at places like Michelman & Samson. Many more would have accepted such offers if made. Economic necessity motivated most of them: they needed to begin repaying student loans. Some became enthralled with the notion of gaining positions to which many aspired but which only the select achieved.

Few new associates realized that Wilson's prescient observations about the profession's dark side during his interview with Daniel Schmidt became even more apropos during the next twenty-five years. In their regular lunch and dinner sessions that no longer included Sam Wilson,

Hopkins and Merritt gave such issues only passing consideration.

"I read an interesting article last week," Hopkins began as he drank his Johnnie Walker Black on the rocks while Merritt sipped iced tea in the Chicago Club dining room. "Apparently, lawyers exceed all other occupations in clinical depression, and we rank near the top in alcoholism and substance abuse."

"Whose fault is that?" Merritt responded. "If they don't like what they do, they should move on."

"Apparently, many are," Hopkins continued. "Attrition from a large law firm's typical class of new associates now exceeds eighty percent after five years."

"So what?" Merritt answered. "Our average equity partner profits surpassed $2 million last year. As long as that trend continues, who cares how many unhappy lawyers there are in the world. I'm happy. Aren't you? The attorneys who come here earn good money for their efforts. They understand the rules before they start playing the game."

Hopkins knew better, but he liked his friend's articulation of the issue. The truth was that the rules kept changing to keep average equity partner profits moving ever skyward. That's how an attorney's required tenure at the firm for equity partner consideration went from ten years to twelve or more; that's how the equity partner entry level compensation became lower; that's how those at the top retained allocations that no newly hired attorney could ever reach.

"You're right," Hopkins agreed. "We're just trying to run a business here."

"By the way, diversity has become part of the new business creed. I think we have to add a woman to the Exec Com," Merritt suggested. "We have so few female equity partners, especially at the higher levels. Are there any viable candidates other than Deborah Rush?"

"I think not," Hopkins answered. "I'll talk to her."

"You do that, and I'll talk to Scott Canby," Merritt said. "They'll take the two seats that open up this year as the old guard retires. Eventually, we'll have one more seat to fill after that. Then the firm's leadership will be set for the next decade."

"Right. Meanwhile, you figure out who we have to put on the nominating committee to make sure Rush and Canby get selected. The key to the entire process is to make sure we never have a contested election. Participatory democracy is not our friend."

* * *

The continued growth of the firm worked to Knight's advantage. As M&S grew to two thousand attorneys worldwide, the size of the Ex Com held firm at a magnificent seven. Such a concentration of power propelled Knight to embrace the MBA takeover, but it was a short trip for him anyway. Throughout his life, hard work had produced success. Even as an associate at M&S, high billable hours had been an early measure of his relative prowess. Using the metrics of revenues, billings, and leverage ratios meshed with Knight's natural predilections, so he drove protégés to protect themselves from criticism by following his path. If they didn't, he'd cut them loose. He felt himself becoming tougher, harder, better.

"Every year—as an associate, non-equity partner, and now as an equity partner—I've averaged almost three thousand billable hours," he often told younger litigators. "If you want to know what it takes to make it here, there's your answer."

He never disclosed what he also knew: for most of them, even that level of dedication would be insufficient. The demands of an ever-increasing associate-partner leverage ratio permitted the advance of fewer and fewer capable candidates.

Even success became a limited concept. Home-grown attorneys found it increasingly difficult to make the business case required to move them to the top levels of the equity partnership. So outsiders entered the breach. Every year, high-profile lateral hires from other big firms and the government joined the top tier of M&S. Knight understood the business justification for every such acquisition. Such people were the rainmakers; they provided M&S's lifeblood—more billings. Sure, the firm he'd joined three decades earlier was disappearing, but that was just progress. Concepts of community yielded to a system of free agency. As marquee players sold themselves and their independent books of business to the highest bidder, M&S's stratospheric partner profits gave it the financial power to win almost every competition for talent that it entered. Michelman & Samson was rapidly becoming a collection of the legal profession's biggest winners.

That's how William Drakow joined the firm as the most recent Exec Com member of the new millennium. He was a forty-nine-year-old lateral hire whose divorce settlement with his third ex-wife required him to earn more than his prior firm could afford. Head of a self-contained bankruptcy practice, he brought his own clients, matters, and team of attorneys with him. His motive for leaving his former firm of twenty-four years was no secret: he needed the money and was available to whoever offered the most.

Knight suppressed his vague sense that Drakow personified a potentially troubling phenomenon. The rainmaker laterals were an odd assortment of personalities who lacked deep connections to any particular firm ethos. Their characters were largely unknown; their agendas revolved exclusively around money. Drakow was a good example: rumors abounded that the scar on the left side of his face had resulted from a knife fight with one of his ex-wives. Knight certainly wasn't going to ask him about it.

Still, Knight didn't pause to ponder at length these longer-term trends, the corporate department's ongoing consolidation of its power, or even whether he was happy with his life. The contest allowed no time for such distractions. When Ratkin had taken the lead in gaining entrance to the Exec Com room, Knight worked hard to catch him two years later. The pace of the race only accelerated thereafter. There was neither light at the end of the tunnel nor an oncoming train, just more tunnel. Meanwhile, every other Tuesday night at ten o'clock, he met Fran Ratkin for their rendezvous at the Four Seasons Hotel. It provided a respite that he found nowhere else, probably because he never looked for it.

CHAPTER 15

The crash of 2008 stalled a great run for most large firm equity partners. A year earlier, Michelman & Samson's average partner profits had grown to almost $3 million. The reasons were obvious: The ratio of all attorneys to equity partners—a number that managers called *leverage*—doubled from three to six in only ten years. The firm tripled in size to more than two thousand attorneys in a dozen offices around the world. Average hours climbed as yearly billing rate increases far outstripped inflation. Trees, it seemed, really did grow to the sky.

Michelman & Samson's balanced portfolio of client work had historically provided protection against the vagaries of the business cycle. Massive lawsuits employing armies of litigation attorneys billing their time at high hourly rates usually resulted in steady and predictable revenue streams even during the worst of times. During economic booms, the corporate transactional practice could charge premium rates for its work because dealmakers themselves were getting even richer than their lawyers. Severe downturns usually benefited Michelman's contingent in the incestuous bankruptcy and restructuring club. Its fee petitions seeking court approval for work billed at extraordinary hourly rates rarely generated scrutiny or objection.

For some reason that mystified the Exec Com, diversification wasn't working as well this time. Michelman & Samson's lucrative corporate venture capital practice had led the firm's fortunes upward, and it experienced the leading edge of the coming collapse. The transactional pipeline dried up first. Attorneys who had maintained a frenetic pace for six years found themselves with little to do. Bristling at hourly rates that had reached a thousand dollars, litigation clients instructed their lawyers to settle cases that would have countered the precipitous decline in corporate work. Almost all clients sought billing rate rollbacks to deal with their own economic challenges. The restructuring group picked up some of the slack, but not enough to maintain the historic profits of earlier times. Even worse, the uproar over executive compensation threatened to spill over into bankruptcy courts, where judges making less than $200,000 a year began taking a closer look at fee petitions and slashed billing rates of attorneys who, according to the latest *Am Law* 100 listings, were still making millions. Inside M&S, leverage boomeranged as it now created a reverse multiplier effect for every idle equity partner.

"What we must do without hesitation," Hopkins said at the first Exec Com meeting after the crash began, "is meet this crisis head-on. The objective must always be the preservation of equity partner profits. Because revenues are down, we must cut costs, starting with the non-equity partners and then proceeding through associates and staff. At year-end, we'll scrutinize carefully the relative contributions of all equity partners, as we always do. No one is off-limits."

For the next six months, the hammer fell everywhere. The recruiting department received a firmwide directive to cut summer associate programs in half. Graduating students expecting to begin full-time work in

September received letters stating that they could either arrive three months later or take year-long public interest jobs for which M&S would pay them one-third of the salary previously promised for its new associate positions. The firm announced the layoff of non-equity partners—more than one-fifth in all. It joined a dozen other large firms in contributing to what the profession would call "Black Thursday," a mid-February day in 2009 when more than eight hundred big firm attorneys lost their jobs in a single twenty-four-hour period. During the subsequent three months, more than three thousand lawyers nationally were fired. The total number of unemployed lawyers had jumped to a ten-year high of twenty thousand. The only good news was also a mixed blessing: voluntary associate attrition from all big firms came to a standstill because even the unhappiest lawyers had nowhere else to go.

It was just the visible beginning. Behind the scenes, the M&S Exec Com demoted equity partners whose billing metrics no longer justified their allocations under tightening criteria. Secretaries and administrative staff went to work wondering if they would be bringing home all of their personal effects in a banker's box at the end of the day. Even the most seasoned veterans, like Helen Peterson, feared that each morning commute to the office might be the last. Peterson hoped that her position as Charles Hopkins's longtime secretary and executive assistant would give her sufficient cover to get through a few more years. But Hopkins himself was retiring soon, so where would that leave her? That question haunted her as she watched lifelong colleagues pack their belongings after getting the fateful word that Michelman & Samson no longer required their services.

"All of this destruction to keep average equity partner profits above $2 million a year," she mused as she watched a friend depart in April. "It's obscene. In other companies throughout America, you read about employees accepting pay cuts so that their fellow workers can keep their jobs. Not here. The millionaire equity partners still get richer while the rest of us hang on by our fingernails."

Knight felt conflicted about the cutbacks. At one level, he understood there were real people behind the numbers on the sheets reporting cost savings that resulted from the widespread terminations. Still, he supported the expense-reduction programs because the firm needed to remain competitive. Michelman & Samson had to protect its enviable position near the top of the *Am Law* 100. It couldn't risk allowing partner profits to drop because that would endanger the entire franchise and cost everyone their jobs. To attract and keep talent that kept the big money flowing, even average equity partner profits of a million dollars a year were not enough. Two million provided a safer margin, but more was always better.

So when Charles Hopkins told the Exec Com that he wanted to increase the firm's leverage ratio from six to eight and get average profits back on track toward $3 million even in a down economy, Knight voiced his approval. Such sterile words—*leverage ratio*—camouflaged harsh reality: some longtime equity partners would lose their jobs, and the admission threshold would become higher for future aspirants. "Putting profits back on track" sounded better than firing more staff to reduce costs while squeezing even more billable hours out of all attorneys. Rhetoric could not hide reality, but it sometimes rendered truth less offensive. Still, Knight saw no alternative. The growing profits beast required regular meals.

* * *

When the aftermath of the crash endured longer than anyone had expected, the ongoing economic turmoil brought into sharp focus the question of how Hopkins's retirement would affect the firm. As the morning sunlight streamed through the window of his Four Seasons Hotel room, Knight pondered the issue alone in the bed that he and Fran had shared the previous evening. Only four days had passed since Charles Hopkins had posed the question that now drove every player at the top of the firm: who would succeed him as chairman?

Knight viewed himself as the only answer. He'd be the steady presence necessary to assure continuity in this critical period. His rival, Ratkin, was too temperamental, unpredictable, and vindictive. He'd lead the firm into endless and paralyzing personality conflicts. Knight could be conciliatory; he was a mediator. He'd demonstrated Hopkins's ability to get along with the corporate people by voting their way whenever they wanted to demote a litigation equity partner. Of course, Ratkin had obliged them, too.

Yet Knight remained oddly uncertain of himself. As he stood at the threshold of achieving all he'd sought for a lifetime, disturbing thoughts once again penetrated his consciousness. The guilt side of his psyche had evidently preserved just enough for one final battle with his sense of entitlement. Sam Wilson's earlier wisdom once again resonated in ways he found difficult to ignore: "What's the point?"

"Shake it off," he said to himself. "Shake it off and get back to work."

Then he remembered that he hadn't lunched with Wilson for a while. Perhaps his former sage could offer one last burst of wisdom to counter the confusion that was swamping him.

As Knight left the hotel lobby an hour later, a stocky man chewed on an unlit cigar as he folded his newspaper, rose from an overstuffed chair, and walked to a private booth. He'd aged very little in fifteen years.

PART III

COMPUCOM Corporation, Plaintiff,

v.

EDELWISE TECHNOLOGY, Defendant,

. . .

WHEREFORE, COMPUCOM requests entry of an order in its favor against EDELWISE in the amount to be proven at trial, but which COMPUCOM estimates to be in excess of $100 billion, plus interest, costs, and reasonable attorneys' fees . . ."

CHAPTER 16

Ronald Ratkin had no inkling of a problem with his marriage. It had never been a priority for him, so he ignored it. Whenever he was home, which was rarely because of his nationwide trial schedule, Fran was there. He thought she'd kept herself looking fit and attractive, especially for a woman her age. He didn't know how she occupied her days, but he thought her advanced courses at the University of Chicago's downtown facility every Tuesday were a good use of her evenings. The two agreed that it made sense for her to stay in the city after the late-night classes. Ratkin himself was usually out of town anyway, so it made no difference to him where she slept.

Immediately after the June Exec Com meeting during which Charles Hopkins had complicated the contest for his successor, a private limousine took Ratkin to a remote area of LaGuardia where a hangar housed an Edelwise private jet.

"Mr. Ratkin," said the desk operator as he walked through the main lobby on the way to the tarmac, "there's been a change in your flight plan. I assume Mr. McGinty notified you."

"Yes," Ratkin responded curtly. He'd already spent twenty minutes on his cell phone trying to calm his client. So far, he hadn't succeeded.

The Edelwise jet took off for the Hayward Executive Airport in northern California. When the plane landed more than six hours later, McGinty was waiting for him. Ratkin got into the front passenger seat of his former protégé's Porsche Cayenne. He could smell the alcohol on McGinty's breath.

"Did you assemble the team?" Ratkin asked.

"Yes."

McGinty felt as though he hadn't progressed at all from his days as an M&S attorney twenty years ago, when he literally carried Ratkin's trial bag. Now he was almost fifty, bald, and unhappily married to a woman he'd met at the Cubby Bear Lounge while he was living near Wrigley Field. When he failed to become an equity partner, she insisted that they move to a better climate. The Edelwise job became the perfect opportunity, although at this moment he wished he'd never heard of the company, Michelman & Samson, Ronald Ratkin, or her.

"And a separate meeting for what remains of his family?" Ratkin continued.

"Yes. Three cousins who haven't seen him in twenty years. They all live in the Bay Area."

"Where are we meeting?"

"My place in Carmel. Sissy is gone for the weekend, so we'll be alone. I told everyone to drive themselves. First the company people, then the three cousins."

"Fine."

McGinty had always marveled at how someone so short managed to position himself so that he was always peering down his nose at people.

"Will there be an easel and whiteboard I can use?"

"Of course," McGinty answered dutifully.

They pulled into the driveway leading to McGinty's modern oceanfront home; two cars were already there. Once inside, Ratkin greeted the president of Edelwise and its chief financial officer. The four men sat at the dining room table as Ratkin approached the whiteboard. With the Pacific Ocean beating against the rocks outside the floor-to-ceiling windows, the teacher began his lecture. McGinty poured himself a tumbler of Jack Daniel's, water, and ice. In accordance with longstanding instructions, an expensive bottle of red wine awaited Ratkin.

"Here's our timeline," Ratkin began as he mapped out in detail and from memory the critical dates that would chronicle Edelwise's fate. The last was three months away, coincidentally one day before the annual Michelman & Samson partnership meeting, Hopkins's last as Exec Com chairman. It was the perfect crescendo to a fitting climax, Ratkin thought as he wrote the final date on the board and then reached for his wine glass.

"Let's take a look at what the world will see next week," he suggested. "Phil, I assume you have your laptop."

"Yes. I've connected it to the LCD monitor on the wall."

"Good evening," said the image of Joshua Egan, founder and chairman of Edelwise.

"My God," said the company's CFO. "I thought he was dead. I thought that was why we all gathered in this emergency session."

McGinty and Ratkin remained silent.

"I know," the image of Egan continued. "You all thought I was dead. Well, I'm someplace where none of you can find me, so please don't try. I assume Ronald has set forth the timeline that will govern our actions over the next three months. He has my complete confidence and all the authority that goes with it. We're all in excellent hands."

Someone off camera handed Egan a note, which he read hurriedly before saying, "I must leave you now, but I'll report back later."

"Now I'm confused," said Edelwise's president. "McGinty called us here because of the supposed emergency relating to Joshua Egan's health, which we assumed meant his death. And I agree: that would be an emergency if it were true. So what's this about?"

"The point Phil and I have tried to make—and we think your reaction proves our success—is that rumors can get out of hand," Ratkin began. "Stock prices rise and fall because someone starts a whisper campaign that can ruin an entire company. Egan has known for months about the market's concern for his health. So he has now positioned the company and all of us to deal with them productively and permanently. He will teach market manipulators a lesson they will never forget."

Ratkin's ability to engage an audience was uncanny, McGinty thought as he tried unsuccessfully to regain sobriety.

"Periodically, Egan will appear throughout the next three months in an effort to impose greater discipline on otherwise wild market forces that could affect the company's financial well-being because of so-called health concerns," Ratkin continued. "Apart from those few webcasts, he will make no public appearances. The first in his series of broadcasts on the subject will be Wednesday morning."

Edelwise's president and chief financial officer were visibly relieved. McGinty had told them that Egan was in perilous shape. In fact, he was far worse than that. Ratkin had not said anything different, but he hadn't revealed the whole truth—namely, that the founder and chairman of Edelwise had died twelve hours earlier. He remained alive only on the hard drive of McGinty's laptop.

After the two Edelwise senior executives left, Ratkin remained at McGinty's home for another half hour, until the three remaining members of Egan's family arrived. McGinty and Ratkin put on the same show, explaining that Joshua Egan would remain in seclusion for the next three months. Egan had never married and had no children. These distant cousins didn't really care about their wealthy relative or what he was doing to preserve money they'd never see anyway.

"It worked!" McGinty said shortly after the last of them departed.

"Of course, it worked," Ratkin replied. "I told you it would work. There will be no tougher audiences than the two we just satisfied. You told them the truth, but they saw and heard what they wanted to see and hear. They believed what they wanted to believe. Psychologists call it confirmation bias."

"Unbelievable."

"We didn't lie to them. You showed them an image on a screen; the image spoke to them. Starting Monday, we'll release the other segments, just as we planned with Egan. In each clip, the founder will announce a new Edelwise breakthrough. With successive iterations, the developments will become increasingly dramatic. Meanwhile, the critical funding date for the new lines of credit that Edelwise needs to survive is sixty days away. Egan will appear to remain in good health until we pass that date. He'll exhibit signs of a noticeable decline thereafter, but he'll maintain sufficient strength to announce the most dramatic breakthrough in the history of modern science and technology."

McGinty asked about securities filings that would be required along the way.

"Those are problematic," Ratkin admitted. "But we'll be fine. We'll draft them to create litigation defenses that we can use later. Edelwise's president and chief financial officer will sign them without even considering the possibility that Egan is dead."

"But how can we submit required documents to the SEC that omit the clearly material fact that the founder and chairman of the company is dead?"

"Your company lives on the cutting edge of technology. I live on the cutting edge of the law. Let me worry about defending what you draft and file, but I need to see every word before Edelwise submits anything to the government. Once I sign off, your only job will be to get the filings done on time. Keep your head through this period, and everything will be just fine. And remember to open and close the insider trading window for Edelwise stock only in accordance with our timeline. We may have to pitch out of some tough jams along the way, and I can't tell you that there's legal precedent for the defense I'll be establishing as we proceed. But let me put it this way. There's an interesting phenomenon in baseball: when a team wins, only the official scorer cares about errors committed during the game. For everyone else, it's the final outcome—game won or lost—that matters."

Ratkin knew that McGinty would obey him. He had no choice. Edelwise's debt totaling $15 billion was coming due. Without replacement financing, the company would become insolvent. His Edelwise stock would be worthless if he didn't follow Ratkin's strategy to save everything. Even the deferred compensation plan to which he'd contributed for retirement would be subject to creditor claims if the company went bankrupt. Unlike traditional 401(k) plans, Edelwise's programs didn't require the company to keep an employee's contributions separate and protected from creditors in the event of Edelwise's insolvency.

Apart from his company stock, McGinty had no other assets. Edelwise had been his life's work and offered his only future. With the real estate market's collapse, his home's value had declined to far below the several mortgages on it. Notwithstanding a paper wealth of more than $50 million, Phil McGinty stood on the brink of financial ruin from which only Ronald Ratkin could rescue him. That was enough to drive any man to drink, he thought as he refilled his tumbler with Jack Daniel's and water.

Ratkin had even more riding on his plan. He and Hopkins had invested in Edelwise to the tune of $20 million they didn't have. It was called leverage. They'd taken out loans to make their initial investments when it was still a start-up company and a minor Michelman & Samson client. That had been easy because every lending institution in the world regarded M&S equity partners as the safest of all credit risks. One perk of their seven-figure incomes was access to seemingly unlimited personal debt. The investment seemed to be a win-win for everyone as Edelwise grew from a penny stock to per share values that now exceeded five hundred dollars. As the price soared, Ratkin and Hopkins used their winnings to increase their loans, buy more stock, and lead a life of unrestrained excess. If the company went under, both men faced financial Armageddon—a prospect that wouldn't help Ratkin gain Hopkins's support as the next Exec Com chairman.

Equally important to Ratkin, he claimed credit for all of Edelwise's annual M&S billings that had grown to more than $100 million since he'd taken them from Knight. Those billings were the linchpin of his economic case for income and power in the firm. Without them, he was nothing. Meanwhile, he also had a trial of the century to win.

*   *   *

After the Carmel sessions, Ratkin boarded the Edelwise jet at midnight. He landed at Boston's Logan Airport early Sunday morning. His immediate task now was to determine how to handle the loss of Egan as a witness in a way that didn't damage his case. Winning always meant everything.

National newspapers were calling it one of the most important early trials of the new millennium. Edelwise and its principal competitor had squared off in a dispute over who'd first developed the technology necessary for operating every laptop computer in the world. Billions of dollars and the future existence of both companies hung in the balance. For Ratkin, life did not get any better than these bet-the-company cases, but he knew this week would be especially tough.

At ten o'clock Sunday evening, he notified his opposing counsel that, contrary to the witness disclosure he'd made on Friday, Joshua Egan would not be testifying when the trial resumed. Instead, Ratkin would read deposition testimony to the jury. When the parties convened Monday morning, he shifted into what many in the profession called full-fledged Ratkin mode.

"As I told opposing counsel over the weekend," he addressed the judge smoothly, "Mr. Egan will not be taking the stand this morning. We haven't reached a final decision as to when he might. Frankly, given the flimsy nature of the plaintiff's evidence, I'm not sure Edelwise will be presenting very much at all in the way of live defense witnesses."

"Well, your Honor," Ratkin's adversary responded, "when Mr. Ratkin says he notified us over the weekend, I want to make clear that he uses that temporal phrase quite loosely. If it had arrived two hours later, his notification would have come on Monday—today. We received it late Sunday evening, only ten hours ago."

The judge didn't care about such bickering. Few things annoyed him more than attorneys fighting about what time they'd told each other about witnesses scheduled to appear the next day. Back when he was arguing cases in state court, trial by ambush was the rule. You never knew who was taking the stand until the opposing lawyer stood up and announced it as that person was walking into the courtroom. He knew all about pretrial orders and notice and all the things that the rules said civilized adversaries were supposed to do, but in forty years on the bench, he'd never seen a trial go as planned.

As a former Marine, the judge likened judicial combat to the haze of battle: troops and materiel in place and ready to execute detailed strategies; then the action began and the terrain became unrecognizable to the warriors. Even more to the point of current contention, if a judge wanted an appellate court to reverse a case, all he had to do was enforce a pretrial order barring some insignificant witness from testifying on grounds that the other side hadn't received sufficient notice of the appearance. He wouldn't make that mistake again.

The judge had grown especially weary of this case. After almost ten years of pretrial wrangling and interlocutory appeals, he just wanted the most unpleasant litigation of his three decades on the bench to end. Whatever happened here was headed for another ten years of appeals, and he'd die long before there was a final outcome. Put it on someone else's docket for awhile, he thought. In the end, the thing would settle anyway; they all did. Civil trials had become rarities during his legal career. In 1960, slightly more than ten percent of all federal civil cases went to trial; forty years later that percentage had dropped to under two. Trial outcomes were never definitive, either. They just set the parameters and negotiating positions that developed while appellate dockets remained clogged.

"Talk to me about something that matters," said the judge. "If you don't have anything else, let's get the jury in here and get going."

*   *   *

As Ratkin left the courtroom at day's end, he was sure that the plan he'd outlined in Carmel would work. There was only one loose end: Egan's nurse. He'd told McGinty to handle it but worried that his former lackey still didn't have what it took to finish the task competently. Sometimes, Ratkin felt as though he had to do everything himself—if he wanted certainty of its timely and definitive completion, that is.

CHAPTER 17

"What's Hopkins up to?" Knight asked Sam Wilson.

As he was leaving the Four Seasons Hotel, Knight had used his cell phone to schedule lunch with his former mentor. Fortunately, the seventy-five-year-old retired lion of the bar was not at his London flat, where he spent half the year. They met at the University Club the same day.

"I don't know," Wilson answered while eating his salad in the Cathedral Room that held so many bad memories for Knight. "But Hopkins will try to play this to some advantage. What we have to figure out is what that could be."

"If he wanted Ratkin to succeed him, he'd just let the nominating process go forward," Knight continued while sipping his Tanqueray and tonic. "Ratkin has the thing locked up if it goes that way. So if he doesn't want Ratkin, he must want me, right?"

"No offense, but I don't think so. Look, I don't like Ratkin any more than you do. He'll spend the rest of his life seeking the love his mother never gave him as a child, and he'll never find it. But he's the smartest person I've ever met, and he's got a way with juries that's remarkable. Compared to what you and I see, he must wear a completely different face when he's trying a case. Maybe he's got multiple personalities—I don't know. But in every other setting, he's interpersonally impossible and about as far from likeable as a human being can get."

"So why did Hopkins support me for the Exec Com?"

"As a neutralizer. Hopkins always regarded you as someone he needed to keep Ratkin in line. I can't imagine that he thinks you should succeed him. But I'll say this about the whole situation you're describing: something just doesn't fit."

Contemplating the puzzle Knight outlined, Wilson devised a simple inquiry: "Here's the way to think about it: What's in this for Hopkins? What's his goal at the end of the process? It seems to me that he wants the next chairman to feel beholden to him. But why? He's retiring. He's relinquishing his equity position. He's leaving the firm . . . Or is he? I don't know how he'll pull it off, but I think Charles O. Hopkins III doesn't want to step down. I don't see any way for him to avoid it, but that has to be behind what's happening here."

"I'll keep that in mind. But I don't think there's anything he or I can do about that inevitable outcome."

"Just don't get caught in the cross fire. People are going to get hurt in this one. I can smell it," Wilson said with a wry smile.

There was a reason Sam Wilson had won all those trials, Knight thought. As a premier Michelman & Samson litigation attorney, he'd possessed uncommon insight and an instinct for the jugular. A dozen years after his retirement, those qualities persisted.

CHAPTER 18

After his lunch with Wilson, Knight returned to his office, planning to resume work on a draft brief due in two weeks. As always, he logged onto CNN.com, where he saw a "BREAKING NEWS" item at the top of the home page:

"Joshua Egan announces advance toward technological breakthrough; Edelwise stock soars."

Perfect, thought Knight. As he and Ratkin jockeyed for position in the race for Exec Com chairman, the firm's biggest client belonged to his nemesis and was getting bigger. He then read the accompanying article that mentioned Ratkin's ongoing performance in the *Compucom v. Edelwise* trial.

"Win or lose, love him or hate him," the article read, "there's no denying Ronald Ratkin's power in a courtroom. The jurors hang on his every word. With a beguiling smile and an unflappable manner, he's a cross between the world's best high school teacher and Albert Einstein."

The language had come directly from Michelman & Samson press releases. Knight didn't know which to hate more when he read such pandering pieces, Ratkin or the firm's publicity machine that generated such fodder for a press that simply parroted it. Still, the progress toward

Edelwise's breakthrough held his interest. He clicked on a video link to a demonstration:

"Voice recognition software has become more sophisticated in recent years, and Edelwise is developing a new twist," the reporter began. "Edelwise founder Joshua Egan himself announced that his company is working on a process that would allow people to talk to computers and enable computers to talk back—in the same voice. In a demonstration that was just released on the Edelwise website, Egan showed how it would work. Here it is."

The video clip then cut to an image of Joshua Egan looking at his laptop computer as he posed a simple question:

"How much is two plus two?" Egan asked the screen.

"Four," came the response that precisely mimicked Egan's voice.

"What is the square root of sixteen?"

"Four."

"What is the capital of Minnesota?"

"St. Paul."

Egan's conversation with the computer ended after about ninety seconds, at which point he turned to the camera and said, "This is just the beginning."

"Knowing Joshua Egan and Edelwise, you can count on that," said the news reporter off camera. "Meanwhile, the market continues to love Egan and his company. The stock price has moved up twenty percent today and is now at an all-time high of six hundred dollars a share."

Knight closed his web browser and returned to editing an appellate brief. He'd owned a little Edelwise common stock when the company first went public. When it moved up more than one hundred percent after only six months, Knight thought the jump from five to twelve dollars a share was a nice gain and sold it all. Today, its stratospheric price became just one more item on a long list of reasons to hate himself.

*   *   *

Daniel Schmidt watched the CNN BREAKING NEWS item about Edelwise, too. Pulling out his personal Edelwise/Ratkin file, he reviewed his notes.

6/8/98: Trading window declared; Hop. and Rat. purchase more E. stock. Est. value of holdings: $100,000 each.

8/99: Compucom sued Edel; major case threatening Edel existence and future. Rat. comments on suit: "Without merit."

9/8/03: Trading window declared; Hop. and Rat. purchase more Edel. stock. Est. value of holdings: $1 million each.

12/4/07: Trading window declared; Hop. and Rat. purchase more Edel. stock. Est. value of holdings: $4 million each.

3/5/08: Trading window declared; Hop. and Rat. purchase more Edel. stock. Est. value of holdings: $20 million each.

4/6/09: Compucom v. Edel. trial begins.

Meanwhile, he repeatedly reviewed the clip showing Joshua Egan's demonstration of his new technology. Between replays, he checked the company's stock price; it was skyrocketing. He also located a blog from a reporter who was posting daily online observations from the *Compucom v. Edelwise* trial. Schmidt added to his notes with the week's developments.

6/09: Defense begins. Mon.—Egan out as witness; Wed. webcast—Egan media display. Pieces don't fit???

He hoped a later review of Edelwise's stock transactions would show Ratkin selling into the stock's remarkable rally. Disappointment overcame him when it didn't. Ratkin and Hopkins still held Edelwise stock that was now worth $25 million to each of them.

"Eventually, Ratkin will sell some of it," Schmidt mumbled to himself. "He has to. He has to."

CHAPTER 19

Two more weeks had passed, and Knight still didn't know how to vote on the three alternatives that Charles Hopkins had offered. His current inclination was to back off and let history take its course. For some reason, Hopkins seemed determined to remove himself from the kingmaker role. It was an odd development for someone whose quest for power had taken him to the top of M&S. Why would he back away from the chance to select the firm's leader for the next decade? It made no sense to Knight. He was grateful that it was one of his biweekly Four Seasons Tuesday nights. Maybe Fran had some insights into what was happening. After all, she was married to his chief rival.

"Ronald has told me that he's a lock to become the next chairman," Fran told Knight that evening. "He says that no matter which path the Exec Com takes, all roads lead to him."

"Has he mentioned to you that Hopkins opened up this can of worms when he said he'd prefer not to vote in the selection of the next chairman?"

"No. The truth is we don't talk very much. He gives me only conclusions, never his thoughts or reasoning. He speaks in grandiose terms, like three months ago when he said, 'Fran, say hello to M&S's next chairman.' And then I said 'Congratulations. How do you know that already? Isn't Hopkins still in charge?' And then he said, 'Not for long. All roads now lead to me.'"

That fits, Knight thought. It would coincide with the time that the Exec Com finalized the nominating committee's membership. Once those who would select Hopkins's replacement were in place, the necessary fourth vote for chairman became his, even if Hopkins himself declined to cast it. But why was Hopkins now charting everyone along such a circuitous route to the inevitable?

As he decided most things, Knight went through a process of elimination in developing his course of action on the leadership succession alternatives. Hopkins didn't support the approach that allowed him to choose his successor directly, so that was a nonstarter because Knight couldn't defy him. Ratkin had rigged the nominating committee, so allowing Hopkins's replacement on the Exec Com to vote on the next chairman would get Knight nowhere. That left the third and most radical option: a secret ballot vote of the entire equity partnership. Knight thought that Ratkin most feared this final option and would fight it, so that made Knight's position easy: the opposite. A lawyer's most common response to an adversary's position came with a jerk of the knee: resist whatever the other side wants. This rule of behavior was often accompanied by a corollary that had helped to create peculiar and transitory alliances throughout human history.

"The enemy of my enemy is my friend," Knight reminded himself.

CHAPTER 20

Ratkin continued to work his magic with the jury in Boston. Almost a month after he'd told the judge that Joshua Egan would not testify in the case, the defense rested. He'd called only two live witnesses from the company: its president and its chief financial officer. An impressive roster of paid experts completed his lineup. All performed well, Ratkin thought. But not as well as he himself would have done on the stand.

He wished the system allowed lawyers, rather than witnesses, to do all the talking in courtrooms. The attorneys knew their clients' positions better than anyone else. Why bother with the subterfuge of putting people on the stand after spending weeks getting them ready for the ordeal? Like all large firms, Michelman & Samson had a mock courtroom in which frightened witnesses learned to become confident advocates. After enduring days of grueling practice examinations, only the best performers advanced to the real show. Stakes were too high for any client to take a chance on a witness who was not fully prepared and well rehearsed.

"Some potential witnesses are problematic," Ratkin once said while giving an M&S instructional presentation to young litigation attorneys during one of the firm's in-house training seminars. "If they cannot be retrained, you have to jettison them and search for someone else to take their places. In large cases, there are usually many candidates for the courtroom. Keep the auditions going until you find those who will do the job you need done. When all else fails, retain an expert who will carry the load. Apart from the quality of the trial lawyers themselves, the most important difference that money makes in the outcome of a case shows up in the experts. A litigant who can afford to hire the best expert witnesses has a tremendous advantage over an adversary who can't. What you're really buying when you hire a testifying expert is someone who can confidently articulate all the things you as an attorney would like to tell the jury yourself, but can't. After all, everyone knows lawyers can't testify, right?"

Forced laughter from the gallery of sycophants followed Ratkin's attempt at humor. Ambitious young associates were always the best audiences for any senior partner.

Following his own advice had served Ratkin well in the Compucom trial. As he boarded Edelwise's private jet to Chicago for the July Exec Com meeting, he wondered what his adversaries would do to rehabilitate themselves during their rebuttal case.

"We've got them by the b-a-a-a-l-l-l-s-s-s," he told a young partner on the plane, who, of course, agreed. Everyone in the firm knew that no one crossed Ronald Ratkin.

Outside Chicago, Edelwise's plane landed at Palwaukee Airport, where a limousine waited to take Ratkin to M&S's downtown headquarters. Most of his underlings on the flight were going to the same place, but he told them to find their own transportation. An hour later, John Merritt sat across from Ratkin's desk as they discussed the following day's Exec Com meeting.

"So where are we going with all this?" Ratkin asked his corporate department ally.

"It depends on how others feel about Hopkins's proposed alternatives," Merritt answered. "But let's assume Knight's people vote with him. That means that if our three votes remain aligned, Hopkins will still have to cast the deciding ballot. But instead of determining who the next chairman will be, he'll be deciding the process by which that person will be chosen. It's very strange, and I don't really get it. But I think we have to assume that Knight and his people realize that their only real shot at the chairmanship is the open election process combined with a secret ballot."

"So now what?"

"Now, I think we just have to see what happens tomorrow," Merritt tried to be reassuring. "The momentum seems to be firmly in your favor, especially with the latest Edelwise announcement and your ongoing trial. I don't see how you can lose, even if we're stuck with democracy."

"Fine," Ratkin said as he dismissed Merritt with a wave. Everyone is useless, he thought. He had to do everything himself; it was a tremendous burden. He picked up the phone to call his wife.

"I'll be home tonight around eight," he said before hanging up without listening for a response. He knew she'd be waiting for him.

CHAPTER 21

The July Exec Com meeting was in M&S's Chicago office on Wacker Drive. As usual, all seven members were present that evening, although William Drakow, the firm's most recent lateral acquisition, said he had to leave early.

"I hope you'll excuse me," Drakow began as Hopkins called the meeting to order. "But I have a client commitment that I must honor. So I have to leave in about a half hour."

"We'll try to accomplish our tasks quickly," Hopkins responded.

Hopkins engineered the deal that had brought Drakow to the firm, so Drakow owed him. If the process for selecting a successor-chairman came to a vote, Drakow would probably help orchestrate Hopkins's desired outcome, but he was unpredictable. Based upon the obvious interpersonal tension between Drakow and Ratkin, Knight regarded Drakow as his third vote—along with himself and Deborah Rush—to succeed Hopkins.

"Let's start where we left off last time," Hopkins began. "I assume we're all agreed that I should not vote on the election of the next chairman. Is there any serious disagreement with that?"

"Yes, Charles, I disagree. I think you should vote," said Deborah Rush.

Great, thought Ratkin, now we're going to have twenty minutes of discussion that will lead nowhere because there are already at least four votes in the room against her position. She needs to learn to count, he grumbled to himself, although everyone else heard only Ratkin's typically disparaging grunt.

"You've served the firm well for many years," she continued. "You've brought M&S into a new era of financial prosperity. We've become the most profitable law firm in the country, thanks to you. Everyone in the room owes you a great debt. And I think it would be most fitting, indeed essential, that you voice your preference for chairman through your final vote as Exec Com chairman."

"I agree," said Drakow.

Ratkin had no use for Drakow, whom he regarded as a Hopkins stooge. Drakow spoke for ten minutes on the contrasts between M&S and the disaster that he thought his old firm had become.

"My former partners don't even average a million bucks a year anymore," he concluded. "Charles, I can't imagine that anyone here would want you to abdicate your last and most important act after making M&S the best firm in the country."

"I think we should respect your concerns, Charles," said Merritt. "You have a great sense of this partnership, and if you believe that abstaining from a vote on your successor best serves the interests of this firm, I'm in no position to second-guess you."

Scott Canby and Ronald Ratkin nodded approvingly. Knight remained silent. He didn't understand any of this until Drakow got up and left.

"As I mentioned," he said, "I have to go. Given the importance of this matter, I don't feel comfortable giving my proxy to anyone. I'm sure you all understand."

With Drakow's vote no longer in the room, Knight's position now mattered. Ratkin and his two allies lined up against allowing Hopkins to vote on the next chairman. With Drakow gone, Hopkins, Knight, and Rush could create a three-three deadlock on the question.

The son-of-a-bitch had planned Drakow's early departure as a loyalty test, Knight thought. Even though Hopkins himself had said he was reluctant to cast the deciding vote for his successor, he wanted the people in the room to beg him to do just that. Now he wanted to see if Knight would join the sycophants, which of course he did.

"Albert, where are you in all of this?" Hopkins asked.

"I agree with Deborah and Bill," he answered dutifully. "You should be participating in the choice of your successor."

"Well, I disagree," Hopkins said with a tone reminiscent of Knight's third-grade teacher, who'd regularly scolded him. Knight had tried to do right by Hopkins but apparently had gotten it wrong. "I didn't raise the issue last month lightly. Either the full partnership should select the next Exec Com chairman, or the committee itself should do it after I'm gone. So let's proceed to the other two options."

Knight was irritated that he'd been set up again. In the Hopkins-arranged contest between Ratkin and Knight, Ratkin had made the selfish choice, and it had been correct. There was no nobility left anywhere, Knight thought. He retaliated in ways that made things worse.

"Well, with Drakow gone, we shouldn't be voting on the remaining two options," Knight suggested.

As if he hadn't heard Knight at all, Ratkin used a parliamentary tactic to gain the advantage: "I move that we adopt option number two, namely, that the Exec Com selects the next chairman after the upcoming election of Charles Hopkins's replacement on the committee," he said.

"There is a motion," said Hopkins, who always followed *Robert's Rules of Order.* "Is there a second?"

"Second," Merritt chimed in quickly.

"Any discussion?" Hopkins continued swiftly.

Screw it, mumbled Knight. I don't need this. Deborah Rush raised her hand.

"Let's get real about this," she began. "Ratkin, Merritt, and Canby are a three-vote block in favor of this motion because the nominating committee—their nominating committee—will select a person who will become Ratkin's fourth vote for chairman. Voting for this motion is voting to make Ratkin the next chairman. It's that simple. Let's stop playing games."

"Well, I appreciate your vote of confidence, Deborah," said Ratkin wryly. "But I think you've gotten about three steps ahead of yourself. Maybe you have a crystal ball that allows you to divine the future with such clarity. But we mere mortals are not so blessed."

"You know, Deborah, that kind of outburst doesn't serve you or the firm very well," Merritt picked up Ratkin's baton. "We try to conduct ourselves with a high degree of professionalism and civility, especially in this room. You're not making things any easier."

Rush couldn't have cared less about making things easier for Ronald Ratkin or John Merritt. She had never liked Merritt, and Ratkin had infuriated her during an Exec Com meeting three years earlier, when the committee was considering candidates for partner promotion and Ratkin called her out. He made the accurate observation that Rush was systematically tougher on younger female attorneys than were their male reviewers. She also consistently rated male associates and partners at all levels higher than the women working for her.

"What's that about?" Ratkin had asked. "Are we never again to see a female M&S attorney who can match your unprecedented and, apparently, never-to-be-equaled abilities, Deborah? You must carry quite a burden, knowing that you're the last in your line of truly gifted large law firm female senior partners."

"You would know more about the subject of pretenders to the throne of unrivaled genius than I," she shot back.

Knight laughed. Deborah Rush's tongue-lashings were always entertaining, especially if she'd had a few vodka martinis.

Ratkin let the matter drop until that evening. After downing a bottle of Chateau Lafite Rothschild from his extensive collection, he called her at home.

"You're an embarrassment to this firm, Deborah. You don't deserve to sit on the Exec Com, and I'm making it my personal mission to drive you out of here."

Now, three years later, he still hadn't succeeded, and she was getting even. As Ratkin and Rush again traded blows, Knight noticed that Hopkins was smiling. Maybe he'd staged this episode, too, Knight thought.

"Is there any further discussion?" Hopkins asked.

Hearing no response, he asked for a vote on the motion. As Rush had predicted, Ratkin, Merritt, and Canby raised their hands in support. With Drakow still gone, only Hopkins himself could now stop the juggernaut.

"Opposed?" Hopkins asked.

After Knight and Rush lifted their hands, Hopkins joined them.

"Three to three," he announced. "Motion fails. I think that leaves all of us with option number three. The entire partnership will vote on the next chairman. We can make that final decision today, or we can wait until next month."

"I move that we adjourn the meeting," Merritt interjected.

"Second," said Ratkin.

"Very well." Hopkins knew he'd accomplished all he could for today. "All those in favor."

All hands shot into the air. The meeting was over.

CHAPTER 22

By mid-July, Ratkin knew it was time for another dramatic Edelwise announcement, so he reminded McGinty to start the process.

"Seems like you've done a nice job with our loose end," he told McGinty before beginning another morning in court. "We've not seen or heard anything from Egan's nurse since you cut her from our roster. It's a classic case of no news is good news."

"She'll remain quiet," McGinty answered solemnly, pouring a drink from the bottle of Jack Daniel's he kept in his desk drawer as he muttered to himself, "It must be noon somewhere in the world."

For his entire legal career, McGinty had found himself crossing lines for Ratkin's clients that went far beyond zealous advocacy. He'd break more laws in dealing with this nurse, Alvarez. What he hated most was that Ratkin somehow knew McGinty was capable of things that surprised even McGinty himself.

"I'll post the webcast now," McGinty said as he opened a special file on his laptop and put it on the Edelwise website. Once again, Joshua Egan would announce publicly the company's progress on its greatest initiative ever.

*   *   *

As he did every morning, Knight began his workday in the office by logging into his computer and opening his web browser to check the latest news. Today, the screen again greeted him with another "BREAKING NEWS" item from Edelwise:

"Progress Toward Monumental Breakthrough Continues At Edelwise; Stock Soars At Market Open."

Yet another video release from Edelwise showed Joshua Egan demonstrating a new development, this one in artificial intelligence.

"Unlike other Internet search engines," Egan began, "which canvass the Internet for particular words, Edelthink takes it a step farther. I'll demonstrate."

Egan then turned to his laptop and typed in a question. A large overhead screen displayed his words as he typed them; they also appeared as an inset on the webcast: "At this moment, what is the exact distance of the earth from the sun?"

Instantaneously, the computer produced the answer that changed every second to remain accurate. He then typed another question: "If you were a participant in the television game *Jeopardy,* what response would you give to this answer: 'November 22, 1963'?"

The screen showed an immediate answer: "What was the date of President John F. Kennedy's assassination?"

Egan typed again: "Retrieve the video file for my most recent golf swing. How can I improve it?"

Again, the answer came without hesitation: "You're not drawing your club back in a straight line from the ball. Slow everything down and concentrate on following that imaginary line all the way through your backswing and then to the ball. I have other suggestions, but work on that one first. Then we can turn to your other problems."

Unbelievable, Knight thought as the demonstration mesmerized him. Although Egan looked tired, he responded to live questions that appeared online throughout the demonstration. He appeared personally on the conference room screen and the webcast insert. Still, something seemed amiss.

Then he heard a reporter ask if Edelwise's stock price could remain at its current seven-hundred-dollar level, and Egan answered, "I could ask the computer, but I know what it will tell us. Before this is all over, it will go much, much higher."

Knight had heard enough. He didn't need to be reminded of the fortune he'd foregone by selling his Edelwise stock almost fifteen years ago.

*　　　　　　*　　　　　　*

As the webcast ended, Phil McGinty finished his fourth drink and returned the bottle of Jack Daniel's to his desk drawer. He was an angry drunk. Every time he thought about the years of abuse that Ratkin had inflicted on him, he became livid. Trying to keep himself in check, he feared that too much whiskey on this morning had left him with too little strength to keep his animosities at bay. He picked up the phone and dialed a number he'd never before called.

"I'm giving you a name," he said. "The rest is up to you. Lucinda Alvarez."

Then he hung up, wondering if he'd be able to live with himself when this nightmarish ordeal was over. He reopened his desk drawer and poured another drink in a futile pursuit: trying to escape from the person he'd become.

CHAPTER 23

Ratkin's trial in Boston continued for the rest of July. Compucom would have the last word in its rebuttal case, beginning on the first Monday in August.

"It's totally unfair," Ratkin complained to young partners regularly. "We represent the defendant, and the plaintiff gets to go first and last. It's like giving the home team the first and last at bats in a baseball game. The whole system is rigged against defendants. It will be a miracle if I win this case."

Of course, they all agreed; pandering is not a spectator sport.

On the first Monday in August, Compucom's counsel presented his request to supplement his witness list with a person not previously identified in any of the pretrial submissions. He handed Ratkin the formal motion as they approached the bench. Ratkin scanned it quickly. The color left his face when he saw the proposed new witness's name.

"Your Honor, Compucom respectfully requests leave to supplement the trial witness list to add a person who recently came to our attention," Ratkin's opposing counsel began. "Her name is Lucinda Alvarez."

Ratkin's heart raced as he struggled to maintain his poker face.

"Your Honor," Ratkin responded, "this comes as a complete surprise. Who is this person? And why are we hearing about her for the first time just as the plaintiff is set to begin presenting evidence during its rebuttal case?"

In pressing his adversary about Alvarez's identity, he was running a bluff. He knew perfectly well that she was the nurse McGinty had hired to tend Joshua Egan during his final months. He convinced himself that his opening reaction to her disclosure was not misleading because, after all, Ratkin wasn't saying that he didn't know who she was. He was just asking the judge to determine if Compucom's lawyer knew anything about her. Such were the fine distinctions that made Ronald Ratkin the effective litigator he was.

"They never identified her in response to interrogatories we served in the case," Ratkin continued. "Nor did her name appear in any of the documents either side produced."

Ratkin didn't mention that he'd never identified Alvarez in response to Compucom's requests for information about persons with potential knowledge about the case, either. He'd concluded that disclosing her name wasn't necessary because she didn't have any relevant information. Ratkin viewed that as one of the ultimate beauties of the Federal Rules of Civil Procedure. Though the rules required extensive pretrial exchange of information to eliminate procedural gamesmanship and trials by surprise, each lawyer made a threshold relevance determination with respect to what his or her own client would produce to an adversary. The rules themselves operated on an honor system, so there was no meaningful remedy for materials improperly withheld on relevance grounds—unless they somehow turned up later. Ratkin had learned that lesson twenty-five years earlier when he came across clearly pertinent documents in the case that he and Knight had worked on as Hopkins's associates. The other side had withheld key reports that inadvertently made their way into Ratkin's hands. He countered by slipping them into a box of useless invoices. From there, they eventually made their way into the trial that Hopkins won.

"Your Honor," Compucom's lead counsel continued, "I'm not sure what her role is. We received an anonymous call from someone who gave us her name and nothing more. The caller didn't identify himself, nor did he explain what information she had. But we've now conducted enough of an investigation to conclude that she might have useful information that this jury should hear."

Ratkin still hadn't heard an answer to the question that vexed him: what did Compucom's lawyer know about Alvarez and her connection to Egan, McGinty, Ratkin, and Edelwise? He took a deep breath while trying to gauge the judge's reaction. Mostly, he saw boredom. Ratkin quickly realized that if he suppressed his own intense reaction to the potential new witness, the judge would take care of his immediate concern—namely, Lucinda Alvarez's possible trial appearance.

"Well," Ratkin said nonchalantly, "I have no idea what this person will say or what relevance her testimony may have to the issues in this case, and neither do you, Judge. I do object to this grandstand play."

"Your Honor, we just found out about her," Compucom's lawyer answered. "We understand that she was in this country for a while but then left quite unexpectedly two months ago. We haven't spoken to her yet, but we expect to do so shortly. We have taken this tip seriously and are pursuing every lead aggressively."

"Wait a minute, wait a minute, wait a minute," the judge interrupted. "You mean to tell me that you want to add a witness to the list now, as we're ending this thing, even though you haven't even met with her yet?"

"That's correct, Judge."

"And you have no idea where she is at this moment?" he continued incredulously.

"That's correct, Judge."

"And, if you find her, you have no idea what she'll say or how, if at all, it will relate to this case?" The wily old judge knew when he had a lawyer twisting in the wind.

"That's correct, Judge."

"And so when, might I ask, do you plan to put her on the stand?" The judge had changed his mocking tone to irritation. Ratkin was sure that anger followed close behind.

"That leads to my next request," said Compucom's lawyer. He was usually effective, just not as smooth as Ratkin. His position, however, was untenable. "We're very close to nailing this down definitively, and we're asking that the court order a two-week recess while we get to the bottom of this."

Bingo, thought Ratkin as he rolled his eyes and shook his head in feigned disbelief. He knew the judge would now go ballistic.

"You're kidding," the judge barked. His voice became louder as he leaned forward in his chair above the two combatants. "I've had this case for ten years. We've had this jury here for almost three months. And you want to give them a summer vacation for two weeks so they can then come back and maybe hear additional evidence that you know nothing about from a witness you've never met or spoken to?"

"I know it's extraordinary, your Honor, but we can see no other way to proceed," said the attorney, who faced an impossible uphill climb.

Ratkin knew he'd won this round. With the judge already on his side, anything he said or did now would only slow the momentum to victory. In such situations, it was always better to continue letting out the rope as an adversary constructed his own noose.

"What say you, Mr. Ratkin?" the judge asked as he sat back in his chair.

"I say 'extraordinary' doesn't quite capture the moment," Ratkin accepted the baton with a broad smile. "I also say that we'd never finish a trial in our system if a litigant had the latitude to string a case along in the way my learned opponent is now requesting. This isn't like baseball, a game that theoretically can continue forever." It was pitch-perfect for the one-man audience that mattered.

"I agree," the judge announced briskly as he sprung forward. "If you have more you want to tell me about this supposed witness and what she might have to say, do it now. Otherwise, you're wasting everyone's time with this one."

"I wish I knew more myself," said Compucom's attorney as he resigned himself to the fate he'd assumed would be his from the beginning. "All I can tell you is that she is a woman who we reasonably believe may have information that could matter to this case. She's been out of the country for the past month or so. More than that, I don't know."

"Motion denied. Do you have anything else before proceeding with your final evidence?"

"No, sir," said both attorneys simultaneously.

"Very well," the judge concluded. "Mr. Ratkin, could I have your thoughts on the likely schedule from this point?"

Ratkin knew that after an incident such as this one, the judge would remain on his side for the rest of the trial. Judicial confidence in an attorney can be tenuous; Compucom's lawyer had just blown his forever. Ratkin specialized in putting the opposing lawyer's credibility on trial at least as much as any hostile witness. By the end of any long case, judges always deferred to him. As difficult and time-consuming as they were, his were the most interesting matters on any judge's docket. And he knew how to work the room in ways few others could.

"If, as opposing counsel has indicated, he has another three weeks of evidence, that means we'll have our jury instruction conference in late August, closing arguments shortly thereafter, and deliberations can begin around Labor Day. If the jury follows past practice based on my previous experience in long trials like this one, they'll pick a foreman and start looking at evidence before adjourning for the long weekend. They'll then resume deliberations the following Tuesday."

"All right," the judge agreed. "All counsel should anticipate a timetable according to Mr. Ratkin's suggestions. Let's get this case to the jury before Labor Day. We'll break for fifteen minutes and then resume with the jury."

"Thank you, your Honor," they said in unison as the judge rose from his chair and returned to his chambers.

Ratkin walked briskly from the courtroom and took the elevator to the ground floor. As he left the building, he called McGinty on his cell phone. His timeline was still intact, but he had a new concern.

"Tell me more about Egan's nurse," he said quietly to Edelwise's general counsel, who, with his trusty bottle of Jack Daniel's, had once again commenced his daily self-medication regimen.

CHAPTER 24

When the court day ended, Ratkin returned to what litigators called the *war room*. In cities where Michelman & Samson didn't have an office, the firm created a temporary one at client expense. In the Compucom case, it had leased two floors of a downtown office building just off the Boston Common. Staffed with attorneys, secretaries, legal assistants, messengers, IT specialists, and an office manager, it had everything necessary to create the firm's vaunted culture of excellence. For the duration of the trial and several months preceding it, the hundred-person operation would make M&S's war room alone one of the largest law firms in the city.

As at the conclusion of every trial day, Ratkin met alone with the attorneys working for him on the case. Senior trial lawyers at M&S typically operated according to one of two models: pyramid or hub and spokes. The hub-and-spokes system put the lead courtroom lawyer in the middle of everything. He delegated directly to attorneys at all experience levels and maintained personal control over every detail. Younger attorneys preferred this to the pyramid model, in which the senior partner interacted only with the next most senior partner on the case who, in turn, adhered to a strict chain of command with respect to those reporting to him. Ratkin followed the pyramid approach. He had no use for underlings, except to abuse them if they committed the error of crossing him. Still, he thought making an appearance to the larger group at day's end helped team morale. He viewed himself as an energizing force and a charismatic leader. Although he overestimated his personal appeal in some settings, even skeptics regarded him with fear and awe.

"We had an interesting day," Ratkin began to address the large group of lawyers under his command. "But before we get into that, I want to know who among the team here speaks fluent Spanish."

Four hands shot into the air; three others went up more slowly.

"I'd like to meet with the seven of you while someone else briefs the rest of the group on the day's developments," he continued. That someone else was the non-equity partner whom Ratkin had selected to remain in the back row of the gallery and take extensive notes of each day's proceedings. Whenever Ronald Ratkin tried a case, he was the only attorney for his client who ever passed through the swinging courtroom gate separating spectators from the arena of battle.

The seven who'd raised their hands followed Ratkin into a small conference room, where he gave a simple assignment.

"I need to know who among you is the most fluent Spanish speaker," he said. "And I need to know it in fifteen minutes."

The candidates looked quizzically at each other, wondering how to choose a winner. As always, Ratkin had the solution.

"So here's what we're going to do. I'm going to sit here and watch all of you converse in Spanish. Then, I'll ask each of you who is the most fluent. So please begin."

Ratkin watched the seven, who ranged from a first-year associate to a thirty-eight-year-old non-equity partner. Even though he couldn't understand a word they spoke, he knew excellence in anything when he saw it. A young female associate, Maria Morales, would certainly be the group's designee, he concluded. Fifteen minutes later, Ratkin brought the room to silence.

"It's Maria Morales, isn't it?" he announced.

Surprised, they all nodded in agreement. They realized they were witnessing firsthand an aspect of the genius that accounted for Ratkin's success.

"Do you have your passport with you?" Ratkin asked.

"Yes, sir," she said without any trace of a Spanish accent.

"The rest of you may return to the daily review meeting. Maria, I'd like to speak with you about a special assignment."

* * *

Maria Morales was a first-generation American. Her parents had emigrated from Mexico to southern California as teenagers. Now twenty-eight, Morales had graduated with honors from Stanford Law School and found a second home in Chicago's large Latino community. Single and unattached, she'd worked seventy-hour weeks during each of her first two years at Michelman & Samson. Observing her long dark hair, black eyes, and remarkable physical beauty, Ratkin thought it seemed almost tragic that she hadn't become a fashion model.

"The assignment I have is extremely important and highly confidential," he began. "You are to discuss it with no one but me."

Excitement surged through Morales as he spoke. As a third-year associate working directly on an important task for Ronald Ratkin, she'd be the envy of every associate in the firm. In addition to her intellect, Morales had street smarts. She knew that having Ratkin as an advocate assured her of great things at M&S.

"Edelwise has retained a consulting expert who's now living in Costa Rica," he continued. "What I need you to do is go down there, meet with her, and try to get her to compromise herself. You can't tell her that you work for Edelwise or its law firm. We need to know whether she can be trusted to remain quiet if the other side approaches her. As you know, consulting experts occupy a special place in our trial rules. We never have to disclose them to anyone. They're not permitted to speak with anyone about their work for us. They're essentially off limits to the world."

Morales hung on his every word. She'd hoped that she'd learn a lot working on his case, but this was a tutorial she'd never imagined.

"She lives in Costa Rica. You'll go and see if you can trick her into telling you anything at all about her connection to Edelwise. If she does, she'll have violated her duties as a consulting expert. You must report that to me immediately so we can take appropriate action."

"I assume you have her address," Morales braved a verbal reaction.

"Yes, she lives in Las Mesas de Pejibaye. Her name is Lucinda Alvarez. Get a flight to San Jose as soon as possible, and keep me advised every step of the way."

CHAPTER 25

At five-thirty Tuesday morning, Morales boarded her flight to Miami, where she'd change planes and arrive in San Jose shortly after eleven o'clock local time, logging almost 2,400 miles before noon. Throughout the trip, she was preoccupied with the thrill of her new assignment. Euphoria diverted her attention from the short, stocky man chewing his unlit cigar in the gate area of her flights. They had the same itinerary.

On the plane, she focused on the only portion of the consulting agreement between Lucinda Alvarez and Edelwise that Ratkin had given her:

"Alvarez agrees that she will not disclose the fact of her Edelwise retention, employment, or service in any capacity to any person or entity. Alvarez further and specifically agrees that she will not aid, assist, or cooperate in any manner with any person or entity (including attorneys and agents) who has claims against Edelwise or who may bring any claim against the Company."

Did this mean that Alvarez could not even disclose her work to Edelwise personnel? What about the IRS when she filled out her income tax return? Did that constitute disclosure? Or was the concept "except as required by law" implied in any contract of this nature? Morales certainly had limited experience in such matters, but this provision seemed remarkably broad.

After landing in San Jose, she grabbed a sandwich that she ate at the rental counter as she picked up a car. Once behind the wheel, she found her way to the Pan-American Highway. South of San Isidro, she passed Chirripo National Park before reaching a dirt road on the right that took her to San Miguel.

Adrenaline overcame exhaustion as she proceeded to the small village Ratkin had identified. She quizzed the blonde, blue-eyed Tican men and women about Lucinda Alvarez. The children, she thought, were especially beautiful.

The strength of the small village's community was evident, even to a brief interloper like Morales. All families lived within severely limited financial means and without things that most Americans took for granted. Still, they exuded an energy and enthusiasm that was infectious. They worked; they laughed; they supported each other. It was, she thought, the opposite of the feeling she had most days at Michelman & Samson. But then again, no one ever accused any big firm of being warm, fuzzy, or a substitute for a healthy family. After an hour of questions to these open and friendly people, she found what she believed was the Alvarez home. She stepped onto the porch and knocked on the door. An elderly woman answered.

"Buenos días, donde está Lucinda Alvarez?" she asked, explaining that she was looking for the young woman who lived there.

"She's not here," the woman answered in Spanish, the language in which they completed their conversation. "She might be back later today. I don't know. She comes and goes."

"May I wait for her?"

"As you like," the old woman shrugged and pointed to a chair on the porch.

Morales sat and pulled out a research memorandum she'd been writing before Ratkin gave her the special assignment. Ratkin had told her that she shouldn't identify her whereabouts on her time entries, referring instead simply to "special project." She wondered if Ratkin had been serious when he said she could double-bill any time spent on the special project when it overlapped with other billable activities. On the plane, she'd worked on other things. Did that mean she could bill both those and her special project travel time for the same hour? He must have been joking, she concluded. After less than an hour, Lucinda Alvarez approached the porch.

"Who are you, and what are you doing on my mother's porch?" she asked Morales in her native tongue.

Ratkin had cautioned Morales to develop a strategy that included a false name in seeking to test Alvarez's integrity.

"My name is Mercedes Diaz," Morales answered in English. "I'm here to ask you about your recent time in America. You worked for Edelwise, didn't you? Can you tell me about it?"

"I'm not required to answer any questions," Alvarez shot back the phrase that Phil McGinty had pounded into her head.

"That, of course, is correct," Morales replied. They continued and concluded the rest of their conversation in English. "But I have to inform you that it will be better for you to answer my questions now than if I have to involve other authorities. At this point, it's all quite routine. But your failure to cooperate can change all of that immediately."

"I didn't kill him," Alvarez blurted. "He died a natural death."

"Who died a natural death?" Morales wondered what kind of consulting expert Ratkin had hired in Alvarez.

"I have already told you too much," she said. "I have nothing more to say to you or to anyone else. Let the authorities do whatever they will with me."

With that, Alvarez slammed the front door. Morales walked slowly away from the porch and back to her rental car. Consulting expert—Edelwise—natural death—special assignment from Ratkin; none of it made any sense.

*   *   *

Without any particular destination in mind, Morales drove north along the Pan-American Highway. Needing to clear her head, she looked for a beach and hoped that the sea air would help solve the mystery that her trip had become. Several hours had passed since she'd left the poverty of the Alvarez's porch when she encountered the Papagayo Peninsula and one of the most fabulous resorts she'd ever seen. She pulled up to the entrance, and the valet opened her car door.

Entering the lobby, she saw real-life vignettes depicting all phases of life. In a remote corner, newlyweds gazed at each other in contemplation of their lives ahead. Near the concierge desk, a man in his thirties was so transfixed to his BlackBerry that he was oblivious to the futile attempts of his wife and two young children to get his attention as they tried to plan the upcoming days of the family's annual summer vacation. Near the reception area, a forty-something lawyer spoke on a cell phone as he checked with his office in New York, talking so loudly as to leave no doubt about his occupation or self-importance. One of the hotel's representatives tried to quiet him with a gentle finger to his own lips after the man's wife and teenage son had failed in similar efforts. Walking toward Morales and the front entrance through which she'd just passed, a middle-aged woman carried a briefcase as a nanny followed three steps behind and held the hand of the woman's young daughter, who was about eight. Walking out to the pool, she saw a man in his mid-fifties typing feverishly on a laptop computer while his toddler used her thumbs to operate a handheld game. He had to be on his second marriage, if not his third.

Morales had seen first-rate hotels before. In fact, she'd stayed in some of the best when she traveled for Michelman & Samson's clients. She'd also seen contrasts between rich and poor as striking as the differences between this resort and Alvarez's village, but somehow the moment and its juxtaposition with the village she'd just left swallowed her. The resort and its guests awakened and disgusted her. She realized that if she succeeded on her current career track, it would someday take her metaphorically, if not literally, to this very spot, insufficiently remote to avoid BlackBerrys, cell phones, nannies, and multiple marriages. Terrorized by her own thoughts, she wanted to escape and rid herself of the resort's residue. Needing something more than a shower, she wanted to cleanse her body so thoroughly that it might penetrate her soul, too.

Morales walked briskly back to the valet, retrieved her car, and drove until she discovered a nearby public beach. After pulling off the road, she removed her clothes, opened the car door, and sprinted across the gold-sand beach into the ocean. She didn't see the car that had been following her with its lights off. The driver was the same man chewing on his unlit cigar whom she hadn't noticed on her flight to Central America. Ever patient, he pulled over and waited.

*   *   *

The next morning, Morales awoke in the backseat of her rental car, put on her tailored business suit, and began the long drive back to the San Jose International Airport. She knew that persuasive argumentation had always been one of her greatest strengths. From childhood, her parents had told her that particular skill would make her a great lawyer someday. So she turned those formidable guns on herself and took careful aim.

She attributed the previous day's overreaction to the resort inhabitants as the product of fatigue and stress. They'd combined to drive her temporarily insane. In the calm light of day, she could see that she'd worked hard to attain her current position. No one just gives all that up. No job is perfect; that's why they call it work. Whether she'd ultimately succeed according to Michelman & Samson's definition remained to be seen and, to a large degree, was out of her hands. Meanwhile, she'd honor her professional code and do the best she could for her clients. If fortune smiled upon her, she'd tackle its challenges just as she'd conquered equally formidable obstacles that life had erected. She could write her own story, and it need not include the chapters that so troubled her as she'd looked briefly into the windows of disconnected lives at the Papagayo Peninsula resort.

Reoriented to her immediate mission, she sat at the airport gate and called Ratkin. He'd given her his private cell phone number and told her to use it any time, day or night, whenever she had anything to report. Calculating the time difference, Morales concluded that the trial was probably in the middle of a lunch break. It was noon in Boston when Ratkin's cell phone rang; he'd set it on vibrate. When he saw the call was coming from Morales, he told his trial team members to leave his office and close the door on their way out.

"Yes, Maria," he began. "So how's it going?"

"Fine, Mr. Ratkin. I'm in the San Jose Airport and preparing to return to the United States."

"Did you speak with Alvarez?"

"Yes. But she didn't want to talk to me. She said I could send the authorities for her if I wanted to, but she had no intention of speaking with anyone about anything relating to Edelwise."

Perfect, Ratkin thought. So McGinty hadn't screwed it up after all.

"She blurted out something peculiar, though," Morales continued. "It still makes no sense to me."

"What's that?"

"She said, 'I didn't kill him. He died a natural death.' Do you have any idea what that means?"

Ratkin felt his pulse accelerate. Those words alone would not matter, provided no one other than Morales ever heard them and provided he could give a persuasive answer to her question.

"It's hard to say," he said cautiously, "but it sounds like she might have been emotionally overwrought. Perhaps someone in her family died recently. Grief can be overwhelming and powerful."

"That makes sense. She did seem quite upset. But one thing is clear, Mr. Ratkin, she's certainly not telling anyone about her status as an Edelwise consulting expert. You can breathe easily on that one."

He smiled at his efficiency. A third-year associate was not going to second-guess Ronald Ratkin's explanation of an innocuous comment from an irrelevant witness. He was having a good week. Monday had begun with an adversary's motion that had caused high anxiety, but only two days later he'd dealt with it completely and definitively. Ratkin could close the book on this chapter; his doubts about McGinty's disposition of Lucinda Alvarez had been resolved. He'd earned the Ritz-Carlton's finest bottle of Bordeaux that he'd order with his room service dinner that evening.

Morales turned off her cell phone and placed it in her purse. For the first time, she noticed a short man chewing on an unlit cigar as they waited for the next plane to Miami. He smiled at her, and she smiled back.

PART IV

OBITUARIES

SAMUEL G. WILSON, longtime partner in the law firm of Michelman & Samson, died of a sudden heart attack yesterday in his home at the age of seventy-five. Born in Minneapolis, he graduated with honors from the University of Minnesota and Harvard Law School. He spent his career at Michelman & Samson, retiring after thirty-eight years. A fellow of the American College of Trial Lawyers, he tried cases throughout the country.

Some of Wilson's adversaries became his greatest admirers. "He was a consummate professional," said Gordon Swenson, an opponent whose client lost a three-month jury trial to Wilson twenty years ago. "I suspect if you interviewed every lawyer who tried a case against him, they'd all say the same thing. He knew how to do an effective job for his client without wading into the acrimonious swamp where many of us find ourselves mired. By the sheer force of his example, he made us better."

Colleagues at his former firm remembered how he described his most important accomplishments. Michelman & Samson senior partner Albert Knight noted, "He bragged to people that he was still married to his first wife and their adult children still talked to him. He also quoted Supreme Court Justice Joseph Story: 'The law is a jealous mistress.' But he insisted that there was no reason to give in to her every demand. Sam was a special person. When young lawyers asked him about career success that he'd sacrificed to maintain a balanced life, he said, 'No one on their death bed ever wished they'd spent more time at the office. I'm as successful as I need to be. That's enough.' More of us should have listened to him—and we should still heed his words."

Survived by his wife of fifty-three years, three children, and five grandchildren, Wilson will be honored at a memorial service to be held on Tuesday, August 11, at 1:00 PM.

CHAPTER 26

A mahogany casket rested in the center aisle between the lectern and the pulpit. A velvet cord isolated the front nineteen pews: "Reserved." Immediate family members sat in the first two rows; the next seventeen were empty. The rest of the church had filled to capacity with friends, extended family, and forty-somethings who had played on the little league baseball and girls' softball teams that Sam Wilson had coached a long time ago. As the musical prelude ended, the equity partners of Michelman & Samson assembled in the foyer. They would enter based upon their current equity allocations in the firm. The magnificent seven led the way.

One by one, men in dark suits and far fewer women in black dresses filed down the aisle and past the mourners. Anyone watching had to be impressed that, at least for this moment, death stopped even M&S. The solemn e-mail announcing the funeral arrangements made clear that every equity partner was expected to attend the final farewell for this departed former member of their brethren. As some young attorneys at the firm wryly observed, it was the final perk of equity partnership.

They walked in three-step intervals. All remained standing as they filled the pews behind the immediate family—the third, the fourth, the fifth, and so on. Two hundred seventy-two M&S equity partners from around the world sat together in seventeen pews, eight attorneys on each side of the aisle. Silently, they communicated a single message: a former Michelman & Samson senior partner is dead; long live the firm.

Words were spoken, but nothing more needed to be said as far as Albert Knight was concerned. Michelman & Samson was central to what even Sam Wilson had been. It formed the core of what Albert Knight would always be, all the way to the end.

* * *

Daniel Schmidt sat at his desk as he finished reading Wilson's obituary Friday evening. "He was the only guy in the place worth a damn," he muttered to himself. "The only one." He then resumed his review of the most recent blogger post from the reporter covering the *Compucom v. Edelwise* trial:

"With the artistic flourish of an Olympic fencer, Ronald Ratkin has vanquished every witness taking the stand against his client. Compucom's lawyer has done a yeoman's job in opposition, but he can't compete with this master of his craft. Facing Compucom's eleventh-hour attempt last Monday to add a surprise witness, Lucinda Alvarez, Ratkin showed his deft skills of thrust and parry. Allowing the trial judge to do his work for him, Ratkin offered strategic support to the court's battering of Compucom's attorney. Its tardiness and mystery doomed the motion from the beginning, but Ratkin used it to score more general credibility points that should carry him to the end of the trial. His adversary must feel like the proverbial unarmed man in this seemingly endless duel."

Schmidt printed the report and circled Alvarez's name before putting it in his personal Edelwise/Ratkin file. Although it was probably just another dead end, his years as an M&S associate had taught him that sometimes small details could make or break a case. Anything knowable should be known; nothing controllable should be left to chance.

*　　　　*　　　　*

The dog days of summer, Knight thought as he walked up Michigan Avenue to the Four Seasons Hotel. Even at ten o'clock in the evening, a hot August night in Chicago could be brutal. At such times, people who could summon the strength to move often killed each other. When he'd first arrived thirty years earlier, Knight assumed that the Windy City was always that, not realizing that the phrase originated offhandedly in an 1858 *Chicago Tribune* article and then reappeared as a pejorative reference to its citizens' incessant bragging. When he learned the epithet's true meaning, he thought it captured the ethos of Michelman & Samson perfectly.

Often in August, the heat, humidity, and dead air combined to suffocate everything. Sam Wilson had gotten out of here just in time, Knight mused sacrilegiously, knowing that Wilson himself would have appreciated his joke. By the time he reached the hotel lobby, perspiration soaked Knight's shirt. Despite the ninety-degree heat and unbearable humidity even at night, he'd worn his suit coat throughout the trek. The concept of casual work attire was irrelevant to him. Even his tie remained in place.

"If others want to walk the halls of Michelman & Samson looking like mailroom delivery boys, let them," he often preached. "I am a partner in the greatest law firm in the world and will always dress the part."

After their first year of trysts, his regular rendezvous with Fran had assumed a comfortable routine. A creature of habit, he found that his activities mattered less than the regularity and predictability with which he performed them. He always needed someplace to be. The most surprising aspect of the relationship was that, after fifteen years, Fran remained interested in him. He viewed it mostly as testament to how badly Ratkin must have been ignoring her. Ironically, he hadn't given his own wife any more attention than Ratkin seemed to have provided Fran.

She'd sent him a text message with her room number so he could avoid the front desk. God, how he loved BlackBerrys. Ten years earlier, he had to guess whether at any given moment a client might be trying to reach him. Cell phones were only a partial solution because not everyone had his number. Certainly, any new client wanting the incomparable services of Albert Knight wouldn't have it. His BlackBerry gave him a way to work at maximum effectiveness twenty-four hours a day, seven days a week. Even between shots during a round of golf, he returned to the cart and checked it religiously. As success at Michelman & Samson became an endurance contest, he was perfectly suited to win it.

When he arrived at the hotel room door, he tapped lightly. Fran opened it, and he could see that, as always, she was dressed for a good time—which is to say, she was wearing not very much at all.

"You know Sam Wilson's service was today," he began while adding tonic to the glass of Tanqueray that she always had waiting for him.

"Yes," she answered, wondering if she'd detected a tear in his eye or if the light had caught it at an angle that made it appear so. "I'm sorry. I know you liked him. I'm sure you're quite sad about his passing."

"I'm just not sure I'll be much fun," he continued as she slipped off his coat, removed his tie, and unbuttoned his wet shirt. Lifting his undershirt over his head as he spoke, she couldn't believe how many layers he was wearing on such a sweltering day.

"Why don't you just relax and let me do all the work tonight?"

An offer he couldn't refuse, he thought. Still, what kind of scoundrel would bury a former partner in the afternoon and then screw another partner's wife that evening? He still had no answer to the question of who he was. But he let her do all the work, just as she had suggested.

CHAPTER 27

The Exec Com's August meeting convened on the first Saturday after Sam Wilson's memorial service. This time they all met in the firm's London office. Sometimes, Knight thought, the views from the conference rooms alone made membership on the Exec Com worthwhile and attendance at the monthly sessions tolerable. From this particular venue, he could see the Tower Bridge and the Thames.

"When we met last, this committee was poised to vote on the final remaining option for selecting the next chairman," Hopkins began. "Shall we review the bidding?"

"It seems that we really have no choice," Ratkin's ally, John Merritt began. "Since you, Charles, have declared your unwillingness to cast the deciding fourth vote and break a three-three tie between Ratkin and Knight, and because there is not a majority in favor of allowing your replacement that privilege, we're down to a single possibility: a secret-ballot election in which all equity partners cast their preferences for chairman. But that leaves a further complication."

"Which is?" Hopkins asked.

"Do we permit a plurality alone to elect the chairman? Or do we adopt a process whereby voting continues until a simple majority is achieved?" Merritt continued. "If the latter, then it seems to me we need a system whereby some candidates drop out as balloting rounds proceed; otherwise we could wind up in hopeless deadlock."

Hopkins had counted on Merritt's refinement. No chairman who obtained merely a plurality, rather than a majority, of equity partner support could serve effectively in that role. Ironically, Merritt's observation might have blown Ratkin's best chance to become chairman because a plurality was an easier threshold for the unpopular litigator to cross.

"Very well," Hopkins replied. "Is there a motion?"

Merritt's sidekick, Scott Canby, took the bait: "I move that we adopt the following process for the selection of the next chairman. First, the equity partnership shall vote initially from a ballot listing all members of the Exec Com. Second, upon the failure of any candidate to receive a majority of equity partner support in the first round, the lowest vote-getter shall drop out, and a new vote shall be taken with the remaining members as candidates. Third, that process shall continue, with the lowest vote-getter dropping out in each subsequent round, until one member of the Executive Committee has a simple majority of votes in favor of his or her becoming chairman."

"Second," said Merritt.

"All those in favor?" Hopkins asked.

"Aye," came the unanimous response; none opposed.

"Very well, gentlemen and lady," Hopkins announced with a wink toward Deborah Rush, who smiled and blushed. "We now have our new process in place. I'll send an appropriate notice to the equity partners announcing the Exec Com's unanimous agreement to this approach so they can begin to consider their votes in the election next month. I congratulate all of you in developing a consensus around what I believe is a very appropriate way to resolve a difficult issue."

Knight didn't understand why Ratkin had rolled over so easily. Then he realized that, in the end, Ratkin had no choice. Hopkins had boxed him out of the two options that would have guaranteed his ascent to the chairmanship, so he had nothing to gain in resisting the inevitable. Still, Knight thought he himself now had a greater chance to become chairman than anyone had ever given him.

Ratkin sized things up differently. He could deliver his litigation people; Merritt and Canby could deliver their corporate partners; and he had a special treat in store for the firm's latest lateral superstar, bankruptcy lawyer William Drakow.

CHAPTER 28

Having squeezed the disquieting moments at the Papagayo Peninsula resort out of her mind, Maria Morales returned to the same late-summer anxieties that afflicted all M&S associates: the annual review process. At a time when the demand for top law school graduates was still exploding, she'd begun work with eighty other recent grads in the firm's Chicago office. Three years later, her associate class—as it was called—was already down to fifty and the economy had tanked. The addition of lateral hires and attorneys who'd gone directly from law school to judicial clerkships for a few years supplemented the ranks. But in good economic times and bad, the M&S business model contemplated—even required—associate attrition on a grand scale.

One way or another, the original class would shrink until no more than fifteen of those who'd started with Morales would still be at M&S for non-equity partner consideration at the end of their sixth years. Few associates thought about an M&S career beyond that point. The chances of becoming an equity partner a dozen or more years after law school graduation seemed about the same as winning the lottery. During economic recessions when equity partners tightened everyone else's belt to preserve eye-popping earnings, the odds seemed even more daunting. Even as the Great Recession seemed to ebb, its scars remained, and everyone expected that this year's prospects for advancement at all levels to be among the worst in the firm's history.

"The firm can't really begin to make meaningful distinctions among associates after only one year," the reviewing attorney had told Morales during her first review in a year when the economy boomed and they needed to retain bodies logging billable hours for flush clients. "So except for recruiting mistakes—that is, those who never should have been here in the first place—most people get a pass for their first year or two. Some choose to leave for their own reasons; we can't keep them if they want to do something else. By year three, some people get the boot while others decide in increasing numbers that it's not the place for them. I think the voluntary departures in later associate years correlate to student loan repayment schedules. They get out of debt and out of the firm at about the same time. But that's just my pet theory."

Her second review consisted of a voice-mail message from a partner she'd never met:

"You're doing well. You'll be receiving a $10,000 raise and a $15,000 bonus. If you have any questions, you can call me."

Hoping to get substantive feedback and constructive suggestions for her continued development, she responded with a request to set up a meeting. A week later, she called and left a message with the partner's secretary. After that, she never heard anything more on the subject and gave up.

Now, having completed her third year, Morales hoped that the special assignment for Ronald Ratkin might give her an edge over her classmates, or at least a reasonable chance to keep her job in what promised to be a tough year for any associate's survival. The only problem was that the review year for all associates had ended in June, meaning that only her work and billed time through that month factored explicitly in her upcoming evaluation. Still, Morales knew that unusual events after the cutoff often made their way into associate review committee deliberations. If she played her situation correctly, she could get credit for the special Ratkin project this year and, if she survived, next year as well.

Upon returning from Costa Rica, she sent an e-mail to the associate review committee coordinator:

"This supplements my review materials for the current cycle. I recently completed a highly confidential project for Mr. Ratkin in connection with the *Compucom v. Edelwise* trial. Mr. Ratkin chose me specifically because it required fluency in Spanish and strong interpersonal skills. I worked directly with Mr. Ratkin on this project, and he can provide additional information about my performance. – Maria Morales."

The associate review coordinator received such special messages every day during the two-month review process that began July 1 and continued through the end of August.

"Every lawyer in this friggin' place thinks he or she is something special," muttered Helen Peterson, whose newest additional assignment beyond her secretarial work for Hopkins and five other lawyers was to provide overflow assistance to the associate review committee staff. Whenever the firm announced layoffs, those who kept their jobs had to pick up the slack wherever it appeared. After scanning the message and finding a partner name—Ronald Ratkin—she clicked twice on her computer's mouse to move the message into the appropriate electronic file and generate a notice to Ratkin that he would have to complete an online associate evaluation. She then resumed her private monologue: "A whole generation of associates who think they are special because their starting salaries alone are three times what I make after almost forty years here. Ridiculous. Most of them can't wipe their own noses."

Instantaneously, an electronic message informed Ronald Ratkin that he had another associate evaluation to complete: "Maria Morales."

"This one will be easy," he thought as he followed the link to the file where he alone could decide whether the twenty-eight-year-old woman would remain at Michelman & Samson for another year. He had specifically told her not to mention the special assignment to anyone and was irritated that she'd supplemented her associate review submission to include it. Still, she'd otherwise handled the delicate situation well, and it appeared that the whole episode had ended safely for him and Edelwise.

He felt like a Roman emperor in the Coliseum after watching gladiators fight for their lives: thumbs up or thumbs down? He could pave the way for her future success or send her packing with a review for which there was no appeal. No one second-guessed Ronald Ratkin's assessment of a third-year associate. High-powered lawyers who made millions defending their clients' due process rights ignored the concept when it came to the treatment of their own. Sipping from a glass of fine red wine in one hand, he poked at his keyboard to complete Maria Morales's online review with the other.

CHAPTER 29

Knight was sitting at his desk when the lobby receptionist called on a Wednesday afternoon in late August.

"There's a man here who says he must speak personally with you on a matter of great urgency," she said.

"Who is it?" he asked.

"He says he's an old friend."

"I'll be right there."

Knight walked to the elevator that took him to the main floor. Upon exiting, he saw a man in a dark suit and gray fedora. He was holding a large manila envelope.

"These are for you," he said before turning and walking away.

As Knight returned to the M&S elevator bank, he opened the envelope to find five glossy photographs. As he looked at the first one, he stopped abruptly and looked back in stunned silence for the mysterious man who'd given him the package. Too late; he'd vanished.

His hands trembling, Knight flipped through the other four photographs before returning to the first one, taken at the Four Seasons Hotel many years earlier. Someone had snapped the picture while he and Fran were in bed. Studying it more closely, he cocked his head as he struggled to determine the angle and wondered how it had been taken. Then he realized the photographer had been outside the building. Whether from a helicopter or through a telephoto lens from a neighboring building, someone had penetrated their privacy without physically entering the room. He couldn't believe how young he looked; Fran looked even better.

The second photo was similar, but recent. Comparing it to the first, he realized that when now encountering Fran in their biweekly Tuesday night sessions, he was seeing what he wanted to see—an image from times long gone—and not the harsher reality in the picture he held. In fact, Knight thought, the photograph was probably taken the night after Sam Wilson's memorial service, when Fran had done all the work for both of them. He couldn't recall another time when he and she had assumed those particular positions.

The third photo included three for the price of one: Catherine was in bed at the Knights' summer home with her tennis instructor and landscaper. He couldn't have cared less about it. She'd become irrelevant to his life, and he to hers, long ago.

The fourth photo was taken in a tropical climate. He didn't recognize either of the two female images and had no idea why it was significant.

The fifth and final photo made his jaw drop. It pictured Ronald Ratkin in bed with Joshua Egan, chairman and founder of Edelwise. Someone had taken it a long time ago. Ratkin appeared to be in his late thirties or early forties. Knight paused momentarily to consider what was happening in his life at that time. The answer became obvious: he'd lost Edelwise as a client and gained Fran as a lover. The symmetry had been perfect, but now there was another dimension to the episode that he hadn't contemplated.

Realizing that he'd frozen in place near the lobby receptionist, Knight shoved the photos into the envelope and walked briskly to the elevator. Once in his office, he closed the door, locked it, and removed the pictures again. This time, he spread them across his marble-top desk and studied each one more carefully. They told a story, he thought. Every good litigator knows that the key to effective advocacy is an engaging narrative. He just had to figure out how these pieces added up and what they meant.

Knight's first thought was blackmail. Someone wanted something from him and would soon surface with a demand. When the phone rang shortly after he'd returned to the office, he grabbed it quickly, surprising his secretary, who'd routinely screened all calls for years.

"I've got it," he told her. But it was a false alarm.

"Albert," said Catherine Knight, "why are you answering your own phone? I can't remember the last time you did that."

Flustered, Knight realized that he'd overreacted. He took a deep breath and turned immediately to the task of calming himself.

"Oh, I was just picking up the phone to make a call, and you were already on the line. Can I call you back later? I'm in the middle of something."

"Sure."

He hung up and resumed his analysis of the photos. The next time the phone rang, he let his secretary answer it, just as she always had. As he felt his life turning upside down, he knew everything had to appear normal. For the rest of the afternoon, his anxieties intensified with each succeeding call to his office, but the one he expected and feared never came.

"What's this about?" he wondered aloud. Outside his window and across the horizon, the setting sun blazed reddish hues that seemed to light the early evening skies aflame. He wished Sam Wilson was still around to solve the puzzle. Wilson would know exactly how the pieces fit together and what Knight should do with them. Meanwhile, his recently deceased mentor's earlier wisdom resonated in his head: "Just don't get caught in the cross fire. People are going to get hurt in this one. I can smell it."

* * *

Twenty-four hours after making his delivery to Albert Knight, the short, stocky man returned to the lobby receptionist at Michelman & Samson. Placing his unlit cigar in his coat pocket, he asked for Ronald Ratkin.

"Certainly," she said. "And who shall I tell him is calling?"

"Tell him it's an acquaintance from Costa Rica who wants to talk to Ronnie," he replied with a smile.

Dutifully, she notified Ratkin's secretary, who passed the message on to her boss. He was in town that Friday because his opponents had moved more quickly than anticipated in wrapping up their rebuttal case. Ratkin didn't want the jury to begin its deliberations any earlier than the Friday before Labor Day. So at his request, the judge had given the jury two days off at the end of August. Walking briskly, Ratkin went immediately to the elevator. By the time he reached the lobby, his visitor had disappeared into the Wacker Drive lunch crowd.

"Mr. Ratkin, the man asking for you left this," said the preternaturally chipper receptionist as she handed him a sealed manila envelope with his name on it marked "CONFIDENTIAL."

He opened it and quickly scanned the same five photographs that, unknown to Ratkin, the mysterious man had left for Knight a day earlier. Each now had the ammunition needed to destroy the other, but neither knew his adversary was similarly armed. Overcoming an initial shock at the collection, Ratkin quickly concluded that this cache would secure his rightful position as chairman of the Exec Com. Ronald Ratkin knew how to deal with a fully loaded gun aimed at an adversary: he'd pull the trigger.

CHAPTER 30

"Charles, it's Ronald," Ratkin began their phone conversation. "I need to speak with you on a matter of great urgency."

"Certainly, Ronald. I'm free now," Hopkins replied. "Why don't you drop by my office?"

"I'll be right up."

Breezing past Helen Peterson without even a nod of acknowledgement, Ratkin entered the most impressive work space in all of Michelman & Samson. Although the twenty floors of attorneys in the firm's high-rise building included many corner offices, Hopkins's was metaphorically perfect: at the top. His panoramic view through floor-to-ceiling windows overlooked Lake Michigan to the east and Chicago's financial district to the south. He sat at an antique roll-top desk. Similarly aged eighteenth-century pieces adorned the place, along with paintings he'd purchased at Sotheby's auctions over the prior thirty years. The firm had a special $5 million insurance rider to cover the priceless items surrounding him.

More than a hundred custom-made bound leather volumes of court filings lined ancient bookshelves, complementing two dozen miniature Lucite cubes that encased signed jury verdict forms from each of his trials—the wins, that is—on a matching credenza. All of these carefully selected materials documented an entire career, starting with his first case as an associate.

Most people in the firm knew that, for all of his trial successes and the wealth accompanying his position at the top of Michelman & Samson, Hopkins's personal life was in shambles. The consummate advocate, he'd persuaded himself that none of it had been his fault. Four years ago, his thirty-year-old son from his first marriage had been arrested for dealing drugs and imprisoned after Hopkins had refused to retain a lawyer for him. Hopkins was certain that his absence from his son's life over the previous three decades had not contributed to delinquency that he now regarded as inevitable and unavoidable. Incarceration provided natural consequences that might straighten out his offspring, but he held no real hope for meaningful change as he opined, "People are who they were always meant to be . . . and they don't change very much, ever."

Hopkins's twelve-year-old daughter from his second marriage had sided with her mother during the divorce. That didn't surprise him because everyone knew that females of all ages always banded together in such matters. On the topic of what makes women tick, he'd always regarded himself as an expert. He had underestimated his second wife and her attorney, though. Hopkins thought his prominence in the bar would intimidate them, so took a hard line during the hearing on temporary alimony: she could have their family home, child support, and little else. Twenty-four hours after her attorney sent Hopkins a letter listing the thirty-seven women he intended to subpoena to testify about the money Hopkins had spent on them during the fifteen-year marriage, Hopkins retreated. The final settlement agreement remained under court seal, preserving his secrets from the probing eyes of voyeurs. Hopkins wasn't ashamed of his prolific sexual prowess; he just didn't want to embarrass the many women who'd accommodated him.

So in the end, he'd taken the honorable path and given his ex-wife far more than she deserved. At least, that's how he viewed it.

Ratkin didn't notice the omission of family photos from the stunning décor surrounding mementos marking a life's work. He knew only that he wanted this very office someday soon. And he wanted the power and prestige that went with it.

"Charles," Ratkin began, "I have a matter of grave importance. It involves Knight."

"And what would that be?"

Advocates made their best cases based on evidence consistent with their positions. It was never their job to be fair, balanced, or completely candid. Ratkin had no obligation to show Hopkins all five of the photographs; he needed only two to make his argument: the compromising photographs of Knight with Fran.

"This sickens me," Ratkin said as he tossed the photos on Hopkins's desk. "I can't believe that my own M&S partner would behave in this way. It's scandalous. The question is: what should I do about it? That's why I've come to you. If I take the action that I'd like to pursue—sue Fran for divorce and Knight for alienation of affections—the media will feast on it. The firm will suffer, and none of us wants that."

Hopkins reviewed the pictures closely before eventually commenting, "When do you suppose these were taken?"

"Obviously at two different times. I can't tell for sure, but judging from the physical appearances of the subjects, it looks like one was taken fifteen or twenty years ago. The other could have been taken yesterday for all I know."

"Fran has held up quite remarkably over the years," Hopkins said with a smile. "She's always been quite attractive. You did well for yourself when you spirited her away from Knight."

Ratkin was surprised at the old man's knowledge of his past private intrigues but chagrined that he was missing the more important point.

"So what do you think we should do about this?" Hopkins said as he forced his eyes away from the photo and broke his trance.

"Knight must leave the firm, or I will. The current situation is untenable."

His ultimatum to Hopkins was perfect, Ratkin thought. Hopkins had asked that the cup of choosing his successor pass from his lips, and the result was next month's idiotic all-partner vote on who would lead the firm. Now Ratkin had placed him in an even hotter seat.

"That's a serious threat, Ronald. You don't really mean it, do you?"

"You bet your ass I do. I want you to cut off Knight's b-a-a-a-l-l-l-s-s-s."

"Does anyone else know about these photos?" Hopkins asked.

"Not yet."

"Let's try to do what's best for the firm and keep it that way, Ronald. I would suggest that you give me a little time to consider this. I'm sympathetic to your situation. And I certainly don't condone Knight's behavior. But if we're going to move him out of the firm, we have to do it smoothly so that M&S retains the important clients he bills. I need to investigate that issue to see how well he has positioned others to assume principal relationships with those clients. Let me start on that immediately, and we'll talk again next week."

"Fine. But there's no other option. Knight has to go."

"I'm afraid you may be correct. I'm sorry to see one of my protégés take such a wrong turn. But you may be right."

For a bunch of guys who think they're so smart, they sure are idiots, Helen Peterson thought as she removed her headset and closed her steno pad. Her boss's intercom had been on during the entire session.

CHAPTER 31

Two days after receiving the unwelcome manila envelope, Knight remained baffled. Spread across his desk were the five photographs that told a story he was supposed to construct. He tried organizing them in different ways. Considered chronologically, the photograph of Ratkin and Egan probably went first, although he couldn't be sure that was where it belonged. Then came the two pictures—fifteen years apart—of Fran in bed with him at the Four Seasons Hotel. The photo of Catherine with their landscaper and her tennis instructor could have been taken as recently as last week. The key to the puzzle was the one that held no meaning for him: two young women standing on a dilapidated porch in what was clearly a tropical climate.

He studied the faces that were oblivious to their photographer. The younger and more attractive of the two was unusually well-dressed for the setting. She seemed to be speaking calmly to the woman whose fearful expression haunted the scene. He examined the background, the trees, the nearby shacks. Why did this photo belong with the other four? How did it fit with the narrative they told?

"Mr. Knight, you wanted me to remind you about the office reception this afternoon," his secretary said as she entered his office.

"Thanks. I'll head down there right now," he said, resigned to the possibility that he'd never unravel the mystery of the fifth photograph.

* * *

On Friday before the Labor Day weekend every year, Michelman & Samson held an all-office reception for its Chicago lawyers. The summer associates were gone, and the idea was to get attorneys from every department to meet the newest full-time attorneys and mingle with each other. Associate turnout always approached one hundred percent. Most non-equity partners likewise attended because they didn't want to miss any opportunity to interact with senior partners who decided their fate. In fact, the perpetuation and growth of M&S's pyramid left the non-equity partners feeling the most vulnerable. They billed hourly rates that made them profitable for the equity partners, but they were the most significant components of the cost structure. They were also close to the day of reckoning when senior partners would decide who among them might gain the brass ring of their own equity partnerships. Even after ninety percent attrition from their original entering associate classes, most of those who remained knew they wouldn't advance to that level.

Equity partners usually didn't attend the office reception in large numbers, but Albert Knight thought such appearances were important. The tradition had endured from before he'd started at the firm thirty years ago; he hoped it would continue after he was gone. Knight viewed such institutional events as essential to his identity. He wanted every lawyer occupying a station lower than his to remember how important he'd become—one of a very few who made the place what it was. Homage, respect, and fear were his due. On these occasions, he became the image that he sought to project and protect.

To accommodate all of the six hundred Chicago office lawyers in one place, the staff had folded the collapsible partitions otherwise dividing the several rooms of the firm's conference center into wall pockets. As Knight entered the opulent open space that included a modern chandelier, he gazed upon the massive crowd, proud of the domain that he regarded as largely his. From his perspective, fewer equity partners showing up for this event was better. It freed everyone to focus on him.

Knight recognized no more than half of the attorneys and could name only a small percentage of those. It was a far cry from thirty years earlier, when he was one of a hundred and twenty lawyers in a Chicago office that occupied four floors rather than twenty. As he went to the open bar for his usual drink—a double Tanqueray and tonic—several sycophants greeted him. While holding court with three of them as he recounted his latest victory that had saved yet another of the firm's most important clients from certain disaster, he downed two more cocktails. By the fourth drink, he was telling two younger equity partners joining the conversation why they would never progress to his heights.

"You're a good second chair," he told one of his own protégés while several non-equity partners and two associates observed in horror. "But you have to step forward. You're not aggressive enough to advance to the front of the courtroom. I think you have what it takes intellectually. But you'll never get there unless you step it up a notch."

None of those listening understood his meaning or how the unfortunate target of his comments should behave differently. She was already one of the most accomplished and highly respected young equity partners in the firm. Somehow, she'd even managed to retain a semblance of a family life that included a husband and three kids. She nodded as he spoke, probably wondering how much longer she'd have to work before she could tell him to stick his advice somewhere most unpleasant. He viewed the monologue differently: any younger M&S attorney should cherish his career guidance.

He then turned to a young male equity partner who'd sacrificed his life to Knight's whims in exchange for a million-dollar annual income at M&S.

"What I have to say to you, Robert," Knight began before abruptly stopping in mid-sentence. "Excuse me; I'll be right back."

He moved swiftly past his shaken underlings and in the direction of Maria Morales, who was holding a glass of white wine while speaking with an equally attractive young male associate. As he approached them, their conversation stopped.

"Hello, I'm Albert Knight," he said, extending his right hand toward her.

"Yes, I know who you are, Mr. Knight. I'm Maria Morales."

As a courtesy, Knight also introduced himself to her companion.

"Hello," he said without taking his eyes off Morales. "Pleased to meet you."

"Cory Weinstein," the young man answered hesitatingly. "Nice to meet you, too. I've heard a lot about you. Congratulations on your win last week in the Fifth Circuit."

Knight wasn't interested in Weinstein, but he couldn't resist flattery, particularly when it invited him to elaborate on the importance of something he'd done. He'd become especially proficient in spinning client developments into wins, regardless of the outcome. But this time, he had an unambiguous victory to tout.

"You know," Knight began, "it was in an interesting case. We made new law. It's the first time that any U.S. Court of Appeals has ruled that a plaintiff can't proceed with a lawsuit against a corporation unless the company itself first agrees to be sued. Of course, that's not the way I presented it—I used the doctrine of exhausting pre-litigation remedies. But the effect of the ruling is unambiguous. My oral argument deeply moved the three-judge panel. I could see it in their faces. We moved them. We moved them profoundly. And the ruling will benefit every corporate client we represent. We should send bills to all of them. It will save corporate America billions of dollars in defense costs because they'll all use the ruling in my case to get lawsuits against them summarily dismissed."

"Until the Supreme Court reverses," said Weinstein, realizing almost immediately that his attempted humor would fall flat.

"The Supreme Court will not reverse this case because they will not take it," Knight said without missing a beat. "For the past fifteen years, we've been hiring legions of former Supreme Court clerks to work in our Washington, D.C., office. Collectively, we have an understanding of how those justices think that surpasses even their own awareness of themselves. Sure, a *cert.* petition will be filed, but this issue will not get the four required Supreme Court justice votes for review, which means it's dead. No, Mr. Weinstein, I'm afraid you're wrong. This victory will stick."

Humiliated, Weinstein excused himself, leaving Knight alone with Maria Morales.

"So, Maria, what have you been working on?"

"I've been on the *Compucom v. Edelwise* case since I began at the firm three years ago," she said proudly. She'd heard that Ratkin and Knight didn't get along particularly well, but she had no idea how much they despised each other.

"What sort of work have you been doing on the case?" Knight was certain that hers was the face in the photograph. She was even wearing the same dress.

"For the first year, I reviewed documents at the depository in Boston. After months of that, I still reviewed documents, but they let me observe depositions in the case once in a while. Last year, I began researching and writing legal memoranda on issues that might come up during trial. When the trial began, I kept doing that, although I did get interesting special assignments once in a while. It's all been quite exciting."

The truth was that Morales had found very little excitement in her work. Many times during her year reviewing company documents in a miserable warehouse, she almost quit and looked for another job. Observing depositions was more interesting, but she hadn't done anything other than watch. By the third year, she was writing legal memoranda that reminded her of the research projects she'd completed as a first-year law student at Stanford. Each year, she found the firm's famous in-house mock trial programs useful and entertaining, but they weren't real. She hadn't gone to law school so that she could pretend to be a lawyer.

Her special project for Ratkin had been the most interesting thing she'd done in three years as an attorney, but it had led nowhere, too. She now hoped simply to hang on to her M&S job long enough to finish repaying student loans, which had exceeded $150,000 by the time she received her law degree. After that, she'd do something meaningful with her talents and her life. Michelman & Samson wasn't going to be the end of her road.

"What sort of special assignments?" Knight asked.

"Oh, they're highly confidential," she said solemnly. "I'm sure you understand, but Mr. Ratkin specifically instructed that I not discuss them."

"Well, I don't want you to violate any of Mr. Ratkin's directives," he said mockingly. "But I hope you at least got some interesting travel out of it."

"Yes, indeed," she said. Surely that response didn't constitute discussing the assignment, although the moment she spoke the words, she feared that she'd already said too much. At this point, a graceful exit was her best path away from a difficult topic with one of the firm's senior partners who wielded the power of life and death over her Michelman & Samson career.

"You know, I just realized I have an appointment that I must keep," she said to Knight.

He knew she was lying. Something about the Compucom case, Ratkin, or the special assignment made her nervous. Most associates jumped at any chance to tell him how important their work was and what great things they'd accomplished. He'd done that himself for many years but was glad to have outgrown the tendency—or so he thought. After giving her a skeptical glance that fell just short of a glare, he let her off the hook with a smile.

"It's been nice talking to you," Knight concluded. "I have to leave, too. I'll walk out with you." There was no further discussion of Edelwise.

CHAPTER 32

Daniel Schmidt was still learning about Lucinda Alvarez. A Costa Rican native, she left San Jose early in the year for its American namesake, San Jose, California. She returned home six months later. There was no record of her activities in the United States. If she earned any income, she wouldn't report it until next year. As near as Schmidt could tell, she emerged from the rainforest of Central America, disappeared into the woodwork of northern California, and then returned home.

"You need to find everything you can on her," he told an assistant over the phone. "I have her name and nothing else. See what you can get from INS, IRS, Homeland Security, the Costa Rican embassy, and anywhere else. Go to the goddamned U.N., if you have to."

Schmidt wasn't sure how Alvarez fit in the puzzle that included Edelwise, the trial, and Ronald Ratkin, but he had a hunch she was important. Twenty years of futile efforts to catch Ratkin had led him to distrust his own instincts. Still, this one felt different. Too much was happening at once: the trial, the Edelwise breakthroughs, the company's surging stock. Notwithstanding the bravado with which Ratkin had dispatched Compucom's motion to add

Alvarez to the trial roster, he feared her. Schmidt wanted to know why.

* * *

Ronald Ratkin had stopped worrying about Lucinda Alvarez. He was busy orchestrating the third and final Joshua Egan release of Edelwise's technological breakthroughs while waiting for the jury to return a verdict in the Compucom case. He wished he could clone himself so that every client needing him as its savior could reap the benefits of his unrivaled services. Ratkin couldn't be in two places at the same time, so he remained in Boston for the jury verdict while assuring his client in California that everything was proceeding exactly as it should.

"Ronald, did you review the final securities filing that we prepared for you?" McGinty had called Ratkin's Boston war room office from his Carmel home. "We have to submit it in three days."

"Yes," Ratkin replied. "It says that Egan is on leave as chairman. That should be enough, but just to be safe, I want you to add the following footnote: 'The company regards Joshua Egan as an honorary historical figurehead only, superfluous to the operation and future of Edelwise.' That will give us another argument—namely, that no one could reasonably rely on Egan's physical existence as contributing to the value of Edelwise. We can even argue that the phrase 'honorary historical figurehead' could be interpreted as meaning that he's dead."

"I can't imagine how that language will help," McGinty countered. "Won't investors sue when the truth comes out and their stock plummets?"

"Perhaps, but filing a suit is not the same as winning one. As you know, the law reaches only company statements that are material, meaning that the information must make a difference to a reasonable investor's decision to buy or sell the company's stock. In this filing, you're going to tell the world that Egan is on leave from Edelwise. That means we can argue he's irrelevant to the company's value. Any more information about his health would be immaterial. Period."

"But he's not on leave. He's dead."

"That distinction is legally irrelevant," Ratkin snapped. "'On leave' means gone from the company. The legal inquiry ends there. It makes no difference to the law that his absence is permanent. The important point is that Edelwise is moving forward without him. That's the only legally important fact. At least, that's what we'll argue if Edelwise has to defend itself."

"But what about all these webcasts?" McGinty probed. "He's right at the center of those."

"That's optics, perception, and media reality. That's what the public sees and believes. But none of that matters in a courtroom where the *legal* reality determines the outcome. The obtuse language in this securities filing will exonerate Edelwise. It won't matter that a complaining investor never read it. It won't matter that the Egan webcasts set the world buzzing. The courts will rule that Edelwise's filing told investors that Egan's role had become inconsequential to the company's fortunes, so if any investors thought otherwise, they acted at their peril."

"You're the team captain, Ronald."

"Indeed, I am. Lawsuits like the one you fear usually begin with federal investigators poking around. They pick up steam when plaintiffs' class action lawyers piggyback onto the government's efforts. When my plan plays out in the fullness of its glory, the feds and the class action bar will scrutinize this securities filing and be stupefied. They'll be convinced that something unlawful has occurred, but they won't be able to fit any of their typical theories or standard complaint forms into the Edelwise situation. I've made new law before, and if I have to I'll do it again. Trust me, Phil. Trust me."

McGinty's head spun as Ratkin continued to explain his self-regarded ingenuity. "Think about it this way. For criminal prosecution, the standard for conviction is proof beyond a reasonable doubt. The government will never have that here. When it comes to civil actions, the positions we take in defending any claim don't have to be true. They require only that I, as your advocate, have a good-faith basis for asserting them. It's called Rule 11 of the Federal Rules of Civil Procedure. Once we're in court with a good-faith argument, anything can happen. Even the weakest legal position can become a winner before the right judge. Sometimes, those judicial mistakes have enormous consequences. I've made a career exploiting the vagaries of so-called established legal doctrines. The law is malleable to the outer limits of the most effective advocate's imagination. In my hands, it's like throwing a spitball or molding with silly putty."

"All right," McGinty said, tiring of Ratkin's incessant baseball references and ignoring the obvious retort that the spitball is an illegal pitch. "How about the final webcast? When should we run it?"

"One week from today."

"How about the jury?" McGinty revealed his anxiety as he lurched from topic to topic. "When will we have a verdict?"

"How am I supposed to know the answer to that, Phil? The jury has been out for a week. We might go into extra innings, and the judge said he was thinking about making them deliberate over the Labor Day weekend, which will really piss them off. If they're leaning plaintiffs' way, they'll take their anger out on us. So prepare to get clobbered."

Ratkin specialized in terrorizing clients about possible adverse outcomes, however unlikely he thought them to be. Properly managing client expectations made him seem all the more heroic when he averted such looming disasters through settlement or outright trial victory. It also set him up to hit the client with a request for a premium—an additional payment beyond the hourly rate charges—on the grounds that his remarkable results merited a special bonus. In fact, he knew that the judge was not planning to give up his own Labor Day weekend, so the jury's weekend was safe, too.

"Then what are we going to do?" McGinty worried.

"My God, Phil, you pay me to do a job. Just let me do it. If we lose the case, we post a bond and appeal. This thing will go on for ten more years, so don't get your knickers in a twist, as my British friends say."

"All right. What about Compucom's request to add the nurse as a witness? Anything more on that?"

"Jesus, Phil, will you just pour yourself a drink and relax?"

Ratkin recalled why he'd told the Exec Com that Phil McGinty should never become an equity partner at M&S. The guy was a hopeless worrywart.

"Fine, but remember: I'm the client," McGinty fumed as he uncharacteristically hung up on his lead trial attorney. He couldn't understand why Ratkin thought he could get away with such abuse, especially now that Egan was dead. Then he opened his desk drawer, pulled out his bottle of Jack Daniel's, and began drinking. There was no time to use a glass as a middleman; if he'd had an intravenous line, he'd have pumped it through.

Once the whiskey had sufficiently emboldened him, he picked up the phone and pressed one of his speed-dial buttons, mumbling to himself, "Phil McGinty shouldn't have to take this crap from anyone, even the legendary Ronald Ratkin."

CHAPTER 33

Charles Hopkins knew he was still indispensable to the firm of Michelman & Samson. Ratkin's visit to his office first confirmed it; now Albert Knight wanted to speak with him, too.

"What's the issue, Albert?" Hopkins asked as the two men sat at a small round table in Hopkins's perfectly appointed office. It was eight o'clock Friday evening before the Labor Day weekend. Even so, Helen Peterson sat at her desk outside Hopkins's office.

"I need your advice," Knight replied, but Wilson's final wisdom still haunted him: "Just don't get caught in the cross fire. People are going to get hurt in this one. I can smell it." He decided to play his cards close to the vest with Hopkins.

"I'm concerned about what will happen if we put the question of your successor to a full partnership vote a week from tomorrow," he continued. "Contested elections rarely occur in any large professional partnership, and when they do, it's usually not healthy for the partners or the firm."

"I understand your concerns, Albert," Hopkins said as he sipped his Johnnie Walker Black. He thought that Knight would have been an even better attorney if Sam Wilson hadn't confused him with all of his nonsense. In the end, Hopkins had won Knight over to what Wilson regarded as the dark side. No one could resist market forces and the wealth they created for the firm's equity partners.

"So, what I'm here to discuss with you is whether it makes sense for one of the two leading candidates to drop out of the race, paving the way for the other to get the broad support that he'll require to be effective in the chairman's role. But that can happen only if you initiate the process that leads to that result."

Knight was buckling under the pressure, Hopkins thought. He was looking for a graceful way out. Wilson's influence over him had apparently survived the grave.

"How do you think I should proceed?" the chairman asked.

"You must tell Ratkin to resign from the firm."

Knight surprised himself with the force of his words.

"Why would Ronald agree to do that?" Hopkins responded.

"Because he has to. He's placed himself and the firm at great financial and professional risk. I don't know all the details because I'm still putting the pieces together, but I have reason to believe he's engaged in actions that are certainly unethical and probably illegal."

"You have evidence to support the serious accusation you're making?"

Hopkins knew the answer. Knight never shot from the hip; he'd made his career and reputation by outworking all opponents inside and outside the firm. He had the goods on Ratkin; Hopkins wondered only how damning Knight could make the case sound.

"I'm still gathering information, even as we speak. I don't know when I'll have everything. But if what I have so far persuades you, then you need to visit Ratkin in Boston and convey to him the gravity of the situation."

"What makes you think he'll listen to me, Albert?"

"It doesn't matter if he listens to you, Charles. Once he understands what is at stake, he'll do whatever you ask of him."

"All right. So what is he doing that is jeopardizing the firm?"

"First, his theft of Edelwise from me as an M&S client years ago resulted from an improper relationship with Joshua Egan," Knight had chosen and rehearsed his words carefully. "I have reason to believe that he and Egan engaged in a sexual relationship and, for all I know, it has continued."

"Well, that may offend your puritanical core, Albert, but it hardly rises to the melodramatic level you're suggesting. M&S attorneys pursue client development in many different ways. Traditionalists prefer to entertain with golf outings and symphony tickets. Others use strip clubs and private escort parties. But there's no single correct way to secure and solidify client relationships. If what you say is true, Ratkin simply took his efforts in a somewhat unorthodox direction. But there's nothing illegal about it. Surely you're not going to discuss law firm morals with me, are you Albert? You know what kinds of things happen at Christmas parties around here. Why should what you have told me be especially shocking or even inappropriate as a matter of the firm's culture? And what you're talking about occurred a long time ago, didn't it?"

"There's more."

Once Knight started, no one could stop him.

"Much more. It involves Edelwise and Ratkin's ongoing trial. I can't go into details because I'm still tying up loose ends. But I'm certain that he's crossed lines that no lawyer should ever cross."

"How do you know that?"

"How I know is not important. What's important is that I know. I have the evidence to prove it. And now you have an obligation to inquire further. You've trained me too well, Charles. You know that I don't fly off half-cocked. You know that I wouldn't involve you or anyone else in this unless I had the gravest concern for the future of this partnership."

"What is this evidence you say you have?"

"You know me well enough to know that I have it," Knight answered. "That's all that matters."

"What are you going to do next?"

"That depends on what you do next, Charles. If I have your assurance that you, as the chairman of the firm, will take these allegations seriously and follow up in an appropriate manner—with Ratkin himself—then I'm prepared to yield to your direction. If not, then, as you know, I have an independent legal obligation to report professional wrongdoing to the state bar association. If I don't, then I risk my own license for failing to do so. You now have the same obligation. So the ball is in your court."

"Very well, Albert. Consider your points made. I'll fly to Boston tomorrow, meet with Ronald, and search for some resolution that protects Michelman & Samson."

"I'm sorry to dump this in your lap," Knight explained as he stood up and walked toward the door. "But under the circumstances, I had no choice."

What a load of crap, Hopkins thought while he said the opposite. "I understand, Albert. Consider this matter resolved. I'm confident that if you and Ratkin are in agreement that we should postpone the election of the next chairman, the rest of the Exec Com will go along. That's the first step in what you're proposing, isn't it?"

"I suppose so. It would be better if Ratkin left the firm immediately, but that's too much to expect of him."

Knight knew that his initial demand for his rival's resignation was just that, a starting position for negotiations that would continue. He'd achieved his first goal, which was to engage Hopkins and persuade him to confront Ratkin. At least as important as talent, patience and perseverance had propelled Knight's thirty-year career; success belonged to the last man standing.

* * *

Less than an hour after Knight had left, Hopkins's office phone rang.

"Mr. McGinty is on the line," Helen Peterson said. "Should I tell him you've left for the day?"

"No, put him through."

Hopkins picked up in the middle of the first ring.

"Hello, Phil. How have you been? How's your lovely bride, Sissy?" Hopkins had an unrivaled memory for names. "I gather from Ronald that he's doing a nice job for you out in Boston."

"That's why I called," said McGinty, slurring his words.

Hopkins recalled one of Ratkin's complaints about McGinty as a non-equity partner: he drank too much and, when he did, talked too much.

"Ratkin is an asshole," McGinty continued. "He still treats me like I'm still carrying his trial bag, rather than paying him and your firm more than $100 million in fees every year. I'm sick of it, just sick of it, Charles."

"Well, Ratkin has always been what he is," Hopkins resorted to tautology when words otherwise failed him. "This is nothing new for you, me, or him. The fact is that he gets great results. When he wins, you're a hero to your management. He's brash, arrogant, expensive, condescending, and sometimes abusive. Some of that goes with being a gifted trial lawyer. We all take the bad with the good when it comes to our talents; Ratkin is no exception."

"Maybe, but this time he's gone too far—really too far."

"In what way, Phil? Tell me what you mean."

Phil McGinty then began purging himself of every anxiety that Ratkin's plan had caused him. Hopkins listened as McGinty described the recent death of Joshua Egan, the consulting agreement by which he'd intimidated the nurse and bribed her to return to Costa Rica, the staged release of Edelwise technological breakthroughs—with the most dramatic only seven days away. None of this surprised Hopkins. He knew Ratkin was a genius whose unorthodox approach produced great results. Nothing else mattered. With her headset on, Helen Peterson wrote feverishly in her steno pad.

"I hear what you're saying, Phil," Hopkins eventually interrupted. "But I think you can rest assured that Ratkin knows what he's doing. His track record entitles him to deference. So let's just allow him to play out the hand. I have to go, but keep in touch, and we'll talk soon."

After hanging up, Hopkins unlocked a desk drawer containing a large manila envelope. It contained the same five photographs that a man in a fedora had delivered to Ratkin and Knight less than a week earlier, plus one more. The sixth photograph included Charles O. Hopkins III.

CHAPTER 34

The next morning, Hopkins took the first flight to Boston. He'd phoned in advance.

"I want to discuss progress on your earlier demand to eject Knight from the firm," Hopkins explained.

"Fine. I'm staying downtown at the Ritz-Carlton. We can meet there."

"No," Hopkins answered. "I'll be staying at the Charles."

It was the most luxurious hotel near the Harvard campus, a site to which he returned at every opportunity. Ratkin relented—a final act of deference to an old man who no longer deserved it.

By 1:00 PM, they sat at a booth in Charlie's Kitchen on Eliot Street. Ratkin called the place a dive, but it had been Hopkins's favorite Cambridge dining spot since his undergraduate days. It remained one of the few cherished threads of continuity in his life. Wives, women, children, clients, and almost everything else throughout his six and a half decades of existence seemed fleeting by comparison—except, of course, Michelman & Samson. Forcing Ratkin to travel to Cambridge from downtown Boston also gave Hopkins the subtle upper hand that came with being on his home court: Ratkin never got over the fact that the place where Hopkins had graduated with honors had rejected Ratkin's application for admission. When it came to psychological devices that disarmed an opponent, Ratkin knew most of them, but Hopkins had mastered them all.

"So I assume you've spoken with Knight?" Ratkin asked.

"Indeed, I have," Hopkins replied. "I talked to him yesterday. He's the reason I wanted to see you in person today."

That was true. It was remarkable how lawyers could be dishonest, especially with each other, without actually lying, he thought.

"Well?" Ratkin pressed.

"He's not willing to step aside," Hopkins said with complete honesty and somewhat less candor. "He thinks the question of marital fidelity is important to a person's integrity. But that alone isn't sufficient grounds for anyone to leave the partnership. He also believes that certain core ethical and moral values should result in excommunication from our ranks, but Knight doesn't regard himself as guilty of any."

Again, Hopkins had chosen his words carefully so that everything he said was technically true. Missing was the much different context for Knight's remarks.

"Then he's setting himself up for a brutal election next Saturday," Ratkin fumed. Hopkins had always admired his protégé's instinct for the jugular. The only problem was that he sometimes mishandled the knife and cut himself. "I intend to circulate those photographs to the equity partners so they can judge for themselves the man's integrity. It's shameful. The fact that he doesn't have the decency to step aside also reflects poorly on his judgment. I've got him by his b-a-a-a-l-l-l-s-s-s. He's just too stupid to realize it."

"Perhaps. But before you do anything more, let me have another conversation with him. Maybe there's a way to navigate the partnership through this divisive problem. By the way, how is your trial going? I heard you got a scare from a supposed surprise witness that the judge refused to let the other side call at trial. What was that about?"

"Nothing. Just a red herring," said Ratkin, wondering how Hopkins had become aware of such a minor detail in one of the many M&S trials occurring simultaneously around the country. Then he remembered that, of course, his was the most important.

"I see," Hopkins said slowly. "Red herring, huh? Pretty nice press releases that Edelwise has been providing about its new technology. I assume you've been following those?"

Ratkin became agitated as Hopkins linked these two seemingly unrelated events—a potential trial witness and Edelwise's breakthroughs—in consecutive comments.

"How does the company handle securities filings when dealing with cutting-edge technology that may or may not lead to anything significant in terms of value? I guess that's for the securities lawyers to figure out, not us litigators, right?" Hopkins said with a laugh.

"Not my problem," said Ratkin tersely. Whatever game Hopkins was playing no longer amused him.

"Well, I'll let you get back to work. I have to get back and plan my next vacation. After next Saturday, I'll have a lot of time on my hands. I was thinking I might visit Costa Rica."

All color left Ratkin's face. Hopkins was too smart to have dropped four consecutive bombs without knowing their intended target. But if Hopkins was willing to end the conversation at this point, Ratkin wouldn't prolong it.

"Good luck, Ron. You'll need it."

He even took the final shot, Ratkin thought. Hopkins had called him Ron.

Their discussion concluded, Ratkin got into the limousine that would take him back downtown. Hopkins watched the car pull away before walking toward Mount Auburn Street. He was staying at the Charles, but his recreation for the afternoon and evening awaited him in a king-size bed at the Harvard Square Hotel across the street.

CHAPTER 35

Ratkin used the Sunday before Labor Day to gather and circle his wagons. A month earlier, he'd involved fellow Exec Com member and recent lateral hire William Drakow in a special advisory assignment for Edelwise.

"The company needs a contingency plan to deal with the possibility that it won't successfully refinance its maturing multibillion-dollar debt," Ratkin had told him. "It's a highly confidential matter, but Edelwise has made clear that it wants the bullpen ready for any possible restructuring scenario, up to and including bankruptcy."

Although initially reluctant to involve himself and his team in another equity partner's client, Drakow was won over with an offer of the ultimate Michelman & Samson prize.

"Under the special circumstances of this retention, you'll be the billing attorney for the matter," Ratkin promised. It was a small price to pay for the support of Drakow and his colleagues in a department that otherwise would have no reason to prefer any particular candidate to succeed Charles Hopkins.

Ratkin had already used similar tactics to cement alliances with Merritt and Canby, who together could deliver the rest of the corporate group. Edelwise's various securities filings, along with the extensive documentation relating to the new loans, kept more than twenty-five of its specialized attorneys busy. Unlike the Drakow deal, Ratkin retained those billings himself. Merritt and Canby were glad to have something to keep their corporate attorneys hard at work. They happily served at the pleasure of Ronald Ratkin, who'd promised to protect them.

* * *

Ratkin knew that adding Drakow's allegiance to that of Merritt and Canby secured his future. It left Knight and Deborah Rush alone with each other and rendered Hopkins's vote irrelevant. Adding Rush would have been a nice symbolic blow, forcing Hopkins to side with an isolated Knight. But he didn't want or need her. He'd cast that die long ago.

Rush's internationally renowned intellectual properties practice would have been a perfect fit for Edelwise, but Ratkin made sure the match was never made. When he first took over the Edelwise billings from Knight, she was doing patent work for the company. Ratkin had told McGinty that was a bad idea.

"Allowing Rush to continue that work risks the firm's future disqualification from litigation involving Edelwise's technology," Ratkin urged. "It could make her and her IP people fact witnesses at a trial. That could give the other side a basis for arguing that M&S could not serve as trial counsel, too. The risk might be small, and whether such an argument prevailed would depend upon the jurisdiction where the litigation occurred. At a minimum, it's certainly problematic insofar as it creates even the slightest chance that you'd lose me and Michelman & Samson litigators as your trial lawyers."

No client wanted that result. From Clarence Darrow and F. Lee Bailey to Charles Hopkins and Ronald Ratkin, few skills have ever been as unique as those of a truly talented courtroom attorney. So when Albert Knight lost Edelwise, Rush lost the opportunity to continue serving one of the largest intellectual property clients in modern history.

That's the way the game is played, Ratkin thought at the time. There are winners and losers; there's first place and everybody else. He predicted that Rush would probably still make her way on to the Exec Com as its first woman, mainly because there were no other females remotely close to her in the equity partner ranks, and he could see that the time to crack that glass ceiling was approaching. She'd become a vote on the committee, but she'd never become a real player.

* * *

With his usual loyalists in tow and Drakow newly added to the alliance, Ratkin ordered a bottle of fine wine for his Boston hotel room, where he spent Sunday evening reviewing the M&S equity partner roster. By Monday afternoon, he'd completed a thorough analysis. Of the total 4,500 equity allocation points available, Ratkin predicted he'd garner more than 2,800 on the first ballot. If Drakow and his people came through for him, he was a lock for the chairmanship. Knight would be lucky to get one-third; the only other Exec Com members receiving votes to succeed Hopkins would have cast them for themselves. He could stop thinking about the problem that was going away in six days. Ratkin finished the bottle of wine and went to sleep.

CHAPTER 36

"We've found Lucinda Alvarez," Daniel Schmidt's assistant told him as they met Tuesday morning after the Labor Day weekend. "She's living in a small village called Las Mesas de Pejibaye, near San Isidro. The closest airport is San Jose. Should we send someone down there to talk to her?"

"No," Schmidt answered. "I'll go myself."

He didn't care if the government reimbursed him for this trip. Those details would take care of themselves after he cornered one of the most visible and high-powered attorneys in America. Among other benefits, catching Michelman & Samson partner Ronald Ratkin in a crime would catapult Schmidt's career to a new level. Within twenty-four hours, he was on his way to San Jose International Airport by way of a stopover in Miami. Sleep was out of the question.

Upon arrival, he rented a car. Hours later, he walked toward the porch of Lucinda Alvarez's home as a woman exited through the front door.

"Ms. Alvarez?" Schmidt asked.

"Who are you, and what do you want?" she asked in Spanish.

"My name is Daniel Schmidt, and I work for the United States government," he replied in rough Spanish, the residue of proficiency he'd once possessed in college. He struggled as they continued the conversation in that language. "May I speak with you for a moment?"

"What do you want with me?"

"I'm here to ask about time you spent in the United States earlier this year," he said as he continued up the porch steps and now stood directly before her.

"You're looking for my dead twin sister, Lucinda. I'm Alicia. I have nothing to say," she sobbed. "Nothing."

Schmidt stood in disbelief before asking softly, "I'm so sorry. How did she die?"

"It was a terrible accident. I won't discuss it with you or anyone else."

Schmidt reeled as she slammed the door. Now Lucinda was dead, and he still had no idea what connected her to Ratkin, Egan, or Edelwise. He sensed that he'd advanced to the brink of success, but he couldn't determine what he'd achieved. One thing was certain: when he returned to Washington, he'd find the assistant who had located Alvarez and ask him why he hadn't told Schmidt about her twin sister or the accident that killed the only person who might solve the mystery. He despised sloppy lawyers.

CHAPTER 37

Knight desperately needed his Four Seasons Tuesday night immediately after Labor Day. He hadn't seen Fran since receiving the five photographs that had interrupted his life almost two weeks earlier. When he knocked on the hotel room door, he still hadn't decided whether to mention them to her.

"I'm exhausted," he said. "You'd think after a long weekend, I'd be rested and ready to go, especially with the partner meeting on Saturday. I'm sure you know all about that from your erstwhile husband."

"Ronald hasn't talked to me at all about that. He doesn't talk to me about anything. It makes me wonder if he has a girlfriend."

The irony of her comment made them both laugh, albeit for different reasons. Then she continued with a phrase that brought the levity to an end.

"I can't remember the last time we had sex."

If only she knew the truth, Knight thought. Would it make her happier? Sadder? Would it make any difference at all?

These twice-monthly Tuesday nights had taken an unexpected turn for both of them. For the first two years, his thrill came from the fear that they might be discovered. Few people in the world were as proper and rule bound as Knight. For Fran, it was something fun to do; a relief from the lonely life of a functional widow. She didn't really care if her husband learned about their trysts because she didn't think he cared at all about her. She concluded long ago that she'd just been one of his first victories over Knight in a contest that both men would take to their graves. Ronald Ratkin had wanted Fran only because Knight had her. Once conquered, she was of no interest to him. It was all about the battle, not the spoils of victory.

Knight worried only slightly that his wife, Catherine, might learn the truth. But that concern had faded when he'd discovered that she was similarly unfaithful. Based on the photograph of her with their gardener and her tennis pro, he considered them even. After overcoming the initial shock of seeing the two pictures of Fran and him taken a decade apart, he likewise felt liberated. Once secrets begin to seep out, there was no reason to fret over their potential disclosure.

Still, he wondered what Fran would think if she saw the photograph of her husband in bed with one of the wealthiest men in the world. Would she care? Deciding nothing good could follow disclosure, he vowed to keep that secret. She'd survived more than twenty years of marriage with Ronald Ratkin; that was humiliation enough for anyone.

"Well, Saturday is the big day," Knight said. "Although I wonder if it will turn out that way. Sometimes the days you think will be most important to your life become the least consequential. There's a part of me that doesn't even want to be chairman of the firm. When you're an associate, you think everything will become easier once you make partner. Then, as a non-equity partner, you think an equity share will make your life complete, so you work twelve-hour days, six days a week to achieve it. And on and on it goes . . ."

"I thought you liked to work long hours," Fran interrupted.

"I do. But I worry about what I'll do when I don't have long hours to work anymore. With any luck, I'll die at my desk. But I can't count on it."

"What a morbid thought."

"My point is that the treadmill never ends until you die at your desk. When you arrive at what you think is the finish line—equity partnership in the most lucrative law firm in the world—before long you realize that it's just the beginning of a new race. You have to prove your economic value to the firm constantly, year in and year out. You have to justify yourself according to the metrics of annual billings and leverage. As you move higher up the ranks, the visibility makes you an easier target. Meanwhile, you can't overcome your own ambition. There's always a bigger piece of the firm pie to seek; there's some important committee that will take your career to the next level, if only you can work the politics to reach it; then there's the Exec Com; and finally, chairman."

"So what's your point? Do you wish you'd never gone to law school? Do you wish you were doing something else? Do you wish you weren't making all these millions? Grow up, Albert. This is the real world. You're one of the lucky ones."

"But something is wrong when there is only one good job in the entire organization and the guy at the very top has it. I think that's my point. It wasn't like this when I started law school or began working at M&S. The world has taken a turn that I thought was okay when I reaped its financial rewards. Now I'm not so sure."

"Don't be so melodramatic," Fran protested. "You're telling me that no one at the firm is happy? No one looks forward to going to work and doing their job? I don't believe that for a second. Ronald isn't at the very top, as you put it, and he's happy trying cases all over the country."

"Maybe he's happy. Maybe he isn't. Maybe he's battling demons every day. Maybe his life is an act, a fraud. Maybe he's just playing a part. Maybe, deep in his core, he's among the unhappiest of all. Did you ever think of that, Fran? Well, I have. I've had those thoughts myself. But I push them away. The phone rings, the client beckons, and I move forward. I'm like a great white shark: I have to keep moving forward, or I die. Along the path, I eat everything in my way."

"Too much talking for one night," she said as she pulled him to the bed. As always when combined with his Tanqueray and tonic, she created the perfect distraction.

CHAPTER 38

The *Compucom v. Edelwise* jury had been deliberating for almost two weeks when a secretary entered Ratkin's private office in the Boston war room on the first Friday morning after Labor Day.

"Mr. Ratkin, the judge's clerk just called. It's about the jury."

*　　　　　　*　　　　　　*

"Well, counsel," the judge began as he addressed the lawyers from the bench, "we have interesting news from the jury. They've given me the following note: 'Dear Judge, What happens if we cannot agree on a verdict? We have been deliberating for a long time and can't reach agreement. Please advise.' And it's signed by the foreman."

"Give them the depth charge, Judge," said Ratkin as his adversary agreed. That was his shorthand for the standard instruction that judges had given juries since the 1896 *Allen* case, when the U.S. Supreme Court first upheld the power of a trial judge to break jury deadlocks with a strong admonition during their deliberations. Depending on the jurisdiction, it took different forms, but the *Compucom v.*

Edelwise judge communicated its common essence after bringing the jury back into the courtroom and telling them to resume the seats they'd held for the three-month ordeal:

"The parties, their lawyers, and the court system have invested a great deal in this trial and are counting on you to reach a verdict to resolve this case. You have an obligation to deliberate vigorously, giving due regard for one another's opinions. You must consider your fellow jurors with deference and continue to deliberate until you reach a verdict."

Hearing nothing else from the judge, the jurors exchanged puzzled glances before standing and returning to the jury room. As near as they could tell, the judge had ignored their question.

*   *   *

Ratkin's carefully planned timeline had held. The jury was still deliberating, and the final Joshua Egan webcast was ready to go. At noon on Friday, the press conference began. As before, Egan himself introduced the subject.

"Last month, I demonstrated the remarkable capabilities of the Edelthink," Egan began. "It was the first truly thinking machine. More than simply a calculator or data compiler, it possesses all attributes of critical human reasoning."

Egan looked ill, Knight thought as he watched his video monitor.

"In July, I showed you our next-generation voice-recognition technology," Egan resumed after a brief pause. "Today, you will see the advance that will revolutionize the world. The most important thing for you to know is that I'm dead."

Knight's jaw dropped.

"Now that I have your undivided attention, let me assure you that this is not a tape," Egan's image continued. "Combining voice-recognition technology with true artificial intelligence—intelligence that can actually reason itself through complex situations—led me in interesting directions. For example, when one speaks of intelligence, what is meant by that concept? If human beings are to program computers so that they can think, doesn't someone have to be the source of the thought patterns that the computer will follow? The answer is obvious."

Knight checked the CNN website to see that, as he suspected, Egan's webcast now dominated the international news. No one knew where he was going, but he'd correctly concluded that he had everyone's attention.

"The missing and, I suggest to you, critical piece of the puzzle comes from modern medicine." Egan's voice was weak, but strong enough to make his point. "It comes from the world of brain-scanning devices. I'm pleased to report to you that Edelwise is taking all of us to a new place. Through modification of the brain-scanning apparatus, we're working to replicate an individual's—in this case, my—critical thought patterns and combine it with visual imaging, voice-recognition technology, and Edelthink to create—or re-create, if you will—me. To put it simply, we've downloaded my brain into the laptop computer from which this webcast originates. We've not yet achieved commercial viability, and more must be done, including the development of a better visual image of a healthier me. But the results so far have been, I dare say, promising."

Ratkin watched the same webcast from his laptop in Boston. From July to September, the sequence had played out beautifully. He clicked on the CNN money.com site to watch Edelwise's stock soar above a thousand dollars a share. In a matter of minutes, he'd made himself and Hopkins millions.

"In fact," Egan's image continued, "my body has been dead for two months. The prior two webcasts that I conducted were performed with the Edelthink technology. My mind lives, but only on the hard drive of a computer. Do

I exist? I think. I plan. The essence of who I was remains. It is the closest man can get to immortality."

Egan disappeared as the screen went blank. Edelwise's stock rose to $1,100. Ronald Ratkin picked up the phone and called Charles Hopkins.

"Yes, Ronald," Hopkins said immediately upon answering, "I saw it."

"Coincidentally, Charles, you should know that Edelwise declared a trading window this morning," Ratkin said with a lilt. "I think it would be a good time to sell your stock in the company."

"Are you crazy? That would be like selling Microsoft thirty years ago when it was a new issue. Now is the time to make hay while the sun shines."

"Charles, listen to me and listen carefully. I'm selling my Edelwise stock, all of it. You understand what I'm saying? All of it. Right now."

"Go ahead. I'm not."

Ratkin hung up the phone. You just can't protect some people from themselves, he thought. Especially those who think they know everything.

PART V

DENOUEMENT

CHAPTER 39

"Has the jury reached its verdict?" the judge asked.

Only two hours had passed since Joshua Egan's monumental webcast. The trial combatants had assumed their usual positions in the courtroom. The lead attorneys had been through this ritual before, so they found it easier than their client representatives to deal with the anxiety immediately preceding the rendering of any jury verdict. Still, even Ronald Ratkin could feel adrenaline's effect as his heart pounded under a tailored French-cuff shirt and custom suit. After more than a half century of life, he'd still found no comparable rush.

On this particular day, the judge didn't ache quite as much for the retirement that this case had long ago caused him to defer. Today was his compensation. Overnight, he'd become the ringmaster of a global circus. Throughout the early days of the proceeding, a handful of reporters and a few interested spectators had occupied most of the benches behind the bar. With Egan's latest broadcast, a standing-room-only crowd now flowed out the doors as media representatives from around the world jammed the hallway.

"We have, your Honor," said the foreman.

"Very well. Let's see it."

The foreman passed several sheets to the bailiff, who handed them to the judge. He unfolded the pages, reviewed them, and then began to speak.

"There are three pages of verdict forms, but only three questions and answers that matter to the outcome here," said the judge. "Here are the punch lines. On Count I, we, the jury, find in favor of defendant Edelwise. On Count II, we, the jury, find in favor of defendant Edelwise. On Count III, we, the jury, find in favor of defendant Edelwise. Mr. Ratkin, it appears that you've got another notch for your holster."

"We ask that the jury be polled," Ratkin's opponent said meekly.

Because the case was tried in federal court, the verdict had to be unanimous. The losing attorney now clung to every defeated advocate's dream: the emergence of a Perry Mason moment in which an individual juror might dramatically disavow the verdict in open court. The judge obliged, asking each member of the panel if the jury's conclusions reflected his or her personal decision in the case.

The question made no sense to one of the Compucom holdouts. She'd stood fast against Ratkin's client until four other female jurors threatened her physically. At that point, she agreed to vote with the others and in favor of Edelwise. So when her turn to answer the judge's inquiry came, she responded with a dutiful "Yes" because, based upon her fear of bodily harm at the time, it was, in fact, the decision for which she'd voted. Not knowing that a different response would likely lead to a mistrial, she worried that revealing the truth would mean a resumption of deliberations, during which those earlier threats would come to pass.

The judge then discharged the group, saying, "I join with the parties to this litigation and their lawyers in thanking you for your time and service in this long and difficult case. As I observe the sea of reporters in this courtroom and beyond, my advice to you is to go home and get some rest before you decide whether you want to talk to anyone about it, ever. Whatever you do in that regard, I strongly urge you to proceed slowly and cautiously. Jurors are excused. Court is in recess."

On the way out, one of the jurors approached Ratkin and whispered, "Once we all saw the Joshua Egan press conference today, your client was home free."

As occurred with increasing frequency in trials everywhere, cell phones had given jurors instant access to the Internet, even during deliberations. Ratkin looked away as the juror spoke, pretending not to hear remarks that vindicated his entire strategy. Prior to deliberations, he'd heard the court's standard instruction to the jury, admonishing all members not to view any media reports relating in any way to what was happening in the courtroom:

"Your verdict shall be based solely on the evidence that has been presented to you in this courtroom, together with these instructions of law that I am giving you."

If the judge or opposing counsel learned that three jurors had shared their iPhone video replays with the group as they watched Egan's presentation in the jury room, a mistrial was likely, if not automatic. In that event, Ratkin's hard-fought victory would be lost. The truth might come out later, but by then Ratkin would have polished arguments he'd already begun to outline in defense of the verdict that had resulted from an improper extrajudicial taint. He might have to make new law to preserve his win, but that was a Michelman & Samson specialty at which Ratkin excelled. And even if he lost in a subsequent round and had to try the case again, he'd have the long-standing M&S fallback position to offer his client:

"I'm such a good trial lawyer, I even persuade juries to go my way in cases that I don't deserve to win."

*　　　　*　　　　*

Hundreds of news reporters waited outside the court building to ask Ratkin about the jury's decision. He stepped to a makeshift podium where the media had attached a dozen microphones. The spotlights bathed him in a warm and energizing light.

"Once again, our system is the true victor," he said. "If you respect the jury members and take the time to educate them about the importance of the issues they face, the jurors will do their job. That's what happened in this case. Thoughtful men and woman listened attentively for three months and then deliberated carefully for more than two weeks. They reached a fair verdict based on the evidence they heard."

"Do you think Joshua Egan's bombshell announcement today had any impact?" asked a reporter.

"Certainly not," Ratkin said quickly. "The judge instructed the jurors to decide the case based on the evidence presented in the courtroom. They know that they are not allowed to consider extraneous matters. I have no reason to believe that this jury did anything other than follow the instructions the court gave them in that regard."

"Do you think this will affect Edelwise's stock price?" another asked.

"I'm not a securities analyst. And I have a personal rule: I don't do my own brain surgery; I don't represent myself at trial; and I don't pick stocks for my investment portfolio."

As polite laughter rippled through the crowd, Ratkin concluded the conference, saying, "Neither I nor my client will have any further comment on this matter. Thank you for your interest."

Ratkin then headed for a waiting limousine. He had a plane to catch and an election for Michelman & Samson's next chairman to win.

* * *

When it closed for the day, Edelwise's stock was at $1,200 per share. Ratkin was a fool for selling earlier in the day, Hopkins thought while calculating the increase in his net worth over the prior twenty-four hours. As he sat back in his desk chair and gazed out the window, the phone rang.

"Charles, it's Phil," said McGinty.

"Hello, Phil. Quite a day for Edelwise, wasn't it?"

"Yes. That's why I'm calling. I wanted to apologize for my behavior when I called you last week. I think I was pretty drunk. But, as you assured me, Ratkin managed to pull the whole thing off. I don't know how, but he did it. I was able to sell enough of my stock during today's trading window to set up a comfortable retirement with a Swiss bank account. When Edelwise stock craters on Monday, at least my new nest egg will be safe."

Hopkins's broad smile disappeared as the color drained from his face. "What do you mean, 'When the stock craters on Monday'? Why will it crater on Monday?"

"I assumed you knew the game plan," McGinty continued. "Ratkin set up the whole thing—even the sequence of Edelwise webcast releases—to achieve maximum impact with the jury in his Compucom trial. His only goal all along was to win that case. The guy is a genius, just like you've always said. He even gave the rest of us a nice fringe benefit by setting up the trading window after our quarterly securities filing last week. It allowed us insiders a chance to sell our stock. I assume you got out, too."

"You mean . . ."

"Egan? Dead as a doornail in body and mind for three months."

The lilt in McGinty's voice infuriated Hopkins.

"But give Ratkin credit for that one, too. Six months ago, he had the foresight to hire that Costa Rican nurse and tie her up with a consulting expert agreement that'll keep her quiet for a long, long time."

"But what about the Edelthink webcasts, the next-generation voice-recognition technology, a new kind of artificial intelligence, the brain-scanning to put everything together in a laptop that could think and speak like Egan?"

The always cool and calm Hopkins moved toward uncharacteristic and uncomfortable panic. Rather than selling his Edelwise stock during the trading window that closed at the end of the day, he'd double downed, buying several million dollars in call options on margin. They'd become worthless if the stock plummeted at the market open on Monday morning, and he'd go broke trying to pay off the margin loans.

"You really believed all that stuff? I'm surprised at you, Charles. After all, you trained the guy. He was what he was, but your mentoring took him to a whole new level."

"I have to go," Hopkins cut him off and hung up.

CHAPTER 40

Daniel Schmidt studied the trading activity for Edelwise stock during the day of Joshua Egan's final and dramatic webcast. Amidst the activity, two things stood out: Ronald Ratkin had sold his holdings worth millions; Charles Hopkins had bet the other way, loading up on call options in the belief that the value of Edelwise's stock would continue to rise. The combination made no sense, unless Ratkin had somehow hoodwinked Hopkins, too. There was no way to know, yet.

Schmidt enjoyed new hope that his personal vendetta might still have life, but it would depend on how events unfolded in the coming days and weeks. Ratkin had played the hand shrewdly, undoubtedly decreeing the trading window that allowed him to make tens of millions when he sold his Edelwise stock on Friday. But that window was not necessarily the end of the story. If an insider had material information unknown to the public, even the company's declaration of a permissible trading period would not provide a complete defense. At this point, everything was theoretical. Would Edelwise stock rise or fall? Would later disclosures prove that Ratkin had known and acted on non-public information when he sold his stock?

Would there be an insider trading case against Ronald Ratkin? Or a misrepresentation case against Edelwise based upon inaccurate disclosures—perhaps with Ratkin as a co-conspirator? At this point, there was no way for Daniel Schmidt to reach any definitive conclusions. But he'd keep his private Ratkin/Edelwise file close at hand for whatever came next.

"Sir, I've tracked down the Alvarez information you requested," said Schmidt's assistant as he entered the office.

"You know, I didn't last five years at M&S, but you wouldn't last five minutes there," Schmidt replied. "I can't believe I went on that wild goose chase based on the incomplete information you'd given me."

"Mr. Schmidt, with all due respect . . ."

"Don't 'with all due respect' me. When lawyers start a sentence like that in court, they're about to attack an opponent."

"Yes, well, I'm not going to do that, but I can tell you this. There's no record of any Alicia Alvarez or of any accident or of Lucinda Alvarez's death."

"What are you saying?"

"I'm saying that the person you met in Costa Rica was, in fact, Lucinda Alvarez. She bamboozled you. She threw you off the scent and got you to give up."

Schmidt sank in his chair as the impact hit him in successive waves of despair. He'd been standing before the person who could solve the triangular riddle of Edelwise, Ratkin, and Egan that still stymied him. Stupidly, he'd let the opportunity escape. Then he realized that perhaps all was not lost and she'd given him new leverage that he hadn't previously possessed. In fabricating an identity to avoid questions from a federal agent, she'd obstructed justice, albeit as a foreigner on foreign soil. When he returned to Costa Rica next time, he'd bring local law enforcement officers with him.

*　　　　　*　　　　　*

Lucinda Alvarez explained to her mother that she had to leave Costa Rica for a while. The money that she'd sent home from the United States would be sufficient to support the Costa Rican family for many years, she assured her.

"Don't worry about me," Lucinda said. "I have other money from that job, and it will last me a long time, too."

"How could you have so much money from such a short time in America?" her mother asked.

"I had very grateful clients. They were quite wealthy and could afford to be very generous."

The truth was that Lucinda didn't understand why her employer had overpaid her, either. But the recent attention from strange visitors who'd traveled great distances to inquire about her nursing job in California began to give her the sense that, eventually, she'd earn every penny.

"Where will you go?" her mother wondered.

"It's better that you not know. I'll contact you regularly to tell you I'm okay. Please do not worry about me. I'll be fine."

Lucinda Alvarez took a bus to the San Jose airport, where she boarded a plane to Miami on her way to New York. She planned to lose herself in New Jersey, where the large Tican population would provide ample cover. Reclining in her seat after takeoff, she opened her purse and pulled out her new passport. From that moment, she would be Claudia Montoya.

Mr. McGinty had taken care of everything, she thought. He had wanted her to remain in Central America with her new identity, but she regarded New Jersey as a much better choice. In any event, she certainly was not going to seek his permission to revise her itinerary. He had told her never to contact him again, a command she intended to respect.

CHAPTER 41

The three men at the center of the Exec Com power struggle met in Charles Hopkins's office shortly before midnight on the Friday before the annual Michelman & Samson equity partners' meeting. This time, Helen Peterson wasn't standing guard outside. Ratkin was gloating over his latest trial victory, while Knight wondered if Hopkins would finally take his nemesis down and out of the firm. Hopkins sat erect between them at the round table.

"Here is what's going to happen," Hopkins began.

Knight knew immediately that this was not going to be a negotiation. When Charles Hopkins started a sentence with that phrase, there was nothing for anyone else to do but listen.

"Albert, we'll start with you," he said.

Knight gulped audibly as his trembling hand reached for a tumbler of water that he wished was filled to the rim with Tanqueray and tonic. He couldn't stand the fact that Charles Hopkins's deep baritone still sent involuntary shock waves through his system. The chairman's unblinking blue eyes bore down on him.

"You have demonstrated that you don't have what it takes to be the chairman of this firm. My private investigator gave you all that you needed to destroy your only rival, and you punted it away. Rather than go for the jugular, you came crying to me in an attempt to inflict no more than a flesh wound on your adversary. You didn't even bring your evidence—the photographs—when you made your case. What kind of litigator are you, anyway?"

Knight realized that the five photographs had been Charles Hopkins's most recent test of leadership, and Knight had failed it miserably. Meanwhile, Ratkin understood at once that he and his nemesis had received identical packages. That meant Knight and Hopkins knew everything about his compromising pose with Egan. They probably knew about Maria Morales's Costa Rican trip, too. Confident that he could outmaneuver both men, he remained calm as Hopkins turned toward him.

"As for you, Ron, I'm not sure where to begin," Hopkins continued. "But I can tell you where and when it ends: right here and right now. This time, you've played too fast and too loose. I haven't even begun to add up all the different exposures of joint and several liability that you've created for every partner in this firm, but I remember enough law to know that you're probably on your way to prison."

"How so?" Ratkin's petulant demeanor survived Hopkins's initial assault. "Let's take the relevant points one by one. Egan is dead. I never said otherwise, and neither did any representative of Edelwise. A company is not liable just because investors jump to an erroneous conclusion."

"Too cute by half, Ron. Misrepresentations can be sins of omission or commission," Hopkins interjected, emphasizing a long "o" in both words. "Failure to disclose Egan's death was a material omission, especially when coupled simultaneously with his highly public touting of Edelwise's newest technologies. It's a violation of federal securities laws, and you know it."

"Not so fast, Chuck," Ratkin fired back. Knight had never heard anyone address Charles Hopkins in that way.

Even Hopkins jerked back as if someone had just missed him with a left hook. "A careful review of Edelwise's securities filings will show that there are sufficient qualifiers, caveats, and footnotes to protect the company and its lawyers—namely us—from liability. For example, they describe Egan as being 'on leave' from his position as chairman, and I specifically added language stating that Egan's physical existence was irrelevant to Edelwise's value. Good-faith defenses can be offered against any claim that might be brought. In fact, the stock has continued to climb, so at least through the close of the market today, there's not really anyone out there who can claim to have been damaged by anything the company has or hasn't said or done."

"You're insane," Hopkins retorted. "What about Monday, when the stock tanks because the whole Edelthink–artificial intelligence innovation is a fraud?"

"Who told you that?" Ratkin laughed. "That idiot McGinty? He doesn't know what he's talking about. Trust me on this one, Charles. The Edelthink innovation is quite real. The stock isn't going to tank."

"Then why did you tell me quite firmly that you were planning to sell yesterday before the day was over?"

"Because lawyers have only narrow and limited windows during which they can buy or sell the stock in a company they represent. I was simply making the point that I was planning to take advantage of that window, which has now closed."

"Here's the problem, Ronald. I don't know if I can believe anything you tell me."

"That makes me the perfect candidate to be the next chairman, doesn't it, Charles?"

"No, because the way you've dealt with Egan's death—even if all that you say is true—violates many laws. You've essentially bribed a nurse to leave the country and remain silent."

"She was a consulting expert," Ratkin interrupted. "We hire such people to buy their silence all the time."

"You've misled a judge about your ignorance concerning a mysterious witness when you, in fact, had orchestrated her absence."

"Read the transcript closely. I just asked questions."

"You've done God knows what in trading Edelwise stock at a time when, as the ultimate insider, you certainly knew far more about the company than anyone else. As near as I can tell, you were actually running the company. No, Ronald. You've given it a nice M&S–litigator's try, but I'm not buying it. Maybe you'll be more persuasive when you testify in the criminal and civil cases where you're sure to be a defendant. I don't know what will happen to Edelwise's stock when the markets open on Monday. But I know what will happen at the annual partners' meeting tomorrow."

"Charles, you may not be in any position to dictate to me what happens at the partners' meeting tomorrow. You're the outgoing chairman—a lame duck. You and the firm had a nice run while it lasted, but your era is over."

"No, it's not, Ronnie. Not quite. Here's what's going to happen." Hopkins resumed with the phrase that pushed an automatic reset button on the entire conversation. He then turned to Knight.

"Albert, you're not going to run for chairman. You're not tough enough for the job. You can keep your Exec Com seat, but you'll stay where you are. You've gone farther than anyone, including you, ever expected you to go in this place. Count your blessings and enjoy the big numbers on your personal financial statement. But your illustrious career at Michelman & Samson has reached its zenith. Starting next year, you'll phase down on the way out. You'll leave in five years. So start planning your retirement."

"All right," Knight responded. He could fight, but what was the point? Nobody ever beat Charles O. Hopkins III.

"As for you, Ronnie, at tomorrow's meeting, I'll announce that you've agreed to run our new Beijing office. There are many practical professional and personal reasons for your move, but we'll only share with the partners the one they'll care about most: you'll make them a lot of money there. Professionally, Beijing will be the financial center of the world during the twenty-first century. Every major law firm will need a presence there to maintain the profit levels to which we've all become accustomed. China's richest families are babes in the woods when it comes to accessing American legal expertise. They'll pay hourly rates and special fees of a magnitude that our stateside clients will no longer tolerate. We've squeezed just about all we can out of our domestic sources of income. From now on, the real money will be made in the Far East. You're the perfect person for that mission. You won't leave any money on the table."

"Thanks for the compliment, I guess," Ratkin replied. "But you're assuming that I won't fight you to the death on this one."

"That leads me to the reason for your new assignment that we won't tell our partners, Ron. Notwithstanding your blithe sophistry in wishing away the serious problems you've created for yourself and the partnership, you're looking at big trouble from law enforcement, government agencies, bar disciplinary commissions, and a lot more. In Beijing, you can't be extradited because the United States has no such arrangement with the Chinese government. You'll be safe there, as long as you never leave China. Of course, if you ever think about leaving Michelman & Samson, we'll do everything in our power to put you behind bars. That, it turns out, is a lot; our tentacles reach far beyond American soil."

All color left Ratkin's face as Hopkins continued calmly and sternly. The voice reminded Ratkin of his own father's, meting out harsh punishment to a disobedient child.

"Remember what Sam Wilson said when he first introduced you as a new non-equity partner twenty-five years ago?" Hopkins's commanding presence was unavoidable. "Well, I do. He never wanted anyone in this firm to walk into a courtroom with Ronald Ratkin on the other side of the case. That's still true, and it will remain true for the rest of your life. Your talents are unrivaled, but your ambition is unrestrained. It renders your judgment flawed in ways that might still be fatal to this law firm. Toe the line, and you'll live out a comfortable career at M&S. But if I hear even the hint of a suggestion that you're thinking about leaving, you'll be so far into the depths of a Chinese prison that no search party will ever find you. And trust me, there won't even be one looking for you."

Ratkin's heart sank at the thought that he'd never again try a case in an American courtroom. But he couldn't deny the logic of Hopkins's analysis. Over the years, he'd developed the view that rules were largely an abstraction. He followed them when they suited his clients' purposes; he ignored them when they didn't. He was a hired gun. His job was to accomplish objectives; rules mattered only when they were a means to an end. They had nothing to do with how he conducted his own life. Rules were for everyone else.

"So, Ron, you'll go to Beijing tomorrow before the partners' meeting begins," Hopkins concluded. "I'll let the partners know that you'd prefer not to remain on the Exec Com in light of your new assignment's challenges and that I've accepted your resignation on behalf of the committee. We all expect that there, as here, you'll continue to make all of us M&S equity partners rich."

"So who does that leave to become the next chairman?" Knight dared to ask.

"You see no one qualified to grab the reins," Hopkins answered, "and I see the same. So the two of you will sign proxies in my favor, authorizing me to cast your votes in support of an amendment to the articles of partnership. I already have in hand similar proxies from Deborah Rush, William Drakow, John Merritt, and Scott Canby. You see, they, too received manila envelopes from a short, stocky man who likes to chew on unlit cigars. Their collections were different from yours, much different. But they allowed me to make the same point with them that I've now made with you: no current member of the Michelman & Samson Executive Committee is fit to succeed me at this critical moment for the firm."

Ratkin viewed Hopkins with grudging admiration, although he knew the final chapter of this saga had yet to be written. Wishing he could disappear, Knight slouched deeper into his chair. He'd never been a match for Hopkins or Ratkin. For years, he'd convinced himself that he belonged in their league. Now both were proving him wrong.

"The amendment to the partnership agreement will accomplish two things," Hopkins summarized. "First, it will extend the mandatory retirement age for me by another five years. It will make clear that this is a personal privilege for me alone, rather than a general revision of the partnership agreement. Second, it will allow me as chairman to select a vice-chairman who serves at my pleasure. I'll announce that person after the partnership approves the amendment tomorrow—sorry, I mean later today, since it's now well after midnight. Are we all clear on the protocol?"

Hopkins had won. Although Drakow had been a new and uncertain ally, the desertions of Merritt and Canby stunned Ratkin. Knight was not surprised by any of these developments. The obvious thought that now gripped his mind should have emerged sooner: Wilson had been right all along; Hopkins was never going to retire. Only the noblest mentors voluntarily relinquish power and status to protégés. More often, incumbent leaders become wary of potential successors whom they once supported. When that happens, they begin to see those who embody the future as unwelcome challenges to their power and unpleasant reminders of their own mortality.

*   *   *

After the two men left his office, Charles Hopkins once again unlocked his desk drawer containing six manila envelopes. Removing them one by one, he smiled at his cache.

The Rush collection included her in a photo with an M&S partner taken several years earlier. She was ten years older than her married male paramour, who left the firm pursuant to an arrangement that Hopkins had personally negotiated.

The photos in the Scott Canby collection featured him celebrating the election of several younger male partners into the equity ranks of the firm. In the most incriminating sequence, two female escorts lay naked on a hotel room bed while stripping Canby before engaging in acts that caused even Hopkins to blush. When faced with the photos, Canby initially defended them as typical indoctrination activities for the firm's newest rising stars.

"What's the fucking big deal?" Canby protested when Hopkins confronted him. "This was no different from my old college fraternity parties. We've just advanced to suites at four-star hotels."

"Yes, and I'm sure that's how your second wife would view the situation, Scott."

Canby quickly capitulated. The last thing he needed was another property settlement. It would prolong his journey toward $50 million in personal net worth—the goal he'd set as his definition of success.

William Drakow's sins had been different: he'd embezzled client funds, so his envelope contained expense reports and the underlying documents proving his fraud.

Apparently, a $5 million share of the firm's annual profits hadn't been enough for him.

Hopkins had lied to Ratkin and Knight about having an envelope for John Merritt. No one had anything on him. The truth was that Merritt had controlled Hopkins since the MBA takeover fifteen years earlier but had been content to let Hopkins become his puppet. Sam Wilson had been right about that fateful moment in the saga of Michelman & Samson.

His favorite envelope was marked "Hopkins" and contained five photographs that were also in the Ratkin and Knight deliveries, along with a sixth that he liked best—the one no one else would ever see. It was yet another picture of two infidels romping their way through a room at the Four Seasons Hotel. Fran Ratkin was one of them; the other was Charles O. Hopkins III. Every other Tuesday—the Tuesdays that did not belong to Knight—Fran belonged to the chairman of Michelman & Samson, whose rumors of retirement had been greatly exaggerated, while gossip about his continuing libido was, if anything, understated.

Hopkins thought he looked pretty good for sixty-four. Then again, he'd known that the picture would be taken, and he'd prepared himself accordingly. Poor Fran, he thought. She was so clueless in so many ways. He smiled as he returned the photographs to their proper and secure location.

Outside Hopkins's office, Helen Peterson wasn't at her desk, but one of her locked drawers contained another secret file about which Hopkins knew nothing. It was titled "Job Security," and it had grown larger every day. On Monday, she'd be relieved to learn that she wouldn't need its contents any time soon; her boss would be around for another five years.

CHAPTER 42

An impressive sight, Hopkins thought. From an elevated platform, he scanned the more than two hundred and fifty Michelman & Samson equity partners gathering in the Four Seasons Hotel's Grand Ballroom. As the crowd moved steadily from the coffee and continental breakfast lines in the anteroom to their seats in the main venue for the day's events, he proceeded to the podium. Behind him, Tina Turner's recorded voice blasted "Simply the Best" over a rolling montage of Michelman & Samson's accumulated honors for the prior twelve months:

"NUMBER ONE Firm in Average Equity Partner Profits . . . One of the TOP TEN Corporate Departments in America . . . One of the TOP TEN Restructuring and Bankruptcy Practices . . . One of the TOP TEN Private Equity Practices . . . NUMBER ONE Litigation Department . . ."

Who in the room wouldn't be proud of his or her association with such a remarkable institution? The music faded as he started to speak.

"Welcome to our annual equity partners meeting," his voice boomed. Hopkins never needed a microphone. "I'll give a short report of the state of the partnership, but before that I want to start with our most exciting international initiative. For some time, your Executive Committee has been working on a new office in Beijing. Last year, we presented to you the strong business case for such an expansion into that Far East venue. I'm pleased to report that we recently resolved the last significant obstacle to that new office—namely, a top senior attorney to lead it."

The crowd stilled.

"Ronald Ratkin, one of the best litigators in our history, is currently on his way to Beijing. Starting tomorrow, he'll be there full time, devoting all of his incomparable skill and energy to making the office a success."

The audience gasped. Why would the firm's most acclaimed litigator go to a country where he'd never try another case? Many posed the question to themselves, but none dared ask it aloud. Instead, polite applause began rippling through the room. Although surprised at Hopkins's announcement, most were focused on the main business items of the day: filling Hopkins's seat on the Exec Com, selecting the committee's new chairman, and hearing the partner profits projection for the current year. Even so, his subsequent comments added even more confusion.

"Ronald believes that the firm's best interests would be served if he resigned his position on the Executive Committee. As we all know, the nominators have already chosen the person whom they've recommended to you as my replacement on the Exec Com, Karen Morton. Under the circumstances, the Executive Committee has unanimously recommended that the partnership proceed to put Karen in Ronald's seat. The committee has also requested that I remain chairman for five more years. Although I'm reluctant to delay the retirement that I've been eagerly anticipating, these remarkable developments and the continuing economic challenges we face dictate that I adjust my plans to serve the firm's best interests. Subject to your approval, I'll agree to the Exec Com's request and remain at the helm for another five years. But if there is even a single vote dissenting from this result, I'll step aside and take the Costa Rican vacation that I've already booked."

The room remained silent until his comment about a vacation, at which point nervous laughter peppered the audience. Only Knight knew what was supposed to come next.

"Is it appropriate to make a motion from the floor?" he asked.

"Surely," said Hopkins.

"Then I move that we amend the articles of partnership to permit Charles O. Hopkins III to remain an equity partner and chairman of the Executive Committee until his seventieth birthday. And I'd add the proviso that our chairman be empowered to select a vice-chair so that a smooth and orderly transition can occur five years from now."

"Second," came Deborah Rush's voice from the other side of the room.

"Any discussion?" asked Hopkins, pausing momentarily before calling the vote: "All those in favor?"

The room muttered in unison: "Aye."

His perfunctory "Opposed?" did not elicit a sound; the largest ballroom in the city retained an eerie quiet.

"Motion carries by unanimous vote."

The room burst into applause as every partner stood.

"On the subject of who should be vice-chairman," Hopkins continued after the partners resumed their seats, "it seems that such a person's most important quality will be to possess your overriding confidence. Without that, leadership fails. If I attempted to dictate to you whom the next chairman should be, you would resent me and that person. Your unanimous support of me isn't automatically transferable to someone else of my choosing. The person who becomes vice-chairman must earn your confidence, and

I know he will. If he doesn't, he'll be joining Ratkin in China someday."

Obligatory nervous laughter followed that final sentence. It made a few in attendance wonder if, in fact, the firm's best trial lawyer had done something to deserve exile. Along with everyone else in the room, Knight waited for the punch line.

"And I'm also mindful of the need to accomplish intergenerational transition, which is why I've selected Scott Canby to be the vice-chairman of Michelman & Samson's Executive Committee. He's served the firm well and will continue to do so."

Another standing ovation followed. As he watched the faces of his partners, Knight noticed John Merritt wearing an uncharacteristic grin. At that moment, a fuzzy picture became painfully clear. From the beginning, the battle between Knight and Ratkin for the Exec Com chairmanship had been an illusion. When the Reagan revolution moved America toward blind faith in the wisdom of private-market solutions during the 1980s, unrestrained economic self-interest began to displace other decision-making criteria. Eventually, men like John Merritt absorbed, emulated, and perfected the MBA mentality of their corporate clients. Derided as bean counters in an earlier era, they became the new masters of the legal universe. Firm culture soon followed the money.

When the *American Lawyer* began listing big firms according to their average profits per equity partner, it gave birth to a new metric that itself became both a catalyst and the definition of success. Slavish adherence to the revised mantra—teaching to the test—was easier than critical thought. The subtle shift in the firm's underlying ethos had gone undetected because the lure of increasing wealth proved as irresistible to the few who made the decisions as it did to the few more who benefitted from them. Merritt had played the hand perfectly. It was the success and failure of free market capitalism all at once. None could deny the financial benefits accruing to the few. Equally evident to those looking more closely was the new model's unmeasured failure at a more personal level—reflected in the lifestyles and unhappiness of too many people working there. Knight now numbered himself among them. In the end, John Merritt and his people never had any serious competition in the quest for the ultimate prize: controlling Michelman & Samson's wealth machine. Who among the ranks dared challenge the meritocracy of metrics or a system that was making them rich?

*   *   *

I'm not as good as the best of them and not as bad as the worst of them, Knight rationalized. In a way, he'd prevailed over his old nemesis after all. Charles Hopkins had vanquished Ronald Ratkin to the other side of the world, where he'd remain well paid but in limbo for the rest of his working life. Knight, on the other hand, could continue to attend Exec Com meetings until he retired in five years. Between the two men, he'd become the relative winner in a contest that no longer mattered. The prize had been a mirage, but most equity partners still sought it. The younger lawyers still wanted what he'd already achieved; this certainty would satisfy his continuing need for validation. He had precious little else.

Although Hopkins remained at the top of the firm, even he must have known that his final ploy to retain power had placed his career on life support. Together, Hopkins and Merritt had created the next generation of leaders in their own image—men and woman who would do whatever was necessary to reach the summit, just as their mentors had. Sooner than Hopkins realized, he'd be on the defensive, fighting every aging senior partner's futile battles against time, younger protégés, and the most haunting specter of all: institutional irrelevance. The cannibalistic cycle reminded him of an old joke that Sam Wilson once told him about an ancient society's parable on aging, generational transition, and mortality.

An elderly widower lived with his son's family for many years. As the old man aged, the son's wife became increasingly irritated at his presence in the home.

"He's driving me crazy," she told her husband. "You must get him out of here!"

The son went to speak with his father about the problem, and they agreed that it was time for him to leave. Because he had nowhere else to live and didn't want to burden anyone, the father said that his time on earth should come to an end. Rather than cast him adrift on an ice floe in accordance with false myths about the Eskimos, the son offered to build a box on wheels. When he finished, the father would get inside, and the son would push it to the edge of a cliff and allow it to roll over the side. It was all agreed.

Knowing that the box would be his father's residence for his last mile before becoming a final resting place, the son worked for many months to make it perfect in every way. Once it was completed, the old man climbed inside. The son locked the door and began to push the contraption toward a nearby canyon.

As the son pressed ahead, the old man started pounding on the box.

"Wait!" the old man yelled. "Wait!"

The son assumed that his father was having second thoughts about their plan, so he pushed the box faster and faster in an effort to overcome the sound of the old man's voice.

"Wait!" the shouts continued. "Wait!"

Faster and faster the son ran with the box until they reached the edge of the canyon.

"All right," the son finally relented, but he still refused to unlock the box. "What is it? I'm at the edge of the cliff and ready to push it the last fateful steps. What is it you want to say for the last time?"

"I'm ready to die," the father replied from inside. "But do yourself a favor. You've put so much time and effort into building this fine box. Don't waste it. I'm prepared to jump off the cliff and into the canyon, but save the box. Someday, your son will need it for you."

*   *   *

Knight became resigned to his own fate. For three decades, the treadmill's pace had remained too quick for him to dismount without permanent injury to his own identity. Now Hopkins had decreed that in five years it would stop. He wasn't sure how life had put him in this place, but he knew he was very, very tired. He couldn't wait for his next Tuesday evening session at the Four Seasons. Perhaps Ronald Ratkin was in Beijing, but his wife would remain in Chicago. In the end, living apart can be done from across the dinner table or from separate continents. For the Ratkins, just as for Albert and Catherine Knight, homes, cars, and investment portfolios had become larger over the previous twenty-five years, but the essential qualities of life had gone the other way. Why would their futures break form?

*   *   *

Long before the Edelwise trial was over, Ronald Ratkin had assigned Maria Morales one more task: the standard post-trial juror interviews. Smart lawyers learned from the reactions of those who'd sat in judgment of their clients. Such feedback helped any trial attorney who wanted to improve. Although the judge had urged jurors to wait before speaking with attorneys or anyone else about the case, Ratkin insisted that such efforts commence immediately after the verdict.

For Morales, weekends had become no different from other workdays. The hours were there for the billing; the path of least resistance in M&S led in that direction. So on the same Saturday morning that the Michelman & Samson equity partners were gathering for their annual meeting at a posh Chicago hotel, she sat at her desk two floors below Hopkins's much larger office. She began making her way down the list of jurors who'd delivered Ronald Ratkin's victory in what commentators were still calling a major trial of the relatively new century.

"Mr. Ratkin is a brilliant man," said the first juror, whose words echoed in the refrain of most others. "I can't imagine how he'd ever lose a case."

"I think he had the right approach," said another. "He explains things without talking down to us. He makes things simple without making us feel stupid."

"The visual aides were very helpful," said a juror who then proceeded to explain that television and computer screens had caused Americans to process information exclusively with their eyes. "Particularly effective was his use of colors: he used blue to highlight good news; red always meant something bad."

Morales rolled her eyes when one juror asked if she could get an autographed copy of Ratkin's photograph. Another wondered if he was married, noting he didn't wear a wedding ring. But it was the final call of the day that caused her heart to race.

"You won't like what I have to say," the juror began. "I held out against your client for as long as I could. I saw past Ratkin's innocent choirboy facade and took a cold, hard look at the facts he was trying to obfuscate. What your client did was wrong. Edelwise should have lost the case, and you know it."

Morales feared that the holdout was right. But right and wrong were not the central inquiries of any advocate in our system, she thought. Each side did its job; judges and juries made decisions to produce situational justice. It was the worst system devised by man, except for every other one.

"I stood firm for a long time," the holdout continued, "but other jurors started watching the big Edelwise press conference on their iPhones. I refused. Then they threatened to beat me up if I did anything to prevent the supposedly great Joshua Egan from continuing his pioneering advances. I understand I'm supposed to stick to my guns during deliberations, but when we told the judge we were deadlocked, he basically ignored us. How long would you last if three people threatened to hit you unless you changed your vote? I'm just glad it's over."

"Have you discussed this with anyone else?" Morales's voice trembled.

"Not yet. I haven't figured out who I should tell. I'm sure your boss couldn't care less. I understand his type. It's all about winning, and he doesn't care how he does it."

Morales ended the call as quickly and politely as she could. She understood too well the implications of what she'd heard. The losing party never had an easy time going behind a jury's verdict and reversing it based on events that allegedly transpired during deliberations. But the combination of improper media exposure and physical threats made this situation serious. After hanging up, she called Ratkin's private cell phone. A recorded message told her that the number was no longer in service.

CHAPTER 43

When the markets opened on Monday, rumors circulated that Egan's Friday afternoon webcast had been a hoax or worse. At noon, the company's president issued a public statement that put most fears to rest and stopped the sell-off in Edelwise's stock:

"In response to concerns about the new Edelthink technology discussed on Friday, Edelwise reiterates that it regards the development of this type of artificial intelligence as an important priority. As the webcast explained, more must be done to achieve commercial viability, but we are continuing work toward that end. We have invited an independent panel of experts in the field to review the progress to date, and at an appropriate time it will issue a report of its findings.

"For those who have inquired, Joshua Egan's physical remains have been cremated and a private service held to memorialize his remarkable life and extraordinary legacy. Egan's virtual presence was in attendance, and we can report that he was pleased with the eulogy that he himself gave."

The announcement soothed the market, and Edelwise's stock remained stable, ending the day at $950 per share. Most of Hopkins's fortune remained secure for now.

Still, he wished greed hadn't overtaken him. He should have sold his stock during the now closed trading window because he didn't know when he'd get another opportunity and, even worse, he no longer knew whom to trust. Could he believe what Edelwise's president had said to calm investors? Or was that just the next step of Ratkin's diabolical scenario that would play out over the coming days, months, or even years? When a person is untrustworthy, he knows and fears more acutely the capacity of others for dishonesty. The simple phrase from ancient times is "hoist with your own petard."

The moment Hopkins's concerns entered his consciousness, he realized that notwithstanding all of his bravado, he himself had become Ratkin's most recent Bambi, frozen in the headlights. Despite banishment from the Exec Com to serve a life sentence in Beijing, the protégé had conquered the mentor in the ways that mattered most—inside the mind. Ratkin had placed Hopkins in a psychological limbo that would become his own private hell. It was the worst of all feelings for an aging lion: he didn't know which way to turn. His confident façade masked a fear that produced paralysis. No worse fate can befall a successful, savvy, and seasoned attorney. Fortunately, he continued to have every other Tuesday at the Four Seasons with Fran Ratkin. Knight still didn't know he was sharing her.

*　　　*　　　*

Daniel Schmidt read the Edelwise press release as he pondered whether he had any moves to make. Even if Ronald Ratkin had orchestrated the entire scheme from start to finish, he wasn't sure what to do with it. The stock had continued to climb throughout the summer and showed no signs of a precipitous drop any time soon. Sure, Ratkin had sold his Edelwise stock, but he'd done so during a trading window, and the stock's relatively steady price thereafter made any insider trading case weak. Usually, insiders got out before bad news caused a stock to plummet. He couldn't envision a persuasive prosecution on the facts as he presently understood them.

Perhaps he could argue that all of the information about Edelthink should have been disclosed long before the final September webcast. After all, those who sold in June, July, or August might have held on longer if they'd known about the dramatic announcement that came in September. Still, proving that case would not be easy. Executives running any business typically have wide latitude in deciding what developing products are appropriate for public disclosure. Indeed, premature touting of an untried technology can create problems for companies that later face accusations of wrongly encouraging investors at a time when caution should have ruled, at least for a while longer.

Perhaps the question of Egan's physical health created issues for Edelwise and its lawyers. Schmidt knew that the company's founder had died sometime before the final dramatic webcast in which his taped presence made the posthumous announcement. But the SEC had never prosecuted a company based upon disclosures relating to an employee's health. Was this a good candidate to be the first? Schmidt thought not.

Maybe obstruction of justice would work. The mystery of Egan's nurse had been no mystery to Ratkin. But at the end of the day, what did Schmidt really have on her or Ratkin? Not much. She'd cared for a dying man and then returned to her country after he had passed. When Schmidt had seen her in Costa Rica, she'd lied about her identity, but even assuming he had jurisdiction to pursue and extradite her, where would that issue take him?

"Mr. Schmidt, your interviewee is here," said his secretary as she entered his office with another young lawyer who'd grown weary of life in a big law firm. This one wanted a job that was more personally fulfilling and offered at least the hope of developing a personal life outside of work. Government service had always appealed as a way of giving something back to the country that had given this young attorney's family so much.

He'd seen a lot of these candidates in recent years. Large law firms offered big money to starting associates, but after a couple of years, it wasn't enough for most of them. They soon found that their lives bore no resemblance to what they'd envisioned when they first chose to become lawyers. *One L* and *The Paper Chase* offered insight into the law school experience, but college students usually discounted the negative aspects of such portrayals as unduly pessimistic or simply inapplicable to them. Bad things always happened to someone else.

When they got to law school, many remained equally clueless about life after graduation, too. Herd mentality and the promise of big starting salaries caused most students to develop the ambition to join a large firm. Few of them knew what they'd do when they got there. Those who took such jobs found that the money was good, but it came with an unexpected personal cost. As soon as they made significant dents in their educational loans, many looked for a way out. That's how Daniel Schmidt had his pick of the nation's best and brightest to fill low-level staff positions in the enforcement division of the Securities and Exchange Commission.

"Hello, Mr. Schmidt," the candidate said as she extended her hand to him. "I'm Maria Morales."

"Have a seat, Maria. I see you're with my old firm, Michelman & Samson. We should have a lot to talk about."

*   *   *

Claudia Montoya, formerly Lucinda Alvarez, had never been to Manhattan. Three months after arriving in America, she boarded a train that took her from New Jersey to the land of skyscraper forests. Emerging from Penn Station, she headed for Fifth Avenue on her way to Rockefeller Center. Approaching the building that the Saks Company erected to house its flagship store before the location itself made its way into the name of what became the national retail chain, she saw gigantic white snowflakes of artificial light gracing its eastern façade. She turned left and walked toward the famous skating rink that looked smaller in real life—and the enormous Christmas tree that looked larger. She lingered for awhile before resuming her trek.

Eventually, she passed a long line of black limousines idling near a stunning high-rise office building. It was ten o'clock on a Friday night, but the lights on the fifty-fifth floor burned brightly. For the ambitious young workers billing time after eight o'clock, clients paid for meals and transportation home.

SOME WOULD MAKE IT; MORE WOULDN'T.

ACKNOWLEDGMENTS

As always, my wife, Kit, deserves the first bow in any attempt to express my gratitude to those who made this book possible. She has mastered the difficult walk along a tightrope that connects any writer's pride of authorship to a reluctant willingness to hear from a spouse whose ideas can improve his work. My daughter, Emma, served as the principal initial editor on this project—a prelude to what could certainly become a successful literary career of her own, if she wants one. Her brothers, Ben and Pete, provided insights, guidance, and support at critical moments. Dr. William Schnaper and his wife, Maria, offered helpful perspectives that made this book better in ways they're sure to recognize. Editor Shannon Pennefeather performed her typically magnificent job in producing the finished final product. Finally, without a thirty-year career at a law firm that allowed me to flourish as a lawyer while also pursuing personally fulfilling dreams along the way, my charmed life would have turned out much differently. I am grateful to the continuing encouragement, support, and friendship of my colleagues.

I owe a special debt to several recent classes of undergraduate students at Northwestern University whom I've been privileged to teach. Most got more than they'd expected when signing up for my seminar, "American Lawyers: Demystifying the Profession." Laboring in boxes they'd built for themselves as they'd tracked toward my profession, they had little notion of what awaited them when they got there. Through our ten weeks of reality therapy together, they began to see themselves and their legal ambitions in a different light. Many continued on to law school and, I'm confident, will enjoy distinguished legal careers. Their ongoing journeys inspired me to write this book.

ABOUT THE AUTHOR

Steven J. Harper is the author of *Crossing Hoffa: A Teamster's Story* and *Straddling Worlds: The Jewish-American Journey of Professor Richard W. Leopold*. For thirty years, he was a litigation attorney in a large international law firm that he joined upon graduation from Harvard Law School. He is an adjunct professor at Northwestern University's School of Law and Weinberg College of Arts and Sciences. He and his wife have three adult children and live in suburban Chicago. Visit his website at www.stevenjharper.com.

CPSIA information can be obtained at www.ICGtesting.com
262521BV00001B/43/P